The Shield of Soren

The Shield of Soren

The Light and Shadow Chronicles Book II

D.M. Cain

Dedication

To my wonderful husband, Matt. You have listened to my excited ramblings when ideas spring to mind, shown me encouragement and support when I've felt like giving up, and given me a kick up the backside when I've been too self-absorbed to see everything I've achieved.
Thank you.

The Light and Shadow Chronicles span thousands of years, and each book tells the story of one character in the tale. The books can be read in any order, and characters dip in and out of each novel. One book may tell the story of a man in his adulthood. The next may be set after that character's death or before his birth.

Putting the story together is up to you. The order of events is not important. But each and every story leads the different strands of the legend to the same conclusion...
The final battle...
The apocalypse.

For those who have read *A Chronicle of Chaos*:
This story takes place four years before Chaos Lennox is born, during Callista Nienna's marriage to her fourth husband, Kham Nitaya.

The World of the Light and Shadow Chronicles

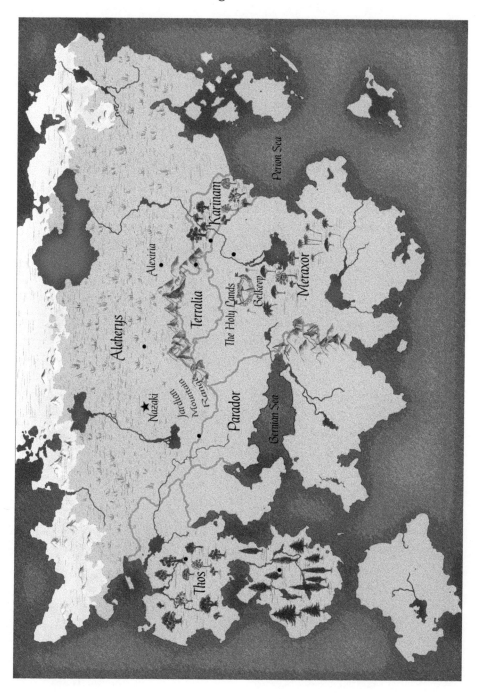

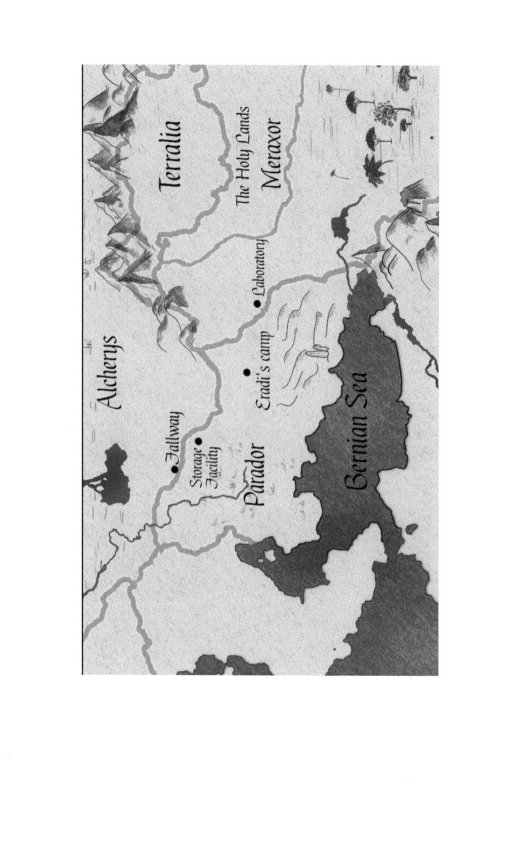

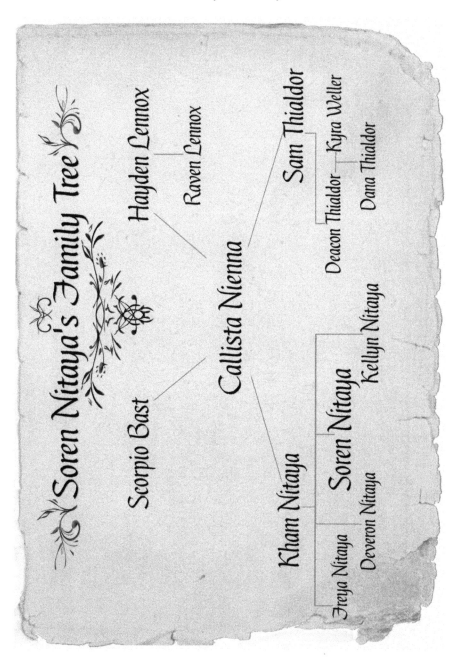

Contents

Chapter One
Experiments (Year 101 of the Second Age)

HE LONG CORRIDORS of the Meraxan research laboratory were cold and sterile. Sickly yellow lights flickered and cast a jaundiced glow across the grey walls. It was quiet tonight with only the occasional guard patrolling the silent passageways. Nobody entered the laboratory. There was little reason to, so why would they? Nobody even knew it existed; the classification of the building as a top-secret location ensured that. Vincent Wilder strode through the corridors with an uncomfortable heaviness hanging over his heart. It should have been an exciting prospect, being called to a top-secret laboratory in the middle of the night with the promise of something game-changing awaiting him.

But Vincent had learnt long ago to treat "ground-breaking" advances in science with scepticism. His last few projects had either fallen flat and produced only minimal results or failed completely. What made this one any different? It didn't help that the state-of-the-art technology and highly expensive research materials were almost entirely under the control of a psychotic scientist by the name of Reign. An unhinged human at loose in a laboratory would have been dangerous enough, but giving that level of control to a Rhygun was insane. Vincent himself would never have allowed a half-human-half-demon access to something so important to their cause, but it hadn't been up to him. No matter how much he liked to think he was in control, Vincent knew who pulled the strings.

Vincent sighed. It was a mess. His whole operation was a mess at the moment. Though he hated to admit it, the Children of Light were stronger than his army. If things continued this way, this war of centuries would finally be over, and not with a pleasing result. For one hundred and eleven years, he had been fighting this damn war against Callista and her people. He never aged, never withered and died, but without growing old he felt like there was no progress. He almost regretted the fact that he and his people had gotten a hold of the Children of Light's elixir at all. Sometimes all he wanted was to grow old naturally and die an old man. Alas, it would never happen. So he was forced to continue fighting a war he wasn't sure he could survive.

It seemed that at every turn the Children of Light were winning. Merely seven years ago, Callista's army had attacked a crucial schooling encampment and destroyed an entire academy of learning, killing many innocents in the process. Not to mention what Callista herself had recently done to his most-beloved child.

Vincent clenched his fists as fury threatened to engulf him. Trying to convince himself that the memories were just that, memories, he tried to calm down. He needed to keep his head, at least until Reign told him what had excited him so much in the middle of the night.

Vincent shook his head to clear his mind and straightened his black collar. The suit jacket usually fit him perfectly, but for some reason this evening it felt snug and restrictive. It was no surprise to him really. He had pushed his body harder than ever over the past few weeks. Since *that incident*, he had thrown himself into sparring with every fibre of his being. Maybe he had bulked up a bit, which could only be a good thing. Every ounce of muscle was an extra ounce that could be used against Callista and her damn people. Vincent smirked at the thought and undid the buttons on his jet-black shirt, so the sleeves didn't dig so much into his muscular forearms.

Maybe whatever Reign brought for him today would be worth something after all. It wasn't as if everything Reign did was a failure. There was always Caleb Maddox. That young man looked to be an interesting addition to their army, if he grew up to fulfil his potential.

Vincent was empowered by the thought that maybe, just maybe, something would start to go their way. By the time he approached the laboratory at the centre of the complex, he was feeling a little more positive.

He waited outside the door and took a deep breath to ready himself for Reign's overbearing presence. No sooner had he set foot inside the room than Reign was directly in front of him, grinning insanely with manic, blazing eyes.

"This is it, Vincent! Oh yes, this is it! You won't believe the beauty I've got for you!" Reign was literally hopping from one foot to the other. Vincent screwed his nose up in annoyance.

"Can you at least let me enter the room?" Vincent mumbled, as he pulled the door closed behind him. There was a peculiar smell in the room, like the faint aroma of burning sulphur or a match that had been lit then extinguished. The human part of Reign ruled over his appearance. At first glance, it was unlikely anybody would notice anything amiss about the kindly-looking middle-aged man. But step too close to him, and nobody could avoid the lingering stench of Hell, the almost tangible wafts of brimstone and ash that clung to him.

Looking away to avoid the smell, Vincent gave a half-hearted smile. "Show me what you've got that was so important at this unreasonable hour."

Reign grinned. "Oh, you won't be disappointed. The boss wasn't." He waved a dismissive hand in the direction of the far corner of the lab. It was only upon closer inspection that Vincent saw the twisting, tumultuous shadow of the Bavelize, lurking in the darkness.

He immediately dropped to one knee and lowered his head. "Oh Great One, forgive my insolence. I did not realise you were here and would not have acted in such a way had I known."

The room was silent, but an eerie echo of breathing reverberated against Vincent's eardrums, as if the noise came from nowhere and everywhere at once. "Stand, Vincent."

Vincent slowly rose to his feet and met the Bavelize face-to-face, if one could call what the shadowy creature had a face. A swirling mass of writhing smoke, there were no features to speak of, but more an ever-changing, undulating mask of darkness.

The voice of the Bavelize echoed through Vincent's head again. "Listen to what the Rhygun has to say. It could change everything."

Vincent was still sceptical, but he could not argue with the deity that watched over the Brotherhood of Shadow's every move. Giving a low, courteous bow, he turned to Reign and indicated that he was ready to hear whatever the scientist had to say.

Reign's eyes glowed with enthusiasm once more. He waved Vincent over to another door and Vincent followed him into a second room. There, in a line, standing strictly to attention, were at least twenty young people from Vincent's kingdom of Meraxor. He frowned. Many of them were his own children, and he looked down the line with a growing sense of uncertainty.

But Reign waved him right by the line of people to a huge glass tube in the centre of the room. An immense cylinder, there was a heavily bolted sliding door at the front, but the rest was completely enclosed. It didn't take Vincent long to realise it was a prison cell.

He pressed his face up to the glass and inside, cowering on the floor of the cell, he saw a young girl, surely no more than ten years old, with flowing silver hair and ragged clothing.

Reign sidled up beside him and placed his chin on Vincent's shoulder, making him jerk back in surprise and a fair amount of annoyance. Reign chuckled and then pressed both hands up against the glass and peered in.

"Look at this beauty, Vincent. We found the specimen a few days ago, out on the edges of the Meraxan rainforest and brought it here." He licked his lips as he looked at her, and it made Vincent feel somewhat queasy.

"She's just a kid. Why did you bring her here? Go and release her."

Reign laughed again and shook his head slowly from side to side. "I think you'll find she holds great potential for our military interests."

Vincent sighed with impatience and began to walk from the room, but a hiss penetrated his hearing suddenly, forcing him to cover his ears to save his eardrums from being perforated.

"You will stay," the Bavelize snarled from the corner, the sounds echoing through the laboratory.

Vincent spun on his heels and tentatively removed his hands. He rejoined Reign and tried to keep his mouth shut as the Rhygun scientist resumed hopping from one foot to the other.

Reign began to unfasten the heavy door of the glass cage, flicking back catches and sliding back weighty iron bolts. With a loud clang of metal slamming into metal, the final bolt was undone. Reign slowly pulled the door open, and Vincent found his breath catching in his throat.

High-pitched whimpering came from the tiny bundle of rags cowering at the back of the cage. Her long silver hair parted for a moment and Vincent could see her wide, silver eyes, terrified and innocent. Vincent's skin prickled with

4

discomfort. He hoped that Reign had a damned good reason for capturing a small child like this.

Beside the glass cage were two oil lamps, both resting unlit. Reign reached up and took one down. Then, in a single savage moment, he slammed the lamp onto the floor of her cage. The girl screamed in terror and covered her head with her hands, but he hadn't been aiming for her.

The shattered glass gave way to a stream of oil that spread out in a pool across the floor. This seemed to scare the girl even more, and she began to cry quietly, sobbing into her clenched hands.

Reign looked back at Vincent. Excitement flashed in his eyes as he drew a match from a box in his pocket. A small flare of light, a flicker of sulphur and a small flame danced on top of the match. With another laugh, Reign tossed the match into the glass cage.

Vincent gasped as the oil ignited in a rush of intense heat. The entire floor of the cage burst into flames. Vincent tried to rush forwards to save the girl from a fiery death, but the heat was too intense. A hand tapped incessantly at his shoulder, and he tried to brush it away, but Reign grabbed hold of his hand.

"Look! Look!" Reign shouted excitedly, pointing at the cage.

When his eyes fell upon the cage, Vincent froze to the spot, his eyes nearly popping from their sockets. "But...how?"

The girl, who Vincent had assumed would be burning in agony, was somehow floating above the flames, hovering at the top of her cage. From her back sprouted two enormous wings of the purest white feathers Vincent had ever seen. The two beautiful white fans could only just fit within the confines of the cage, and as she beat them to stay afloat they fanned the flames beneath her.

It wasn't just her wings that dazzled Vincent with their purity. Her whole body had adopted an ethereal, almost ghostly, silver aura, her hair shimmering with radiance. She didn't seem too frightened any more, but there was a definite hint of sadness in her gentle eyes.

Vincent studied her carefully, struggling to catch his breath, which he hadn't realised he had been holding. "What is she?" he managed to croak.

Reign grinned and draped an arm across Vincent's shoulder. "She, my friend, is an angel." He paused to allow Vincent a chance to absorb the surprising revelation before continuing. "I could sense something in the air when we first picked her up, a kind of sour smell, a tingling on the tip of my tongue—the reek of an angel. The demon in me is repulsed by and attracted to her at the same time. Our species have been at war since the dawn of time, so the temptation to rip her to shreds is rather overwhelming." He chuckled again, sending shivers down Vincent's spine. "But, of course, my duty is to you, the Bavelize, and my mission in your realm, so I think we should utilise her skills instead."

Vincent nodded, his eyes still locked onto the bewildering sight of the angel, rhythmically flapping her wings to float above the dwindling fire. The flames were beginning to die down now that the fuel was running low, but thick, black smoke swirled at the top of the cage and the angel was beginning to cough and choke on the oppressive fumes.

Reign grabbed a bucket of water that he had presumably prepared, ready for this occasion, and hurled it into the cage. The freezing liquid hit the flames and extinguished them immediately.

The angel collapsed to the floor, wet and gasping for breath, her energy seemingly sapped. Her grand, beautiful wings slowly folded back into her shoulder blades and her eerie glow faded until she was nothing more than a cowering, terrified child again.

"I don't understand," Vincent said, frowning. "I've heard of angels before. The legends of the first age are full of them. The stories claim that angels possess incredible strength and speed and that they can heal themselves. This one should be able to break free of this cage and kill me easily. Maybe not you with your demon genes, but definitely me. Why doesn't she at least defend herself?" He stepped in closer and examined the cuts on her body, where whip lashes and knives had sliced her skin.

"It looks like you've been taking chunks out of her already." Vincent turned and glared at Reign, who grinned back at him. "Why doesn't she heal? I thought all angels healed."

Reign tapped absently at the glass, eyeing her as one would an interesting museum exhibit. "Yes, usually they do. We think that this one may be damaged. I don't know, but she seems...incomplete, somehow. She is strong and fast, or at least she was when we first captured her. She tried to escape a number of times. When she gets her wings out, we have to be careful because she can fly quickly. But her power or energy or something seems to be dwindling and she's getting weaker and weaker, so she isn't as much of a threat anymore. Besides, we've found a few ways to deter her from attempting escape. She responds well to drugs, electric shocks and, as you've seen, fire. With those at our disposal, we've managed to suppress her and keep her under control."

Fascination had replaced Vincent's concern for the girl. Now that he knew she wasn't human, his mind was racing with possibilities.

"Could we train her up as a weapon? If we could use her in battle to fight for us, we'd have a huge advantage." All the recent defeats he'd suffered echoed in Vincent's memory, and he relished the idea of a weapon to neutralise the Children of Light.

Reign grimaced. "Yes, and no. She has all the power and skills, but not the constitution. She's far too meek and gentle to be any use in battle, and her power seems to be weakening with every test we do anyway. I think we need to take the best of her and put it into somebody else."

Vincent stared at him for a moment as the words sunk in. His eyes flickered to the twisting, turning cloud of shadow in the corner. The dark plumes formed into the shape of a human long enough for the Bavelize to nod his head in encouragement, and then it dispersed into a tumultuous cloud of ever-shifting smoke again.

Vincent knew he couldn't argue with the Bavelize, and he had to admit the prospect of utilising her power was exciting to him. "OK. How do we do that?"

Reign sniggered. "We need to find a suitable body to host the angel's DNA. If we give it to one of our young soldiers, we may be able to replicate her traits, but without her irritating calmness. What we need is a ruthless killer, a powerful weapon who will benefit from her strength and use it to his or her advantage."

He had failed to deliver upon his promises so many times that Vincent was reluctant to rely upon him again. The idea of blindly taking some DNA from a completely strange creature and injecting it into a human being was dangerous and idiotic. He was quite sure that there were so many scientific inaccuracies with the theory that it wasn't even worth considering. However, Vincent was beginning to run out of other options. The Brotherhood of Shadow simply had nothing that could rival the Children of Light and their elite warriors. Maybe this could work after all, and if it didn't, one person would be lost, not an entire army.

Something else was nagging at Vincent though. Reign had brought this group of young men to present before Vincent and the Bavelize, and those he had chosen included some that Vincent was simply not willing to sacrifice.

Reaching up to wipe a bead of nervous sweat from his forehead, Vincent frowned. "I don't like this. It's too risky, and we risk losing the lives of soldiers and of my children in the process."

If the idea of sacrificing a child's life bothered Reign, he didn't show it. An all-too-familiar manic grin crept across his lips as he slyly looked towards the Bavelize, lurking in the shadows beside them.

In a voice as thick and dark as smoke, the Bavelize answered, "Then choose wisely..."

Reign cackled and rubbed his hands together, wandering up and down the line of potential candidates. "The person you choose will need to be strong enough to withstand the experiments, which will be harsh and gruelling and, at times, agonising. Despite the strength, they should also be disposable if all this fails."

Vincent looked up and down the line of young men to see if anybody adequately met the requirements. Who could withstand such torrents of abuse, and who was Vincent willing to forfeit?

They stood, hands locked behind their backs, chins raised, tall and proud. The candidates Reign had chosen varied hugely in their value. Terralian slaves, weak and disposable, were easily the obvious choice if somebody was to be sacrificed. However, their blood was inferior. By nature, Vincent recoiled in the presence of a Terralian. He could never entrust something so important to a member of a race he considered no greater than insects.

He scoffed as he walked past the Terralian slaves in their simple brown robes, their vibrant red hair tied back from their pale faces, and continued down the line.

Some of Reign's choices were downright ludicrous. He raised his eyebrows at the Rhygun to show his dissatisfaction. "Obviously, this is a brand-new experiment, isn't it?" Vincent snapped. "Why have you chosen those you already know have another fate awaiting them? Valentine, Amadeus, Horus—their destinies are already sealed. And Caleb? Do you not think his genes are muddled enough?"

The next two candidates in the line gave Vincent pause. Two of his own sons, but those who had yet to impress him. Drake Wilder, aged twenty-eight, was undoubtedly powerful, a behemoth, in fact. His rippling muscles bulged beneath the dark T-shirt he wore. Vincent was aware that boosting Drake even further with angel DNA could make him unstoppable. However, there was no way Vincent would be willing to sacrifice a man with so much potential, even if he hadn't shown his true value and probably never would.

The twenty-one-year-old Silas Wilder was the last in the line. Even when asked to stand alongside his brothers and remain still, Silas jigged from one foot to the other, a misplaced grin dancing upon his lips. The young man had shown talent in training, but he was inconsistent and clearly preferred entertaining himself above completing his duty. If a trustworthy apprentice was what Vincent was looking for, Silas definitely was not it.

Hopelessness was plaguing Vincent once again, the all-too-familiar feeling that fate was simply conspiring against him. All he needed was to select somebody he was willing to sacrifice. How difficult could that be?

He threw his hands into the air with frustration. "None of them! None of them are right. How can you expect me to choose for my children to die?"

"Because," Reign hissed, "through sacrificing the lives of your children, you bring the end of hers."

Ah, Callista Nienna, his idol and enemy all in one. Frankly, Vincent would sacrifice every member of his family if he could be one hundred percent sure he could either obtain or destroy her. One life, even of his own flesh and blood, was more than worth it for the impact it would have upon the fabled Callista and her army of light. He gritted his teeth as he thought about her, and it was then that an idea came to him.

"Of course," he murmured. "I know exactly who we can use. It's obvious."

He wandered backwards and forwards muttering beneath his breath. "He is weak, of course, and ill. His pathetic blood, so useless for everything else, might just be good enough for this. He is definitely not strong enough to withstand anything substantial, but what does it matter if he dies? What possible use will we ever have for him?"

"Who?" asked Reign. "Who do you speak of?"

The confidence was back in Vincent's smile as he waved a commanding arm towards the guard stationed by the door. "Guardian. Bring me Guardian."

Chapter Two
Ruins of the Gods (Year 106 of the Second Age)

COLD SLAB OF STONE. That was all that was left of fifteen-year-old Freya Nitaya. The bells around the city of Nazaki chimed, their mournful tune echoing across the kingdom of Alcherys like ripples across a calm lake.

The usually vibrant and majestic city had been brought to a standstill when Freya's body had been taken through the streets, followed by a stream of mourners. The funeral procession finished its slow march at the Nazaki Cathedral, an immense marble temple right in the centre of the capital city.

At least two hundred members of Freya's family attended, all of her siblings, aunts and uncles, and distant cousins who had come from miles away. Everybody. They were all part of the largest family on the planet, the Children of Light. When one of their own died, they all turned out to say goodbye. On top of that, there were a huge number of ordinary citizens of Alcherys who had turned up to pay their respects to the fallen princess.

The ceremony was short but beautiful, a fitting tribute to the tragically short life of the beautiful teenage girl for whom life had only just begun. When it was finished, the Alcherans trudged back to their homes with their heads drooped in sadness. Their grief at the loss of one of the royal family was profound. It always was every time the war claimed one of their leaders, but at least they could return to their lives and leave the conflict behind. When the halls were emptied of mourners, only the family was left behind in the cold, marble temple. It was Freya's parents, her brothers and sister who would have to live with the loss.

There were still fifty people or more in the grand cathedral where the funeral had taken place, but now that the villagers had left, it seemed deserted.

Soren Nitaya was just five years old, and he was angrier than he had ever been in his life. He stood, rigid as a post, his fists clenched tightly together and his chin tucked in to his chest. He glared furiously at any who tried to come near him, any who tried to comfort him about the death of his sister. And there were many who tried. '

A hand rested gently on Soren's shoulder, but he bristled at the touch and shook it away. He cast a bitter scowl up at his older brother. Deveron was still a child himself, only nine years old, but he had taken it upon himself to look after Soren and their baby sister, Kellyn.

Their parents were too grief-stricken at the moment to help anybody.

Soren glared at them from across the hall, where they clung to one another, tears marking their faces.

"Let's go home now, Soren," Deveron said and tried to lead him away, but Soren stood his ground.

"No!" He crossed his arms over his chest but kept his eyes locked onto his mother and father.

"Come on. Mummy and Daddy will come later." Deveron reached out to hold Soren's hand, but he held his arms crossed even more tightly together.

"Don't care. I hate Mum and Dad."

Deveron paused, taken aback by his brother's words, but he tried not to let it show.

"Don't be silly. You don't hate Mum and Dad. Come home, and I'll play soldiers with you."

Soren stamped his feet in quick succession. "No, no, no!"

His angry voice echoed across the hall, causing his mother and father to snap out of their catatonic grief. With slow, shaky steps, they walked over to their sons together.

"Hey, little buddy," their mother said, as she knelt down in front of Soren. He resolutely looked away from her. Tears welled in his eyes, but he wouldn't make eye contact with his mother.

She stood up and looked to Deveron instead, whose face was ashen and full of sadness.

"You holding up OK?"

Deveron tried to answer, but he couldn't get his words out so he merely gave a hurried nod. His mother pulled him into a warm and comforting embrace, and he nestled his face into her long, platinum hair. The familiar smell of his mother, of roses and leather, clearly comforted Deveron's frayed nerves. He gently pulled out of her arms and looked to his father, Kham, but although he stood beside them, he wasn't really there. His eyes were distant and unfocused, his dark skin pale and sunken.

Kham Nitaya had been a powerful warrior once, strong and dedicated to their cause, but the loss of his daughter had destroyed his will to fight, to survive even. He was a shadow of the man he had once been.

It unnerved Soren and Deveron to see their father like this, and they both looked away. The children's mother, Callista Nienna, Queen of Alcherys and the leader of the Children of Light, looked as radiant as ever. Her long white-blonde hair cascaded in rivers down to the small of her back. Her hazel eyes glistened with pain, but her expression remained stoic, the hardened shell of a strong leader.

"Everything's finished now, boys," Callista said in a warm but authoritative voice. "Let's go home."

She moved to put an arm around each of her boys, but Soren ducked away from her embrace and crossed his arms again, high upon his chest. He wore a deep purple uniform with the silver symbol of the Children of Light stitched onto it. He looked down at it and screwed his nose up in distaste, making sure he crossed his arms to hide the badge. His bottom lip was firmly stuck out in defiance.

"Come on, Soren," said Callista.

"I don't want to go anywhere!" he shrieked. He frantically shook his head from side to side. His messy black hair fell across his face, and he angrily swept it aside.

"Come on. You'll feel better back at home."

"No, I won't!" He clenched his fists by his side and glowered at his mother.

"I know you're upset, but—"

"No! You don't know anything!"

Callista looked to her husband for support, but his face was blank and distant, as if he wasn't even aware they were in the room.

"Tell me what's wrong," she said softly and reached out to stroke Soren's cheek.

Soren clenched his jaw, grinding his little teeth together. When his mother reached out to him, he waved her hand away and sat down on the floor with a loud huff.

Callista nodded to Deveron, and he sat down in front of his brother.

"What's up?" Deveron asked in a calm, friendly voice, blatantly trying to put Soren at ease, which aggravated him further.

Soren cast a cross frown at his mum again before looking back at his brother. He mumbled something under his breath.

"What was that?" Deveron leaned in more closely.

"It's Mum's fault. She let Freya die."

Deveron glanced up at his mother with wide eyes. "Why do you think that?" he asked. "Mum had nothing to do with it."

"She didn't save her."

Callista crossed her arms and turned away, but not before Soren saw her trying to hide the burning tears that glistened in her eyes.

"Don't be silly. Mum couldn't have done anything," Deveron said.

"She could! Mum has that potion. She can give it to anybody whenever she likes. It can bring people back. She could have saved her."

"It's not like that, Soren," Callista said quietly with her back still turned to the boys.

"It is! That magical potion makes people live forever. You live forever. Daddy lives forever. Everybody does! When I reach sixteen, I will take it and live forever. Why didn't you give it to Freya?"

"I couldn't...," Callista murmured.

"You could too!"

There was an uncomfortable silence, broken only by a barely audible sniff as Callista held back tears.

Deveron straightened up. "He's right, Mum. Why didn't you just give Freya the elixir? Then she *could* have lived forever."

Callista's eyes were wracked with pain. "I wish I could have, but it doesn't work that way. You don't understand..."

"So tell us!" Deveron cried.

"You're too young to understand..."

"We're not babies!" Soren shouted, and he leapt up to his feet. "We're big now! We can understand."

Callista frowned, unsure.

"Come on, Mum. We need to know why this happened. We want to know why you didn't save our sister."

Callista gave a sad smile. The boys could tell she knew they were right. Their ability to believe in her, to believe in the world again, rested on this.

She turned to her gaunt and exhausted husband.

"Kham, I'll do it. I'll take the boys to Alexiria and show them the book, where it all began. Then they'll understand."

Their father snapped out of his silence. "You can't, Callista. It's too dangerous, and the boys will be at risk. What if the Brotherhood of Shadow have spies on the roads? They could target you and hurt the boys."

"It'll be fine. We'll take a cart tomorrow morning and be back by evening. We'll bring a dryll as well, so we have a way of communicating with home. We'll be discreet and stick to the main roads, and I can defend the kids. Please, they need this. You stay here and look after baby Kellyn."

"Soren's too young to travel so far."

Callista rested a hand on Soren's head. "Something tells me Soren will be just fine."

The following morning, Callista, Deveron and Soren made their way through the thriving streets of Nazaki, Alcherys's capital city, with canvas bags of food and water strung over their backs for the long journey. A wooden cart was waiting for them, and an elderly driver sat at the front with the horses' reins in his hands.

As the ruler of Alcherys, Callista had easily persuaded the elderly driver to cart them across the country, even if it would take all day. She paid him well, as the royal family were tremendously wealthy, and that gave him the encouragement he needed to forsake other jobs for the day.

Soren clambered up onto the cart, eager and ready for the long trip across Alcherys. He didn't know where his mother was taking him, but despite the prickling of anger he still felt towards her, he couldn't help feeling excited about their adventure.

That excitement doubled when he first caught sight of the palace dryll they were taking with them. It was twice the size of the drylls Soren had seen flapping around the fields on the city's outskirts. His fascination with the proud and impressive birds of prey had begun on his first journey out of Nazaki's walls, watching them soaring high above, mere dots in the sky, before hurtling towards the ground at break-neck speed to catch an unsuspecting victim.

But this particular dryll was nothing like those wild birds. This one was a pedigree, bred for speed and efficiency, and it had developed its striking plumage somewhere along the way. Its grand, royal-blue feathers ruffled haughtily around its neck as the bird's handler placed it carefully on the edge of the cart and tied the rope around its feet to a hook on the wooden panels.

Soren was intimidated by the dryll's piercing yellow eyes and edged back towards his mother, but he couldn't stop staring at the incredible creature. He shifted his position to make sure he was out of range of those deadly sharp talons, while retaining a good view of them.

When Soren had finished fussing and fidgeting, they finally set off, and the cart trundled along the shale pathway out of Nazaki.

At eight hours' travelling time, the trip was boring and exhausting for the children. Even the dryll became boring to Soren after it tucked its head inside an enormous wing and slept for the majority of the journey. So Deveron made up games to play with Soren along the way. They sang songs and challenged each other to be the first to spot various items. Traversing from one side of the nation to the other should have been exciting for the two young boys, but Alcherys wasn't the most interesting country. Ninety percent of the landscape was largely featureless plains and wastelands, and only the vast and impressive settlements of the Children of Light broke the monotony.

A journey across the country of Meraxor with its vibrant rainforests and dramatic mountain vistas would have been far more exciting, but as the land of the Brotherhood of Shadow, Meraxor was far too dangerous. They would have to make do with the dull plains of Alcherys instead.

When trying to entertain himself became boring, Soren drifted in and out of sleep, curled up in his mother's arms, his belly full of the bread and cheese they had brought along with them. Deveron was quiet, seemingly content to simply watch the scenery passing by.

After what felt like an eternity, the cart began to slow as it approached Alexiria. The boys had heard of the place before. Everybody in Alcherys had.

It was the place where everything had begun, where Callista had formed their nation and where the ghosts of their ancestors still stalked the skeletal ruins of a lost civilisation.

Soren didn't believe in ghosts, but if he had done, Alexiria is where they would do their haunting.

He was still feeling groggy from his intermittent naps, but, as they approached the ruins, excited butterflies began to dance in his stomach. Even the dryll pulled its head from under its wing and eyed everything suspiciously with its beady yellow eyes.

"Deveron, is there anybody up ahead?" Callista asked.

Deveron focused on the wall ahead, his forehead creased into a frown. To a passer-by, it might look like he was staring at nothing, but Soren knew different. His brother was special.

"No, I can't detect any life forces."

Callista nodded, and they continued on their journey. Soren stared at his big brother in admiration and wished he had a special power. Nobody knew why Deveron could do what he could do. He had just been different ever since birth. He could literally see life. He could discover traces of living beings when all other signs failed. It was as if he were fundamentally entwined with the planet, synchronised with the life force itself, its conduit. Others saw it as a great gift, and it certainly came in handy for Deveron when he was hiding from other kids or playing chase games. But, the darker side of his "gift" had become clear the day he saw Freya's body stretched out on a stone slab. His beloved big sister, who had always cared for him, who had always possessed such a vibrant and strong life force, was now empty and cold. His power had been stronger since then.

They were drawing near to Alexiria. Soren just knew it, but all he could see in front of him was a blank grey wall, dilapidated and covered in moss and creeping ivy. The cart didn't stop as it got closer and Soren's eyes widened. They were going to hit the wall. Preparing himself for a big crash, Soren covered his face with his hands, but at the last minute, the walls seemed to open up before them. As the angle of their approach changed, Soren saw that there was a thin crack running between two steep cliffs made by the walls. Nature had provided the city of Alexiria with natural camouflage.

Soren, Deveron and Callista watched in silence as the cart slowly passed through the wall and into the ruins of the city. Soren's excited eyes widened with wonder as they trundled along the cobblestone paths and past ruined, overgrown buildings on either side.

Callista called for the driver to stop as they approached the tallest building. It was a huge, colonnaded mastery of architecture. Marble columns supported elaborately carved friezes showing parades of people, animals and what looked like humans with wings.

A large archway at the front appeared to be the main doorway. This was where Callista chose to release the dryll. Soren stayed as still as possible, watching his mother closely as she untied the rope with tentative movements. They all knew better than to startle a dryll. People had lost fingers that way.

When the bird of prey was untethered, Callista took a small note from her bag. Soren assumed it was the usual note to their father telling him of their safe arrival. It didn't take much to set Kham to worrying, and Soren was pretty sure he would be worrying right now.

Tucking the note safely inside a small brace on the bird's leg just above its right claw, Callista ran a piece of cloth from one of Kham's old shirts under its nose. The dryll's eyes focused on something in the distance, and then it was off, flapping its gigantic wings with a great rush of air.

Callista, Soren and Deveron gathered their things together and asked the cart's driver to wait for them. As they dismounted from the cart, Soren ran ahead, bounding up the steps, oblivious to any danger.

"Soren! Wait for us!" Callista called, as she helped Deveron down from the cart.

They jogged after Soren, and together passed into the building. Whatever Soren had been expecting, it wasn't this. The hall they stepped into was the size of a cavern. The ceiling, stretching at least twenty-five metres above their heads, was covered in splinters of coloured glass. The bright sun shone through in tiny scattered rays, casting kaleidoscope emeralds, rubies and sapphires across the floor.

Soren and Deveron stopped in the centre of the room, their eyes cast up to the awe-inspiring ceiling and their jaws nearly hit the patterned grey stone floor.

"Welcome to the library of Alexiria, boys," Callista said with a smile.

The children tore their eyes from the ceiling and looked around the room. They were inside an immense cylinder. The ceiling was a patterned disc sitting on top of the rounded walls, which the boys had only just noticed were lined with bookshelves at least eight metres high.

Hundreds of thousands of crinkly old tomes were stacked neatly along the shelves, their covers grey with a film of dust.

"What are all these?" Deveron asked, as he pulled a dark-brown leather-bound book from the shelf.

"These are documents written thousands of years ago by an ancient unknown civilisation. When the war first started, I came here with my friends. They were the only people I had left in the world. We found this library, and I began to read those books. Over the last hundred years, I have read them all. They tell of ancient history—age-old battles, angels, demons, dragons—all manner of fantastical things."

Soren's eyes were wide with fascination, watching his mother carefully as she ran her hand across the bound spines of the books.

"How much of it is true and how much mere fairy tale, I do not know. But some of these books speak of things no person could possibly know of gods and monsters beyond belief and even of the future."

"The future? That's impossible," Soren said.

Callista smiled. "I thought so too at first, but whoever filled this library knew an awful lot about us, about our way of life, our family, me. How can that be when they were written so long ago? We could only surmise that the person, or people, who wrote them had magical powers of some kind. These books were written by something greater than a human. Something superior, something we should bow down to and follow."

Deveron gasped. "Is this where you found *The Book of Alcherys*?"

Callista's eyes twinkled. "Yes. Right here."

She pointed to an empty marble plinth which held pride of place in the centre of the room. "I knew it was special immediately. The other books were amazing, but this was different. I could feel the magic oozing from the pages and knew once I read it, life would never be the same again."

She slung her bag off her shoulder and tugged at the drawstrings. They came open, and she reached carefully inside and withdrew a large, dusty book with frayed edges and stitching so old it looked like it would fall apart at a touch.

"Is that it? The real book? I've only seen copies." Deveron's voice was filled with wonder.

Callista nodded and sat on the floor with her legs tucked beneath her. She opened the book carefully, and the leather cover creaked. A waft of musk hit them, and a smell of old papyrus hung in the air.

Soren screwed his nose up in disgust and waved the dusty air away from his face, but Deveron soaked up the smell of the paper, closed his eyes and tried to get a feel for the time when the Book was written.

Callista ran her fingers over the pages fondly, as if caressing a much-loved pet. "When I was lost, alone, with no idea what to do for my people, this book saved me. I don't know how, but the words in it told me exactly what I should do to keep my friends and family alive. This book has warned me of disasters long before they have happened. It has shown me which path to take when I couldn't choose. I learned long ago that the Book is sacred and we cannot argue with the words inside."

Callista began to flick through the pages, and Soren leaned in further as the sheets of scratchy black writing flitted past. Each page was decorated with patterns running around the edges: swords, shields, feathers, dragons, and flames.

Soren's hand shot out and he pointed excitedly to one of the symbols. "That's ours! That's the badge of the Children of Light!" He jumped to his feet and pulled aside his jacket to reveal his deep purple uniform with the silver badge featuring four daggers upon it.

"That's right, Soren," his mother said. "When we set up our nation, we took our sigil from the Book that had given us so much guidance."

She flicked on again until she landed on a page with the word "elixir" in spiky lettering across the top of the page. She spread the book out on the floor between herself and her two children.

Soren crept forwards and leaned over it eagerly. In the centre of the page was the knot of infinity. It looked like a figure eight lying on its side, and Soren's eyes followed the loops round and around until he began to feel sick. His mother began to read:

"This mystical brew has the power to stop the turning of the tides and the decline of the living. But one sip and the drinker shall never age, never fall victim to withering skin or greying hair. An eternity of youthfulness awaits he who drinks from the potion of life. Even on the verge of death itself, this tonic can bring a person back from impending oblivion. But beware, for once the damage is too great and the icy hand of death clasps around the heart, not even the properties of the elixir can bring life back."

Callista closed the book gently.

"Do you see, boys? The elixir, which every person in Alcherys takes at the age of sixteen, gives eternal youth. That is why we never age. It is why I am nearly one hundred and twenty-seven years old. When you come of age, you shall take it too. It makes your body stronger and natural decay does not ravage you. If you are injured and nearly dead, you could be saved by a dose of elixir. If even a single spark of life remains, you can be saved, but once that spark is gone...once you are dead, it cannot bring you back," she whispered and tears gathered in the corner of her eyes.

"Freya was too far gone...," Deveron said quietly. Callista nodded, biting her lower lip to stop the trembling.

"There was nothing I could do. It was too late to give her the elixir."

Soren trembled and began to cry, as the anger he had been holding inside dissipated. He shuffled over to his mother and threw his arms around her, snuggling into her warm embrace. She put her other arm around Deveron and pulled him in close too. When she spoke again, it was in a warm and comforting voice.

"Everything in our lives is mapped out. It has already been decided by forces bigger than us. *The Book of Alcherys* is proof of that. There was nothing I could do for Freya, nothing any of us could do once she was in the grip of evil. There is only one person to blame for your sister's death—Vincent Wilder."

Chapter Three
That Man (Year 111 of the Second Age)

HE SOUND OF KNIVES and forks scraping against plates was driving Soren mad. Each clink echoed around the room, making the tension all the more glaring. He shifted in his chair, unable to get comfortable, and poked at his bacon with the tip of his knife. He chased it backwards and forwards across the plate, enjoying the high-pitched squeal as it scraped across the porcelain. Eventually, a stern glare from his mother forced him to stop.

The Nitaya family sat for breakfast around the large table in the kitchen. It was the first meal they'd had together for three weeks and the first time Soren had seen his father in two. Kham might as well have been absent this time too as he sat in silence, staring into his untouched breakfast. He had barely made eye contact as they cooked and served the food and hadn't said a word to his three children yet.

Soren and Deveron, at ten and fourteen years respectively, were old enough to accept their father's quietness or at least to understand, even if it made Soren feel bitter and unloved. Their little sister Kellyn, however, was just five—too young to recognise that anything was wrong. She had only been a baby when their sister Freya had died. For as long as she could remember, Kham had always been distant. It wasn't unusual for him to say nothing to her for weeks at a time. This absent parenting made Soren's blood boil, and he wanted to scream at his father to recognise their existence.

It couldn't be easy being the fourth husband of Callista Nienna, but there must have been some strength in him at some point or else his mother, with all her pride and determination, would never have married him. The death of Freya had hit him the hardest of all, and he hadn't even had his wife to console him. She had been busy organising a funeral, comforting the dismayed people of Alcherys, and planning her revenge on Vincent Wilder.

After five minutes of deafening silence, Deveron spoke up in a quiet, detached voice. "So, what's everybody up to today?"

Kellyn was straight in to the conversation. "I'm going around Sella's house after school. She's got a new wooden ship with all the sailors and the crew and everything. We'll destroy that barbarian fleet!"

Deveron and Soren exchanged glances. Soren put his knife down and sat forwards in his chair. "I don't know. That barbarian hoard is merciless. You'd better have the best soldiers on board or they'll commandeer your ship."

"I have!" she squealed, and her eyes widened in excitement. "The very best! I'm taking all of my soldiers round there too. I've got all the Children and Brotherhood figures Freya made me."

At the mention of Freya, the room fell silent again, but Soren refused to let her name become taboo. "That's great! You'll do fine then. They won't stand a chance. Freya made the best figures of all. The strongest soldiers."

"She did! She made Mum and Dad and Raven and Vincent. All the best!"

"No..." Kham's voice was quiet and cracked from disuse. "No. Don't put *his* name in with 'the best.' His name has no place in our house."

"But Vincent Wilder is one of the greatest soldiers ever known. You know that. He's very powerful, Dad." Kellyn's dark eyes were wide and innocent, oblivious to the fire she was stoking.

"NO!" he shouted as he slammed his hands down on the table. "I am well aware of how powerful he is! Don't you *ever* forget what that man has done to me, what he has taken from us. His name is not welcome in our house. Kellyn, you will throw that damn figure away. Today." He angrily poked at the tabletop with a stiff finger. The cutlery rattled.

"But, Daddy..." Her little eyes started to water. "Freya made it for me. I don't want to throw it away."

Kham buried his head in his hands, and Callista rubbed a gentle hand across his shoulders. "Kellyn, just put the figure away, OK? Somewhere we don't need to see it. And let's stop talking about Freya, please. That goes for everybody." She cast threatening glances at her three children.

Kellyn began to sob into her hands, tears running over her fingers. Deveron's cheeks burned red. He was close to tears too, but all Soren felt was anger burning inside.

"No, Mum. We will talk about Freya. We should talk about her every day."

His mother leant towards him and hissed, "Soren! It upsets your father."

"I don't care! He's always upset. What difference does one more mention of her make? She shouldn't be forgotten and pushed aside just because our stupid dad isn't tough enough to handle her death!"

"Don't be a prat, Soren," Deveron said, shaking his head. "Dad, we know you're sad, of course, and we don't want to upset you more. Soren doesn't mean to make it worse, but he does have a point. We should talk about Freya and remember her for all the good times we had with her...like when she made these figures for Kellyn. We shouldn't just remember how she died."

There was a heavy silence again. Soren watched as Callista poked at her breakfast, sneaking glances at his father who sat, still as stone, with his hands in his hair. Kellyn's sobs became quieter, and she pushed her chair backwards and jumped down from the table. She ran over to Deveron and threw herself into his arms. He rubbed her back comfortingly.

With her father being so distant, Kellyn had come to look up to her big brother Deveron as a father figure. Deveron had always been caring and supportive, far more so than Soren, who was often too busy to spend time with her.

That wasn't the only guilt building up inside Soren. He had snapped at his father and now he felt bad. "Sorry, Dad," he muttered and then reached up and gingerly patted his father's shoulder. Kham kept his head down but untangled one hand from his mop of dark hair and held onto Soren's hand tightly. Now Soren felt like he could cry too.

Callista gave the tiniest hint of a smile. "I've got a busy few days ahead of me. It's the memorial service at the council hall tomorrow for the local girl who died. I'll be heading there with Kyra. As our healer, she thought she might be able to help with soothing the hearts of mourners."

Kham slowly dragged himself out of his slump and straightened his back. He looked at his son and gave him the slightest hint of a smile before he dropped his hand.

"Mummy, will you get to burn the paper birds this week?" Kellyn asked, sitting back down at the table.

"I will, sweetie. It's such an honour." Callista smiled at her daughter and reached over to push a strand of dark hair from her eyes.

"Can I come?"

Callista hesitated. Soren knew she was debating whether it was wise to let her daughter see the aftermath of death.

Callista smiled at Kellyn. "Of course, baby. Come over after school."

Kellyn gave a wide grin and started tucking back into her cold bacon and eggs. The tension eased slightly and Soren felt himself relax.

"Hey, guess what I'm doing today? After school, I've got a training session with Raven, and he's bringing Deacon too! I get to train with two of the most talented fighters the Children of Light has ever seen! Isn't that great, Dad?" Soren's eyes flared with excitement.

Callista nodded encouragingly, but Kham said nothing. He made the briefest eye contact with Soren before glancing away. Soren knew he should let it go, but somehow he couldn't.

"Dad? Dad? I said I was training with Raven and Deacon today."

His father still ignored him, and Soren felt anger brewing at the back of his throat, waiting to burst out of his mouth.

"Dad!" he shouted. "Did you hear what I said?!"

Kham gave a heavy sigh. "Sorry, Soren. I just don't like you fighting."

"What? Why not?" Soren was hysterical and his voice rose higher and higher. "You fight! Or at least you used to fight before Freya. You can't tell me I shouldn't fight!"

Kham shook his head sadly. "I know I used to fight, and it didn't do me any good, did it? I couldn't save the people who mattered to me. Learning to fight just puts you at the forefront of all the death and suffering. It just increases the chances of you getting killed in battle."

"Is that how you see it?" Soren pushed his chair out behind him and stood up. "You don't care how well I'm doing? You don't care that I am the youngest person ever to be taken on as an apprentice? That Raven himself trains me? You want me to hide away and never learn to defend myself? That's what you did to Freya! You stopped her from learning anything. You never let her fight, and look what happened to her! If she had learnt to fight back, none of this would have happened. You say Vincent killed her, but he didn't. You killed her by not teaching her anything!" he screamed at his father.

Ignoring the pleas from his mother and Kellyn's sobs, Soren snatched up his bag and ran for the door. He fumbled at the lock and finally wrenched the handle open, slamming the door behind him in a huff.

Chapter Four
Guardian

HE YOUNG BOY was stretched out on an operating table, his long limbs dangling over the edges of the uncomfortable metal. He had slipped into unconsciousness an hour ago when he had begun to shake uncontrollably and the weakness in his legs had become too much for him. His body was pale, almost translucent under the harsh white glow of the lights strung above him. His pink eyelids were so thin his light-blue eyes could be seen beneath the papery skin.

Guardian's fourteen years of life to date had been an agonising journey through one affliction to another. Born with a rare disorder, he haemorrhaged blood frequently, passed out from a mere cut and needed almost continuous blood transfusions to stop his system from drying up and shutting down. Unconsciousness was nothing new to him. A few hours ago he had happily sunk into peaceful darkness yet again.

Now, Guardian stirred and gave a deep groan. As consciousness slowly came back to him, he pried his exhausted eyes open and stared, blinking wildly, at the glaring lights. Hovering over him was his father, Vincent Wilder, and Reign, the scientist in charge of his medication. Guardian's heart leapt in his chest. They must be doing experiments on him again. It was the only time his father ever visited the cold, sterile lab on the edge of Meraxor, the place where he had grown up.

He considered fighting them away, squirming from the table and running as far as his atrophied legs could carry him, but he knew there was no point.

There could be no escape from the leader of the Brotherhood of Shadow and a cold-hearted Rhygun.

So he didn't struggle and he didn't complain. Once the pain started, he knew his body would give way to oblivion anyway. He closed his eyes and waited for the blissful darkness to come, trying to blot out the callous voice of his father.

"Do we need to strap him down for this?" Vincent asked, eyeing his son with distaste.

"No," Reign scoffed with an arrogant laugh. "He's too powerless to put up a fight anyway. That's why I enjoy working with this one. He's as weak as a kitten."

Vincent's eyes narrowed with derision, and he looked down his nose at his child. From his prone position on the table, Guardian watched as Reign cast him a sideways glance.

"Are you sure you give your consent for me to do this to your son?"

Vincent stared at Guardian's weak, frail body. "He's no son of mine. I have plenty of strong children, and he isn't one of them."

The words hurt Guardian, but he couldn't show it. There would be no point anyway. Reign shrugged at Vincent's words and walked over to a small table beside where Guardian lay. His singsong voice drifted over the room, washing over Guardian with a fair amount of menace. Vincent, stood with his arms crossed, frowning as Reign spoke.

"As a subject, Guardian has been unresponsive. The boosters I gave him failed to strengthen his system, and the tonics have caused no significant reduction in his symptoms. His illness is getting worse. The only reason he is alive is because he receives continual transfusions to replace his own diseased blood. I've come to the conclusion that he cannot be healed by conventional methods. Eventually, his disease will take over his system. As he gets older, transfusions will no longer be enough to sustain him."

"He'll die?" Vincent asked with no emotion in his cold voice.

"Most probably." Reign lifted a syringe filled with clear liquid from the table and held it up to the light, tapping the glass with his fingernail. "This is the DNA we managed to isolate from the angel. We know it as Ceresecca agent, and it has some miraculous properties. When injected into other subjects, the Ceresecca agent showed a dramatic increase in endorphins, red cell count and adrenaline. But, for a healthy body, the agent was too strong and sent each test subject's nervous system into overdrive. The patients' bodies couldn't cope with the overload and shut down. Every subject died within three hours of the agent being administered."

Reign shuffled up to Guardian's side and turned the boy's arm over so his palm faced the ceiling. He continued, "But this boy's system is already weak and failing. With the addition of the Ceresecca gene, his cells might become fortified and his body stronger."

Vincent nodded, a distant haze descending over his eyes. "Proceed when ready, Reign."

The scientist nodded and took a firm grasp of Guardian's wrist. Guardian tried to struggle, but he could do nothing as Reign pulled his pale, bony arm towards him. Reign lifted the needle up to the barely visible vein and pushed it deep inside. Guardian squirmed with pain, but Reign ignored him and slowly depressed the syringe, unloading the serum into Guardian's bloodstream. When he was finished, Reign withdrew the needle. "And now we wait."

"What will happen to him?" Vincent asked.

Reign chuckled. "I don't know. Let's wait and see."

Cold shivers wracked Guardian's body His skin began to prickle in random areas, but he was blissfully unaware of much else as a fuzzy darkness descended over him. Through the oppressive blackness, all he was aware of was the conversation that seemed to echo around him.

"What's the situation with the Angelis Ceresecca? Any progress?" Vincent's voice fluctuated in volume as he began to pace back and forth across the room.

"None. She is completely unresponsive, as if turned to stone. She doesn't even flinch when cut and shows no signs of recognising sound or light."

"A coma?"

"I don't know if angels can be put in such a state but certainly something similar. Nothing will rouse her. The tests were too severe, and she has completely cut herself off from the outside world. The tests show her body still functions at a basic level. I suspect she may be hoarding what little energy she has left. She could be dangerous when she comes out of this state."

"Lock her in one of the experimentation tanks then, only accessible externally. Then, she can hide in her little coma as long as she likes."

"Will she stay here?" Reign asked.

"Yes, but dump her in one of the unused labs in the basement, out of the way. Nobody will find her there and we can still use her for whatever we need."

Guardian didn't understand any of the things they talked about. Angelis Ceresecca, angels—

none of it made any sense to him, and his interest was dwindling. His mind was much more preoccupied with the burning sensation that he was experiencing in patches all across his body. Intense searing pain, as if somebody were pressing a scalding iron to his skin. He yearned to scratch at it, but his body was weak and aching, unable to move as his thoughts dictated.

He felt Reign return to him, pressing something to his chest (presumably to check his breathing). "He appears to be developing red lesions on his skin. But that is nothing unusual for a patient with Guardian's blood condition. No other major changes yet. It may take a while."

"Call for me when something happens," Vincent muttered, and Guardian heard the bang of the door as he left the room.

Ignoring the intense yearning to tear his own skin to shreds, Guardian listened as Reign shuffled around the laboratory, muttering under his breath. The scientist talked through each of his experiments, drawing details from his impeccable memory and reeling off the current status of each of his genetic manipulations and chemical trials. Genetics was his area of passion, and anybody could see that he revelled in playing God with his breeding. Mixing races, classes and even species produced all sorts of results that the half-demon was fascinated by. Guardian knew from listening to his mumblings that this was the first time he'd had access to angel genes.

As Guardian's agony began to peak and the searing burns on his skin became too much, he eventually passed out, his weak body unable to take the stress anymore.

When Guardian finally awoke, Reign was hovering over him excitedly. Guardian concentrated on his heartbeat. The incessant thump of his strained heart was conspicuously absent. He was surprised to feel a calm, regulated beat in its place. His skin still burned like crazy and was now weeping with a sticky, yellow pus that stung and smelled bad.

The Rhygun obviously noticed the same changes, as he pressed the cold metal instrument to Guardian's chest again to check his heartbeat. Wandering away, muttering in an excitable voice, he said things that meant nothing to Guardian but that he presumed must have been positive.

"Ninety beats per minute. Amazing. Significant improvement on two hundred. Hmmm, sores still seeping though."

Guardian blinked myopically, trying to force the blur from his eyes. As his vision cleared, he saw Reign scurry to the guard stationed at the door. "Fetch Vincent now," Reign barked and the guard left.

There was another half an hour or more of Guardian lying still, gathering strength and basking in his new healthy condition. He flexed joints that usually riddled him with agony and sucked in deep lungfuls of crisp air that would normally have reduced him to a wheezing mess. Whatever it was that Reign had injected him with this time, it definitely had Guardian's approval.

Reign was still buzzing excitedly around the room when Vincent stormed in. "Did it work?" he barked.

"His vitals have improved." Reign scurried over and poked at Guardian's pale cheek. "But his eyes still look sunken. When the virus was first introduced, he suffered these abscesses and lesions. See? They look a bit like burns, as if the toxin seared his skin from the inside. Interesting."

"Well, the Ceresecca DNA didn't kill him at least," Vincent muttered.

Guardian strained to raise his head from the table as Reign stuck a needle in his forearm and pulled on the syringe, drawing blood slowly into the attached vial. Reign frowned and held it up to the light. "Hmm, still dark in tone and thick. I was hoping his blood might thin and reach average viscosity." He rushed the vial over to the work surface at the side of the room, sucked a single drop of blood into a pipette and dropped it on a slide. With hands quivering from excitement, Guardian watched him place the slide beneath the microscope and peer through.

After ten minutes or more of scanning every millimetre thoroughly, Reign whipped his head back up. "This isn't right, Vincent. Look at this."

Vincent walked over and bent down to peer through the microscope. An irritated frown marked his dark features as he straightened back up. "It's just blood. It means nothing to me."

Reign tutted and rolled his piercing eyes. "Don't you see? The cells have developed a thin membrane. Almost like something has coated each cell, like a support propping them up."

"That's good, right? Isn't that what you wanted to happen?"

Reign scoffed. "Yes, of course, but the cell itself is still weak and diseased. The covering around it will do nothing if the cell itself is still defected." Reign banged a furious fist on the work surface, causing everything to rattle violently.

"It's all been for nothing! All for nothing! If Guardian still has the disease, he will still need blood transfusions. He is a failure."

Vincent's eyes narrowed. "At least some of his symptoms have improved, so there is some hope. Keep him alive for now. Give him his usual transfusion, I suppose."

Guardian was used to hearing himself spoken about in such a way and it had little impact on him, even when he heard Reign muttering beneath his breath about flushing waste away. He was almost surprised when Reign scurried over to the ice barrel in the corner and fetched a vial of clean blood. He attached a clear tube to the vial and the other end to the needle he had used to draw Guardian's diseased blood. He roughly pushed the needle back into Guardian's pale veins and began pumping the blood into him.

The effect was instantaneous. Guardian gasped with shock at the tremors that shook his body. A wave of comfort washed over him and all the pain from the abscesses on his skin was suppressed. Guardian closed his eyes to absorb the pleasant sensations. It usually took at least half an hour for the blood to settle into his system and for him to improve, but this time he felt a rush of energy and strength flood over him immediately.

Reign muttered to himself in delighted surprise. "Pallor rosy. Gaunt cheeks now filled out. Sunken eyes have lost their shadow."

Guardian opened his eyes, desperate to get a look at what he felt was a new and improved body. Reign nearly leapt backwards in shock when Guardian's eyes snapped open. "Incredible! Eyes have changed hue. No longer pale blue but burning red."

The transfusion wasn't even finished when Guardian pulled himself up to a seated position. He fixed his shining red eyes on Reign and Vincent and he smiled. "What did you do to me?"

A satisfied smirk crept across Vincent's face. "It looks like we fixed you."

"Is it gone? My sickness?"

Reign shrugged his shoulders. "Let's see."

Guardian stretched an arm out, noting with amazement that his skin was no longer deathly pale but instead a healthy cream. The remnants of the hideous, weeping sores that had covered his skin were still there, but they no longer hurt and they were scabbing over quickly.

Reign took another vial of blood, the red liquid flowing more easily now. Reign peered into the microscope and made numerous gasps and hums before turning to face Vincent and Guardian.

"This is incredible. The disease still exists. Guardian, your sickness lies dormant deep inside your cells, but the Angelis Ceresecca DNA was activated once you received the clean blood. When your red cell count was low, there was nothing. But top you up and the benefits show. It worked! Your system is fortified. You should be able to do all the things you've never done before!"

Reign's shoulders dipped up and down, and he giggled in a bizarrely high-pitched voice. Guardian's heart leapt in his chest. "Really? Could I run?" he asked his father, but Vincent shrugged his shoulders noncommittally.

"Get up and try it out!" Reign squeaked in excitement. Guardian swung his legs from the table. Since birth, he'd had to be slow and steady when standing. His balance had to adjust and if he was too quick, he would become dizzy and pass out. This time, he jumped down confidently and stood proudly upon legs which suddenly looked athletic and strong.

"Incredible," Reign whispered as Guardian strode around the room.

"How do you feel?" Vincent asked in a gruff, deep voice.

Guardian stopped pacing. A grin crept across his face. "I feel better than I've ever felt before. But my back hurts. Up here at my shoulder blades."

He pointed over his shoulder. Reign ran behind him. Another loud gasp issued from Reign's lips, and he clapped his hands over his mouth.

"What is it?" Vincent asked, but Reign couldn't speak. He nodded at Guardian's back. Vincent walked around to look for himself.

"Amazing," Vincent stammered in a hushed voice.

"What? What's wrong?" Guardian asked.

Reign managed to find his voice. "I think...I think you're growing wings."

They stood behind him and watched, shocked into silence as painful spasms wracked Guardian's shoulder blades. There was a ripping sensation and bony protrusions began to tear through Guardian's shirt with tiny tufts of grey feathers stuck to the ends. Though his superiors were shocked, Guardian felt empowered, unstoppable, and he flexed his shoulders to help the bones break free. When his wings had unfurled completely, Guardian struck an imposing figure, a young boy but with a huge wingspan, spreading out like a fan behind him.

They spent the next two days testing Guardian's new abilities. He could run farther and faster than many of his peers, could lift tremendous weights, and one flap of his enormous wings could propel him high into the sky. But by the end of the second day in his new state, Guardian started to feel nauseous whenever he ran and sick and dizzy when he flew. His body began to shake and shiver and his sickly pale hue returned. His heart pounded furiously, even when he was seated, and the smallest movements made him sluggish and tired again. The hideous sores returned, and, when he clawed at the maddening itch, his skin broke open in bleeding, infected wounds.

His mood changed drastically by the third day. Despite the care and attention Reign paid his subject, Guardian continually felt exhausted and confused. The intense irritation in his skin was pushing him to the edge of his sanity. He didn't understand where his new vigour and strength had gone, but, more than that, he couldn't control his anger. Fury bubbled inside of him, and darkness brewed in his heart, an evil desire for malice. By midday, he had already smashed half of the equipment in the lab.

Although it irritated him, Guardian allowed Reign to observe him at a distance, seeing the interest in the Rhygun's eyes as he watched Guardian's humanity decline. The Ceresecca DNA still coated his cells, so his strength was still impressive, his mind callous and brutal, but the disease he had been born with raged once more beneath the surface.

Reign watched him all the time, with a curious sneer across his lips. Despite the fierce nature of the sickness ravaging Guardian, he knew that Reign could have cured him if he really wanted to, but he was clearly having too much fun watching what the Ceresecca DNA was doing to his young subject. It seemed to be protecting his system. He wouldn't die—he was sure of that—but he could also feel his disease eating at his body and his mind. Eventually, he guessed it would destroy his humanity, but Reign cared little for Guardian's welfare. He never had wanted to help cure him. The disgusting Rhygun's only interest was in research and creating the most efficient human weapons he could.

So Reign held back on treating Guardian and allowed his disease to run rampant. After six days, Guardian's body had withered and shrunk, his skin covered in continually weeping necrotic sores, but it was the ferociousness in his intense red eyes that seemed to interest Reign the most.

With the overbearing stench of sulphur that followed him around, he would lean close to Guardian and observe him carefully. It drove Guardian mad. More and more he felt that he could barely contain his brutality, always on the verge of a vicious assault. His assertion proved to be true when a guard arrived to deliver a message. Guardian was powerless, a slave to his own intense desire for destruction, as his fierce ruby eyes locked onto the guard. The unsuspecting man had barely said the first words of his message when Guardian attacked. His sickness forgotten, he launched himself at the unsuspecting soldier and sent him reeling backwards.

His jagged fingernails clawed frantically at the man's neck, ripping his skin open in deep gashes. Guardian's thin legs wrapped around the guard and locked him in place, as he sat atop the man's struggling body and bent down to his neck. Placing his pale lips on the guard's jugular vein, he lapped thirstily at the blood that dripped from the scratch wounds, ignoring the man's desperate cries for freedom.

When the wounds were clean, Guardian tore at him again, raking more skin and veins open and then drank hungrily, gnawing at the torn flesh, sucking every drop of blood from the ravaged throat. As the man's cries died down, he fell limp, Guardian sat upright and looked at the bemused and fascinated Reign. Guardian's eyes were shining brightly once more, his skin full and rich in colour and his limbs strong and healthy again. He looked down at the blood-ied body of the man beneath him.

"I'm sorry. I didn't mean to kill him. It just happened."

A delighted grin crept across Reign's face. He sent a guard to fetch his master and stood grinning as Vincent entered and froze before the body of the guard. His dark eyes widened.

"What happened here?" His voice was thick with suspicion and distrust.

"Guardian happened," Reign replied and cast another maniacal smile at Guardian, who grinned back, dizzy with the adrenaline of his new-found power.

Reign explained everything to Vincent—Guardian's decline, his increased brutality and his violent attack on the guard. When he explained the effect the blood had on him, the same manic smile flooded Vincent's eyes.

"Are you saying that giving him blood makes him strong and depriving him of blood makes him homicidal?"

That psychotic grin again. "That's exactly what I'm saying."

Guardian felt giddy with excitement as the same look of delight crept across Vincent's face.

"It's like some sort of double-edged weapon. Unleash Guardian upon the Children of Light and they wouldn't stand a chance. Give him blood, and he's too strong to defeat. Deprive him of blood, and he's murderous. They'd have to kill him, and they wouldn't be able to get close enough to him in either state."

Another giggle from Reign. "If we could get him inside their villages and palaces, we'd be unstoppable." He hesitated. "The problem is that he's unpredictable. There's every chance that if we released him, we wouldn't get him back again."

In just a few short days, Guardian's whole life had changed beyond all recognition and his mind was reeling with the opportunities his new condition might bring. Just to be able to run again would have been more than he could have wished for, but flying and containing such incredible power? It was a dream come true. Vincent had given him a gift above all others, and he would happily use his skills as a weapon if that's what his father desired.

"Reign," Vincent asked slowly, turning to the Rhygun, "could you isolate the effects of this new disease in Guardian's blood?"

Guardian stretched an arm out willingly, allowing Reign to extract another syringe of blood and examine it closely. "The virus itself is easy to isolate. The contaminated cells are coated in Ceresecca DNA. That's what's giving him the strength and stopping the disease from killing the host."

Vincent's eyes were wide with excitement. "Could you extract the virus along with the Ceresecca DNA? Could it be given to another person?"

"It might take some work, but, yes, I believe I could."

Vincent's head was reeling with the possibilities. "We may not be able to release Guardian into their towns, but if we could get that virus into members of the Children of Light..."

"They would lose their minds and eventually tear each other to shreds."

Chapter Five
Unity

OREN SLAMMED THE FRONT DOOR of his house behind him in a huff. His fingers were clenched tightly into fists, and he ground his teeth together, cursing the world through angry jaws. His eyes softened as he saw a girl walking towards his house, a warm smile dancing on her lips. All the bitterness and tension drifted away, and he gave her a giddy smile.

"Jade! I didn't know you came this way," Soren called to her, as he skipped lightly down the steps at the front of his house.

She smiled coyly. "I don't usually. I live on the other side of town, but I came this way hoping to find a certain prince to walk in with."

Soren's stomach performed an acrobatic leap, and he felt his cheeks prickle as they flushed red. No other children from their school lived around this part of town. It had been one of the things that had irritated Soren when they had first moved to Fallway from the capital city of Nazaki.

Soren's family had lived in Nazaki for years so that Callista could govern the nation of Alcherys from the capital. They still lived there really, or at least Soren liked to think they did. Their house remained untouched, and they could return to it whenever Callista felt they were finished in Fallway. It had been three years that Soren's family had been living in Fallway, ever since relations had soured with their neighbouring nation, Parador. Callista had left the capital in the capable hands of her second-in-command and had moved her family out to Fallway, a small trading town right on the border between Alcherys and

Parador. It had been a gesture of peace aimed at the Paradoran people to show that the royal family didn't think themselves above the common people.

As far as Soren was concerned, it still looked at little like they thought themselves above the rest though. Most of the children in Fallway attended the ordinary Paradoran schools. Only a select few were part of a special experimental schooling project set up by Callista and Prince Ezra Khaled of Parador. The whole idea was for the children of the two nations to mix, make friendships and pave the way for peace. None of that really mattered to Soren though. The only thing he cared about was the fact that none of his fellow students lived anywhere near him, which meant that Jade had come here looking specifically for Soren. The thought made his head swim.

He cursed his cheeks for burning and tried to act cool and aloof. He cast her a quick sideways glance to see if she had noticed his embarrassment, but her stunning emerald eyes were set ahead. He took the opportunity to examine her exotic features. Those intense green eyes grabbed his attention first, so bright and vivid. Her eyes were a beautiful shape, narrow and piercing, and were made all the more interesting by her heavy, dark eyelids. When she smiled, she looked cunning and intelligent. She was slightly taller than Soren, despite being six months younger. Her light brown hair swished behind her back when she walked, and she brushed it away from her delicate features, exposing creamy skin with light freckles dotted across her nose and cheeks.

She turned to Soren. "What's wrong with you today? You seemed annoyed when you stepped out of your house."

Soren shrugged his shoulders. "Just stupid parents. You know how it is. They never listen."

Jade cast her eyes to the ground. "I know what you mean. My dad can get pretty angry, and my mum's crazy. I mean, literally. She just takes lots of pills and then crashes out asleep. Nothing I say to her goes in."

Soren suddenly felt tremendously guilty. He moaned about his parents, thinking they were dreadful, but he never thought Jade's situation could be worse than his. And the truth was that he knew why his parents were distant and why they didn't always respond to his wishes. They were mourning. Suddenly, he didn't feel as unlucky, and he let his bitterness drift away.

They walked through the narrow, winding streets of Fallway together and headed towards the school. Soren pranced around, trying to make Jade laugh by walking in funny ways and putting on high-pitched voices. Jade giggled at his clowning around but said little in return. She watched him closely, smiling at his blatant attempts to impress her. He knew he was making a fool of himself, but for as long as she was entertained, he'd keep playing the jester.

By the time they reached the school, Jade was laughing hysterically and her pretty, freckled nose was crinkled and flushed pink. Soren, who was now covered in flecks of mud after jumping across every filthy puddle they could find, glowed inside at the sound of her laughter. He made an attempt to wipe off as much mud as possible on the nearby bushes and tried to force his face into a serious, contemplative expression, which just made Jade laugh more.

The School of Unity was surrounded by tall, iron gates which seemed excessive to Soren. They didn't need to keep the children locked in and shouldn't need to keep anybody else out as far as he was concerned. This wasn't a dangerous town, and there were no real threats to his mind. When Callista and Khaled had set the school up, Callista had insisted on the gates, saying that there were radical groups in Parador who didn't approve of the union between the two nations. She said that the school could be a prime target for Brotherhood of Shadow agents who wanted to make a statement. Khaled hadn't seen the problem. He said the groups disagreed with the peace treaty, but they weren't violent. Soren knew this was just another example of his mother overreacting. Since Freya died, she saw danger everywhere.

Soren and Jade passed through the opening in the gates and walked into the schoolyard.

"Oh no," Jade said quietly. "We're late. Everyone's already gone in."

They ran up the steps, and Soren yanked the door open. They thundered down the long corridor and past the two other classes. On their left was the kindergarten. A wave of noise hit them from behind the closed door, the laughter and sounds of children playing. Soren glanced through the glass door as they passed and saw a group of five-year-olds squabbling over a toy.

As Soren and Jade ran further down the passageway, they passed the senior class on their right, where the teenagers worked in silence. Soren's brother Deveron was in the seat nearest to the door, bent over his desk and engrossed in his writing.

At the end of the corridor was the door to the junior class, where the six-to twelve-year-old children studied. Soren and Jade stopped for a moment to compose themselves before they went in. Soren slowly turned the handle, his heart thumping in his chest, mind frantically racing to come up with an acceptable excuse. As soon as they entered, the teacher, a young woman from the next town over, fixed them in a glare.

"Soren Nitaya and Jade Wessel." She tapped her foot on the wooden floor. "What was it this time? A storm held you up, did it? You had to deliver an urgent message to a made-up family member?"

Soren's cheeks flushed red, and he stuttered over his words. "No, we just...well...I had some family issues."

"If you're going to make up an excuse, Soren, at least make it believable. Your brother and sister got in on time, as usual." She raised her eyebrows, challenging him to attempt another lie. He hung his head in shame and said nothing more.

"Jade?" The teacher turned to her, looking for an explanation.

Jade held her head high and met the teacher's eyes with a confident smirk. "Me and Soren were having fun and lost track of time."

The teacher was taken aback by her daring forthrightness. "Well, at least you've been honest, I guess. Hurry up and take your seats. Soren, I'll be writing to your mother. *Again.*"

Soren glanced sheepishly at Jade as they made their way to their tables. The edges of her mouth curled in a proud smile. Soren felt quite sure he had never admired somebody so much in his life.

They took their seats at separate tables. They hadn't been allowed to sit together since Soren had been caught flicking pieces of paper into the ears of other pupils on Jade's orders. The teacher kept them away from each other as much as possible, but they always found new and inventive ways to communicate surreptitiously. Soren sat near to the front of class at a table with three other boys, none of whom he really spoke to. Jade went right to the back of the room and sat next to a boy she detested.

There were only eleven children in Soren's class so far, but every week one or two more would apply for a place. It was arguably the best school in the entire nation of Parador as Callista ensured it was funded with Children of Light gold. Some parents didn't like their children mixing with the sons and daughters of the warring country, while others hoped that making alliances would help to protect their offspring in later years. It had been a political minefield when it was first set up, but the operation had been running for a year with no issues and more people were warming to the idea of the best teachers in Alcherys educating their children.

The morning dragged on for Soren. He barely listened as they worked through mathematics and literature. He gave minimal effort and did only what was necessary to get him through the lessons. The teacher recognised his complacency and began to watch him like a hawk, hovering behind him as he worked. Her constant looming presence grated on Soren's nerves, and he slowed his pace even further, pretending to struggle on the simplest of questions. After half an hour of trying over and over to explain a method Soren understood only too well, the teacher gave up and left him to do it on his own. He rapidly scribbled the correct answers down and then sat back with his arms crossed, whistling loudly.

He earned a detention at morning break and winked smugly to Jade as she filed out with the others into the yard. She grinned at him as he sat back in his seat feeling pleased with himself, until the teacher ordered him to write three hundred words about why he should always try his best. He grumbled as he began to scrawl his ideas down, making sure he used his messiest writing.

After recess, Soren's attitude changed. The lesson was history and politics, something Soren genuinely enjoyed and, more than that, felt was useful to him in his career as a Children of Light soldier. He was quite sure that he would grow up to be one of the greatest generals the army had ever seen and that he would follow in the footsteps of the fabled warriors of Light such as Raven, Deacon and Soren's own mother. If he was to be a great leader of his people, he needed to know their history and how their enemies and allies worked.

The rapid change in his attitude was noticed by the teacher, who assumed her punishment had fixed his behaviour. She smiled at him, pleased with his concentration, and asked him to read aloud to the class from the *Annals of History*, a thick tome which chronicled the history of Alcherys, Meraxor and Parador. Soren took a deep breath and began to read.

"*The great war between the Children of Light and the Brotherhood of Shadow has raged for many years. Over this time, numerous disasters and...atro....atrocities?*" Soren attempted the word and glanced up for the teacher's approval. She nodded her encouragement, and he continued, "*...atrocities have been committed in the name of Alcherys or Meraxor. Many lives have been lost and civ...civilisations destroyed, not...not...notably the destruction of Terralia following the D.U.S.K. crisis. However, during this time there has been sig...significant advancement in the fields of medicine, construction and agriculture. Though there is always the threat of war at the edges of Parador, ordinary civilians have profited greatly from the* *ongoing co...conf...conflict. The standard of living has improved across the nation with Alcheran and Meraxan medicine and goods enriching the lives of Paradoran citizens. Tradesmen and farmers are able to make excellent profits from dealing with the two nations and, as a result, Parador's economy is booming."*

Soren stopped reading and looked up to a wide smile from the teacher.

"Beautifully read, Soren. Thank you." She nodded in his direction and, embarrassed but secretly pleased with himself, he looked away. She continued, "As explained in that extract, we can see that the war between Alcherys and Meraxor, as the nations of the Children of Light and the Brotherhood of Shadow, has been good for Parador. We have been able to profit from the war—that means make money—and our medicine, buildings and education are much better now, thanks to the support from both armies. Paradorans enjoy protection from both armies without actually being ruled by either. So the war is good for Parador.

"However, many lives are lost every day because of this war, and many innocent people's lives are ruined. Now, your job is to decide whether the technology and medicine developed in the name of the war is worth the death and destruction it brings. Get yourself into pairs and discuss it. I'll be expecting a presentation from each group outlining your conclusions."

Within seconds of her finishing the sentence, Soren was on his feet and beside Jade. "Wanna work together?"

She merely smiled in response, and they settled down side by side to discuss the project. Soren got straight into it, tossing out arguments on why the war was good for all civilisations, not just Parador. He fervently defended the way the Children of Light supported the minor nations and offered military aid and resources.

"All of the tiny towns out there living in the Dark Ages would never have developed without our support. That's what Mum's always saying. The Brotherhood only want to kill people and steal their belongings, but we want to help them. Their lives are better as a result of the war, even if some people die sometimes."

Jade listened quietly, watching as the passion grew in his expression. When he finally paused for breath, she gave a wry laugh.

"Who cares? Things are the way they are. Life is as it is. Maybe it helped my family, maybe we'd have been better off without it. I'm not interested right now."

Soren was taken aback. The political edge he'd gained from his mother balked at her dismissal of something so important. But all bitterness disappeared when she reached out with her slender fingers and gently stroked his hand. He immediately blushed and felt awkward in his own skin, but inside, his heart danced.

She ran her hand up to his wrist and gently pulled his sleeve back. "Show me again."

Soren cast a tentative glance around the classroom to check the teacher wasn't watching and then shuffled closer to Jade and pulled his sleeve back enough for her to see the peculiar markings he had been born with. Strange, scratchy lines like bristles marked his wrist in a line down the right side, then three rough, raised circles like the old scars of some awful pox.

"Amazing," she murmured, staring at the marks, her eyes roaming over the ugly patterns. "Did you have an accident?"

"No, I was just born with them."

"Does the rest of your family have them?"

"No, just me. I'm a freak. Everybody says so."

Jade hesitated and then spoke quietly. "Did your sister Freya have them?"

Soren's eyes dropped to the floor. "No, just me."

"How did Freya die?" Jade asked, her eyes roaming over his face.

No matter how much he wanted to tell her, no matter how much the truth was burning inside of him and he yearned to just spit it out, he couldn't. He wasn't ready, even after all this time. It was like there was a physical barrier stopping him form saying the words. So he said nothing at all.

Jade looked at him for a while, waiting for an answer, but when none came she didn't push him. He was thankful for that, and even more thankful when she gently ran her fingers across his birthmarks.

Every instinct in him yearned to pull his hand away, to cover up the marks he detested so much, the marks he'd been mocked for all his life. But he didn't move a muscle because her hand touching his felt so nice he never wanted it to end. Eventually, she let go of his hand and he hurriedly pulled his sleeve back down.

"Anyway, let's get back to this project," Soren muttered and began gathering their papers back up, when Jade's hand slammed down onto the table, pinning their work to the desk.

42

"I know a secret," she whispered. Her eyes widened with excitement. "Wanna know it?"

"Sure."

"Don't worry. It's about the project...in a way. I've heard a rumour. In fact, it's more than a rumour. It's a fact. We're talking about scientific discoveries and stuff. Well, I happen to know of a Brotherhood of Shadow research facility near to here."

Soren frowned sceptically. "The Brotherhood haven't got anything anywhere near here. We're fifty miles from Meraxor."

She threw her head back and laughed. "Yeah, well the Brotherhood doesn't care for boundaries, does it? Trust me, there's an old facility here in Parador, a warehouse where they used to keep dodgy medicines and potions and stuff. It's abandoned. Has been for years. But my cousin Delia said she found a broken window and looked in, and all their old stuff is still there. Just think what amazing things there would be."

Soren scoffed. "Amazing how? Just elixir probably. That's boring. Everybody gets one of those anyway."

Jade laughed again. "Soren, you're so naive! Don't you know what the Brotherhood is working on these days? Tonics that boost strength and speed. Shots that turn an average boy into a super soldier. There's even a story that there's something that gives you special powers, the ability to cast magic. And it's all just left there, unguarded."

Soren couldn't possibly believe what she said was true, but his interest was certainly piqued. "Nobody guards it at all? Not ever?"

She smiled cunningly and shook her head. "Just think, Soren. You're an amazing soldier now. What would you be like with that kind of power?"

He gazed into the distance and his head clouded with visions of what he could achieve for his family and his people. He could save them all. He could win the war for the Children. He could get revenge for his sister's death. When he snapped out of his reverie, Jade was staring at him closely, analysing his expression with her intense eyes.

"Let's do it." He leaned in closely to Jade and hissed the words with excitement. "Let's go together and explore the building tomorrow morning. We could creep out early and both get the magic."

She shook her head slowly. "I've got a better idea. I don't want the powers. I want you to have them."

Soren couldn't help the mocking scepticism that crept into his voice. "You don't want powers? Are you mad? Why wouldn't you want them?"

Shrugging her shoulders, she brushed his questions aside. "I'm not interested. I don't want to be a hero. It must be exhausting. You, however, would be amazing, incredible, the greatest soldier the world has ever known."

Hearing her speak about him like that made Soren's chest swell up with pride. "I want to be a hero."

"I know you do, and you could be one. Easily. But part of being a hero is being brave. That's why you need to go to this facility by yourself. It's part of the challenge."

"You're not even coming with me?"

"I'll never get away with leaving our house in the morning. That's when I have to do all my chores and if I wasn't there Dad would skin me alive."

"I'd get in trouble with my parents too."

"Maybe, but you're a hero, right? So a little telling off from your parents won't bother you. You're a *hero*," she stressed the word. "A *hero*, Soren. I'm not cut out for that, but you are."

Soren nodded, frowning. "You're right. If it's me that wants to be a hero, it should be me that goes. I can do it. I'll sneak out early tomorrow morning."

"You're not brave enough."

"What?"

"Prove you're brave enough by sneaking out of this lesson. Now. Right now. Underneath the teacher's nose. I dare you. I bet you can't sneak out of class this minute. If you do it, I'll know you're brave enough, and then you can go to the facility tomorrow morning."

Soren laughed at her hysterically before noting the serious look in her eye. "Tell me you're joking. What does sneaking out of class now have to do with getting to that laboratory?"

"Because I won't tell you exactly where it is unless I think you're brave enough."

"So, you'll tell me if I sneak out now?"

She nodded, a mischievous look in her eye. "I'll send a dryll in the morning and give you directions if you pass the test. If you do this, it would make me happy. So happy that...I might be your girlfriend."

His laughter stopped abruptly. "I don't want you to be my girlfriend."

"Don't you?" A devilish look glinted in her eye.

"No," he muttered uncertainly.

"OK. Don't do it, and I won't be your girlfriend then." She turned back to the work before them.

"OK. I'll do it." He ducked beneath the table and grabbed the backpack that he used to carry his books. He reached inside and pulled out a small black capsule. "This is a smoke bomb. Me and my mentor Raven use them in training. It makes a big cloud of black smoke. It's for hiding yourself as you attack an enemy, but I could use it to distract the teacher while I escape."

She grinned and her eyes flashed mischievously. "Do it."

He stood up and gripped the capsule in his fist. His heart pounded in his chest. His mother would go mad, but that was something he could deal with later. The fiery excitement in Jade's eyes was all he needed to worry about right now.

He inhaled deeply and then threw the capsule down as hard as he could. The room immediately disappeared in a huge cloud of darkness as plumes of thick smoke erupted around them. The screams and squeals of the other pupils were lost amongst the billowing darkness and Soren wound his way through the tables using his hands to navigate. Used to finding his way around in the blinding smoke, he easily made his way to the door while all around him the other students and the teacher floundered and flapped hysterically.

He found the door handle and yanked it open, causing smoke to flow out into the corridor beyond. As he stepped out, he took a look back over his shoulder but could see nothing through the swirling grey. He pulled the door closed behind him with a mixture of triumph and guilt.

Chapter Six
The Star of Dishonour

 OREN STEPPED out of the classroom and pulled the door shut behind him as quickly as he could. He hurriedly crept away, down the corridor and out through the main exit. The mid-morning warmth shone on him, and he grinned. There were some definite benefits to bunking out of class on a fine day. But there was no time to mess around in the sun. He had proven himself to Jade now, and he had to plan tomorrow's mission.

Pacing back and forth in the woods outside the town, he kicked about in the leaves for a while with the best intentions to put a plan together, but before long he realised he had no idea where to start. What would he need for a journey into the wild lands of a foreign country? Would it be a long way to this facility? Did he need to take food and water?

He wondered if he could make it there and back without needing a pack of supplies because really couldn't be bothered with all that. But one thing was certain. He wasn't going anywhere without his sword. He would never head into unfamiliar territory unarmed. In fact, he'd never head anywhere unarmed if it was up to him. He'd take his sword everywhere if it weren't for the school banning weapons (a rule that Soren thought was ludicrous).

Whatever happened, he needed to have everything ready for the morning. He didn't know how long the journey would take, but being organised was crucial. All he wanted to do was run back home and make plans, gather resources, but it was late morning. He couldn't just walk over to his house. If any Children of Light members saw him, they'd drag him back to school. If his mentor, Raven, caught him he'd be in all sorts of trouble. He knew he'd have to wait a few hours until it was at least plausible that he'd been let out at lunchtime. So he'd have to entertain himself until then.

There wasn't a lot to do in Fallway, especially when all the other kids were at school, so he headed to the market square, which was quiet today with only nine stalls selling their wares. A handful of customers wandered lazily around with canvas bags in tow. Soren casually strolled by the tradesmen, eyeing up their goods. A mischievous thought entered his head. He stopped by a bread store and took a crusty loaf in his hand. The seller shuffled over with a suspicious look in his eyes. Soren weighed him up.

His white shirt was barely fastened over his enormous belly, the buttons nearly popping under the strain. A dark jacket adorned his shoulders but was too small to fasten across his chest. Soren grinned, raised his eyebrows at the man as a challenge and then sprinted off with the loaf in his hand.

The man yelled and cursed as he huffed angrily behind Soren, his great belly wobbling and beads of sweat flying from his hulking form. Soren shot around the edge of the market in a wide arc around the backs of the other stalls. Market sellers and shoppers alike stopped and stared at the young thief and the enormous, red-faced mountain of fury chasing him.

Soren nearly ran into a young couple who strolled arm in arm through the market. They pulled up short with gasps of surprise. Soren sidestepped them and powered on, laughing at the top of his voice as the tradesman went barrelling into them.

All three ended up in a pile on the ground, and Soren slowed his pace and turned to watch. The seller scrambled to his feet, showering the shocked but uninjured couple with apologies. With a roar of anger, he began chasing Soren again, who laughed uproariously. Soren's little legs moved quickly. He continued his great circle, bringing him back to the very store he'd stolen from. Casting a mocking smirk back at the wheezing storekeeper, he dropped the bread back onto the stall. He took off across the centre of the market where he could safely stop and watch the bewildered seller, who placed both hands on his knees and bent over double trying to get his breath back.

Soren laughed so hard that he struggled to breathe. He was taken by surprise when a firm hand grabbed his shoulder.

"What do you think you're doing?" It was the harsh, strong tone of one of the town guards. Known for their zero-tolerance approach to crime, just fear of them kept most people in order. As soon as Soren laid eyes on the guard, he knew this wouldn't be good.

He immediately went on the defensive. "What? I didn't do anything!" His heart pounded, but he held his head high and straightened his back so he stood tall and confident. The spluttering, lumbering stall-owner staggered up to them.

"It was him! He stole my bread, the little..."

The guard squeezed Soren's shoulder, and Soren winced with the pain. "I didn't do anything!" he squealed.

"I saw you, so don't try to lie your way out of this. You know what we do with thieves in this town, don't you? You need marking."

He pulled a short-bladed knife from his pocket and held it up in front of Soren's face.

"No! I didn't steal it. I put it back. If you saw me, you should have seen that I put it back again. I don't have it now, do I?" He held his hands out wide to show they were empty.

"Well, you panicked when you were being chased, and you put it back. But your intention was clear, and that's enough."

The guard dragged Soren by the shoulder until they stood before another stall selling spices and herbs. There was a table which was mostly clear and the guard grabbed Soren's left hand and slammed it onto the table. Twisting it brutally, he flipped Soren's hand over, so the palm was facing upwards.

Soren yelped with pain and discomfort. His senses went into overload, and his instincts screamed for his sword. With all the training he'd had, he could fight them with his bare hands, but it had all happened so quickly that he hadn't had the time to compose himself. Now his stronger hand was trapped, his body skewed at a strange angle. He couldn't move.

The storekeeper smiled coldly, pleased to see justice being carried out. He helped by holding Soren's arm down firmly as the guard yanked Soren's sleeve up to his elbow. The guard paused for a moment, frowning in fascination at the strange red birthmark on Soren's wrist. It was ugly and unusual and the guard had clearly never seen anything like it before.

He stared more closely and screwed his nose up in disgust. "What's wrong with your arm? You're a freak."

Soren felt his face flush scarlet with humiliation. He'd always been sensitive about his birthmark. It had marked him out as different all of his life, and he hated it.

"It's not my fault. I was born with it."

The guard scoffed with distaste. "It's disgusting, you little freak. You look deformed."

He nodded to the storekeeper who pressed down on Soren's forearm even harder, pinning him down with hands like vices. Soren cried out in agony. It felt as if his arm was about to break under the pressure. He didn't dare move an inch.

Taking his knife in his hand again, the guard pressed the razor sharp point to the fleshy part of Soren's thumb. He pushed down until a puddle of blood welled up. Soren cried out in fear, as the guard began to talk him through the punishment.

"In accordance with Paradoran law, anybody caught stealing will be sentenced to appropriate punishment. The thief will have a blade drawn across their hand from the tip of each finger to the centre of the palm to mark them with the star of dishonour. The cuts shall be deep enough that the scars will be visible for life—to let all honest people know they are not to be trusted."

Soren began to shake with fear. "Please, I'm sorry. I was just playing a trick. I never meant to steal. Please believe me," he whimpered.

"Stop lying, you little freak! You can't go through life doing whatever you want without having to face the consequences. This is for your own good, and now your parents will know what you've been doing too."

His parents! The thought hit Soren like a bolt of lightning.

"You can't mark me. My mother will be furious."

The guard and stall owner looked at each other and laughed out loud. "What can she do about it? The law is the law."

"But my mother is Callista Nienna!" he cried.

They froze and looked at each other. Soren saw their surprised expressions and pushed the point further. "I am Soren Nitaya, son of Callista Nienna and Kham Nitaya. I'm part of the inclusion program in Fallway. My mother is in the town hall holding counsel right now. Take me there if you don't believe me."

They hesitated. Soren could see nervous sweat break out on the large storekeeper's brow. The guard pulled the blade away from Soren's hand, and the puddle of blood ran over his finger and onto the table underneath. He released his grip on Soren's hand, and Soren dragged it away as quickly as he could and nursed his sore, dripping finger.

The guard was shifting nervously from one foot to the other, a worried frown creasing his forehead. "I didn't know you were a Child of Light. I would never do anything to hurt or offend the royal family. Please believe me. My loyalty is yours, always. I was just doing my job," he stammered. "If you come with me, I can fetch you a bandage."

The storekeeper, whose face had lost all of its colour, chipped up in a voice far more polite than it had been just minutes before. "You won't tell your mother of this, will you? She might question our loyalty. We honestly didn't know. And you can have the bread. There's no charge for a member of the Nienna bloodline. I'll fetch it for you."

Soren's finger throbbed and he felt hurt and angry. "I don't want the bread! I told you I didn't try to steal it. You can keep your stupid bread!"

He turned and ran back through the market with his hand clutched against his chest. He just wanted to get away to somewhere where nobody could threaten to maim him. He ran until he was on the outskirts of Fallway, which wasn't far, as the town was small, especially compared to the grand scale of Nazaki where he had grown up. He followed a narrow pathway between two rows of trees and found himself at the burial ground.

Paradoran graveyards were different to those in Alcherys, where they were sad, sombre places full of depressing cold stones propped up to mark the departeds' resting place. Here, however, each grave was marked with a mini-shrine to that person. There were paintings of them, their favourite belongings, poems and song lyrics, and jokes and stories from their lives. Each grave was intended to celebrate the life of the deceased, to show appreciation for all they had achieved. Visiting the graveyard in Parador was a journey through the lives of those who had gone before, no matter how much it hurt to have lost the person.

Soren wandered through the brightly coloured shrines, sucking on his cut finger and trying to appreciate the tender messages and pictures, but all he could feel was bitterness clawing at the back of his throat. These people were celebrated and honoured, when all that honoured his sister was a cold grey slab of stone. What did that tell anybody about her life? These people with their decorated memorials would live on in the eyes of everybody who visited, whether they had known them or not.

Tears welled up in Soren's eyes, and he rubbed angrily at them. He missed her, of course he did, but the truth was he hardly remembered his sister at all. He'd just been five when she had died. All he could remember was her chasing him and scooping him up in her arms. He couldn't remember her voice or her smile, and it took all of his concentration just to picture her face. He was sad when he thought of her. He regretted not having more time with her, but the overwhelming feeling that clawed at him was guilt because he hated the way his parents mourned for her every day and forgot to appreciate their children who still lived.

His mother hid behind her work and trapped her sadness behind a wall of diplomatic smiles and fierce battle-planning. She made sure she was so busy that she couldn't dwell on her daughter's tragic death. Unfortunately, that also meant she was too busy to spend time with her living children. And although Soren understood her reasons for that, he was angry at her for neglecting him. It was unfair, but he needed attention too, even more so since Freya had gone. That was something his mother just didn't seem to grasp.

His father was far worse. When Freya died, Soren's strong and loving father had retreated into himself. He was a mere shadow of the man he had once been. It had been the final insult in a lifetime of persecution at the hands of Vincent Wilder, who had an intense obsession with destroying him.

Now Kham was quiet and distant. He did the things that were expected of him, the meetings and greetings, but he was emotionally closed off. He couldn't maintain a proper conversation, ate little and no matter how often Soren tried to get him involved in a discussion or begged his father to train with him, his father always had a mumbled excuse.

Tears burned the back of Soren's throat. *I might as well have been the one who died. They don't pay attention to me anyway*, he thought and kicked through the leaves angrily. Well, he'd have to appeal to the one thing that did make his mother's ears prick up—military prowess. It seemed to be the only way to get Callista's attention, to prove you were strong enough to earn it. He knew he would just have to do something extraordinary.

He was reminded of his mission and snapped out of his swirling thoughts. He left the graveyard and weaved back through the streets to the town hall, where a large wooden clock displayed the time proudly. It was 12:45 PM, and

Soren could get away with going home to pack his bags for the big day to-morrow.

He trudged through the narrow streets, ducking under the brightly coloured linens that were strung out to dry between the buildings. His mind was swirling with a wild array of thoughts. He felt sad and delicate about the uncomfortable memories of his sister and the acknowledgement of his distant parents. His nerves were still raw from his frightening run-in with the storekeeper and the town guard, and his thumb ached where his cut was beginning to scab over. But now there was excitement brewing in his veins. He was going on an adventure—a voyage into mysterious lands. What could be more thrilling?

The early morning sun danced across Soren's pillow, warming his closed eyelids as he slowly pulled out of sleep. It didn't take long for him to snap into being wide awake, sitting up straight and stretching the stiffness from his limbs. He checked his timepiece: 7:00 AM. This was it. The day he would prove himself.

Bending to look over the side of his bed, he checked that his packed bag was still there. The little brown satchel he had organised yesterday contained some rope, a box of matches, a bottle of water and a few packs of treats. He hadn't really known what else to pack, but he was sure this would be enough. Last, but definitely not least, was his sword, which lay in its display stand on the dresser, glinting in the morning sun.

Soren finished dressing and grabbed his short sword and scabbard from the wooden stand where his prized possession always rested. He ran his hand across the carved scabbard with nostalgia. He'd started out with a practice sword since he was old enough to hold it upright, which had been around his fourth birthday. When his dad was satisfied he wouldn't injure himself with it, he presented him with his own sharpened blade. Soren had owned this beauty for a year now and he had never looked back since.

This sword was the answer to everything in Soren's life. It was the answer to his problems, his future and his destiny. He was excellent at wielding it, partly due to the first-rate training he'd had from various people but also due to an innate talent he had just been born with.

Soren dropped to the floor and crawled, as quietly as he could, to open the bedroom door and make his escape. Deveron (who had always been a light sleeper) stirred and sat up, rubbing his eyes. As soon as his sleepy gaze fell upon Soren mid-crawl across the room, he frowned.

"What are you doing?"

Soren jumped to his feet and brushed himself down. "I'm going out."

"Out where?" Deveron replied absently, having lost interest in his brother mere seconds after he'd woken him.

Soren shrugged his shoulders. "I'm going into Parador."

Deveron stared. "Parador? What are you talking about? Are you mental? You can't go to Parador. Is Mum taking you for a meeting or something?"

Soren sighed and rolled his eyes at Deveron.

"I'm going on my own. There's an abandoned Brotherhood facility just over the border in Parador. Somebody at school said. It's empty, no guards or anything. Apparently there are all sorts of things in there, potions and magic. Things that could make us into heroes."

Deveron tumbled out of his covers, shaking a foot to loosen a sheet that had wrapped itself around him. He began pulling on clothes in a rush. "Tell me you're joking. You can't believe that. Anyway, what are you going to do? Are you just going to wander over and check it out? Don't be ridiculous. You can't go without Mother's permission. We don't know what's out there."

Soren scoffed as he scrabbled around in the drawer under his bed, looking for extra weapons—a knife, perhaps—but he could find nothing useful.

"Parador isn't an alien planet or anything, Deveron. We've been there before. What's the problem?"

Deveron leapt up from his bed and blocked Soren's path to the door. "You're not going without an adult. I won't let you."

Soren threw his head back and laughed out loud. "Like *you* can stop me!" Soren tried to push past him, but Deveron put both hands on Soren's shoulders and held him back.

"Come on, Soren. Don't be an idiot! It's dangerous."

Soren wriggled free from his grasp. "I'll be fine. I can look after myself."

"No!" Deveron shouted. "You're not going anywhere. Mum and Dad will go mad."

Soren looked to the floor. "They won't even notice I'm gone, and you know it."

Deveron's chest heaved up and down, and his eyes flicked from left to right as he struggled for ways to convince Soren to stay. "What about Raven? If he finds out, he'll give you hell. In fact, it's Saturday. Aren't you supposed to be training with him and Deacon this morning? They'll notice if you're not there."

Soren's heart leapt in his chest. He'd forgotten they'd scheduled a training session. Well, this was more important. Raven would have to wait until he got back.

"I don't care. I'm going." Soren pushed past Deveron. He grabbed the brass handle and yanked the door open.

"I'll tell Mum where you've gone," Deveron called desperately after him.

"Do it. I'll be long gone by the time she catches up to me."

Deveron cursed under his breath. Soren tried to stop a victorious smirk from crossing his lips. He had put his brother in a tricky position. He couldn't go to Callista and leave him alone. Soren could practically see the cogs turning in Deveron's head.

"Fine. Go, but I'm coming with you. You wouldn't even notice someone's attacking you until they're right on top of you. If I come, I can at least keep us away from soldiers," Deveron said with a deep huff.

"I don't need your freakish *power* to help me. I can handle myself."

Deveron ignored his jibes. "Stay there. I'm getting my jacket."

Soren sighed with impatience, crossed his arms across his chest and waited as his brother ran back into the room. Deveron shot across the room, grabbed a quill and a sheet of paper and wrote a scribbled note to Raven, who would come looking for Soren soon.

He placed the letter on Soren's pillow and then grabbed his coat and dashed back out. Soren turned away and strode down the corridor without a word to his brother. When they reached the top of the stairs, Soren held Deveron back. They watched in silence, hidden behind the banisters whilst the maid scurried by, preparing breakfast. They heard her shoes clopping on the kitchen floor and knew the coast was clear. Soren waved Deveron on, and they crept down the stairs and out of the house.

Chapter Seven
Treachery

ELKEEP HAD BEEN the centre of all Brotherhood of Shadow operations for over one hundred years. The towering, prosperous city was known throughout the world for its culture and vibrant style of life. The buildings were tall and pointed, stretching like spiralling needles into the sky. The houses, shops and theatres were built in concentric circles, spreading outwards like ripples from the drop in the centre, the impressive castle of Belkeep.

Even though it had been built under horrific conditions by thousands of enslaved workers, the beauty of the castle never failed to stun those who looked upon it. Over one hundred thousand golden leaves had been handcrafted and bolted onto the walls and spires. When the sunlight hit the castle at the right angle, shafts of golden light reflected across the city. The Brotherhood's flag, a golden phoenix encased in orange flame, flew from each of the eight immense turrets that towered beyond everything else in the city.

The afternoon was drawing to a close, and the hot Meraxan sun was beginning to dip towards the horizon. The golden city glowed, and the sunset reflected off the roof of every building like a spider web aflame.

Vincent Wilder took long, slow steps backwards and forwards across the marble floor of the grand library. His dark, piercing eyes were locked onto his great-granddaughter as she spoke, his head turning slowly to follow her with every step he took. There was a terrifying intensity in his expression, and his jaw stood out, the muscles bulging as he clamped his teeth together.

"Did you manage to do it, Jade?"

Jade nodded, smiling. "Yes. He'll be there later today."

"Tell me everything."

"We are three months into the operation now, and I have become friends with Soren. We play at break times and eat lunch together. He trusts me, so it was easy to get him to do what I wanted."

Vincent nodded, keeping his eyes fixed upon her. "What have you learned about him?" His voice was deep and rich.

"He is living in a house in Fallway with his family—his mother, father, brother Deveron and sister Kellyn." Vincent's eyes blazed with burning darkness, but he gestured for her to continue. "I think the family has some problems. He tells me that they don't all get along. He fights with his mother, is embarrassed by his older brother and never sees his father. After school, he spends his time training with his mentor, Raven."

Vincent stopped dead in his tracks and glared at her with accusing eyes. She held her ground confidently and met his stare.

"Raven? Are you sure he trains with Raven? That can't be true. In the Children of Light, they don't take on apprentices until they take the elixir at sixteen."

Jade shrugged her shoulders. "Definitely true. Soren tells me at least once a day that he's 'special' because Raven picked him before he was of age. He thinks it means he'll be the strongest soldier in the world." Jade gave a small chuckle, but it wasn't echoed by Vincent, whose expression intensified further.

"If he's being trained now, then in a few years' time he might be. Tell me more."

"He's a nice boy. We have fun together, but he's a bit simple. Quite predictable. Still a baby really. I can manipulate him easily enough. He does whatever I say."

Vincent gave the tiniest hint of a smile. "You've done well, Jade. I'm proud of what you have achieved. Are you sure he's definitely going to the facility?"

"Oh yes. He couldn't wait to get there."

Vincent smirked and continued pacing. "Of course, you'll be rewarded handsomely. If that child does indeed get to the facility, alone, his death will be on your hands. That classes as a high-rank kill, which will guarantee you one dose of elixir when you reach sixteen."

Jade's eyes widened at the prospect of receiving a rare and precious elixir. Every boy and girl in the Children of Light might get one automatically, but in the Brotherhood they had to be earned. Still, she hesitated. "Remind me again why Soren is worth all of this. His older brother is weak and cannot protect himself. Why not take him out instead?"

"Precisely *because* Deveron is weak and, therefore, not a threat. Whereas Soren, I've seen his type before—cocky, unmistakably talented but definitely overconfident. Give it ten years and he'll be another Raven, especially now that he's training him." Vincent began to rub his hands together, and his expression shifted yet another shade darker. "But it's more than that. There is any number of troublesome kids we could kill, but not all of them are Kham's. That infidel, that stain on the face of the planet, will suffer."

"Don't you think he's suffered enough? Soren says he's depressed already," Jade said quietly.

"It's not enough! It's never enough! I will not be satisfied until every one of his children's corpses haunt him at night. Everything is his fault. Everything! What I suffer, day in day out, is due to him. And he gets to share the bed of MY woman! Those damn children of his...they should be mine. He is inferior. His race is inferior. Everything about him is inferior! He is not worthy to father Callista's children. Only I am. I will work through the filthy little scum, killing them one by one until none of their disgusting half-breeds are left." He had stepped right up to Jade and was shouting in her face by the end of his tirade.

Jade didn't flinch when Vincent shouted, but her brow furrowed.

"It wasn't right what that man did to you, Great-Grandfather, but it wasn't Soren's fault." She swallowed heavily and nearly wilted under his fearsome glare, but she kept her head up. "I don't agree that it's the right way to go. I think it'll just inflame Callista further and make her stronger. If Soren dies, they'll come after you with everything they've got."

Vincent's face broke into a malicious smile. He draped an arm over Jade's shoulder, holding onto her slightly too tightly to be comfortable.

"Yes, but you see they won't have as much to come after me with, will they? The thing is, Jade, you don't understand exactly what this toxin does. Soren may end up dead, or he may end up worse. And we're not just going for him. Once we've assessed how well it works on that brat, we can take them all out. If all this goes to plan, there will be total pandemonium, and they'll take themselves out of the equation."

Jade frowned but her eyes grew shade brighter. "So, there's a chance Soren might survive?"

"Oh yes. He might make it out alive, though perhaps he'll be some-what...different afterwards."

"Changed, how?"

"You don't need to worry yourself with that, my dear. Your part of the plan has already been completed. Now I'm handing it over to Reign. You can just sit back and see what happens. Either way, you won't be around for the fallout. You can never go back to Fallway now."

Jade frowned but finally nodded. "OK. I'm glad I could help and be a part of this. If it leads to the destruction of the Children of Light, I'm happy but...I kind of hope Soren survives."

"So do I," Vincent muttered as she left.

As soon as the door closed behind her, the temperature in the room dropped a few degrees and the air began to subtly shift, until a barely noticeable vibration hummed all around Vincent. A thin grey veil was cast over his vision and he took a step back and straightened his dark suit, adjusting the crest of the Brotherhood on his breast pocket.

The air in front of him, thickened like smoke, was being pumped into the room from an unseen source. It whirled and undulated into thick, writhing plumes. The smoke began to gather in one place, to form a body the size and shape of a human, slightly taller than Vincent himself. Long plumes shot out to form arms and legs and a twisting, continually swirling mass became the skull. The shape stood before him and despite its lack of eyes, stared straight at him. The Bavelize, the mysterious, other-worldly advisor to the Brotherhood of Shadow. It began to talk in a voice that issued from everywhere and nowhere at the same time.

"Is everything ready?" The words seemed to come from inside Vincent's skull and his head began to ache, a deep throb behind his eyes.

"Yes. The virus is packed into syringes and ready to go. Jade has directed the boy to the storage facility in Parador, and I'll send Reign to infect him with the virus. From there, the boy will either die under the strain of the virus or carry the madness back to Fallway. Within days, he will become a blood-sucking monster and will murder everybody around him including, hopefully, his mongrel family."

"Good." The sound of the creature's voice rumbled in Vincent's temples.

"Mighty Bavelize, forgive my ignorance, but I must ask. Isn't there a chance this could backfire on us? If Soren doesn't die, if he contracts this...affliction instead, won't he be stronger than before? Won't it be harder to kill him?"

The creature was silent for a moment. Vincent looked down, fear rising in his heart. Eventually, it spoke again.

"Do you not trust my judgement, Wilder?"

"Of course, I do, master. I just don't have your wisdom, so I can't understand."

Silence again, for so long that Vincent began to shudder in his boots involuntarily and beads of sweat formed on his forehead. When the response came, it was cold and quiet.

"When the boy, and all others who will be subjected to it afterwards, fall ill with this virus, it will eat away at their minds and destroy their souls. They will not come out of it the same people. Families will fall apart. Friends will turn against each other. It will do much more than kill a few. It will turn their entire nation into monsters. It will tear apart their cities and towns and make them kill one another, irrespective of age, gender and prior relationships. This is the weapon we've been waiting for. This is the weapon that will dissolve the Children of Light."

Vincent tried to keep his eyes fixed on where the Bavelize's face should have been, but the swirling smoke made it difficult to concentrate upon. His head started to pound, and he was forced to look away.

"Call him. Call the scientist," the Bavelize hissed in a voice that reverberated around Vincent's skull.

Vincent nodded and took three long strides to the wooden door. He wrenched it open, startling the guard who stood outside.

"Fetch Reign. Now," Vincent barked. The guard's eyes flickered over Vincent's shoulder and fell upon the writhing form of the Bavelize. With a sharp intake of breath, the guard tore his eyes away and rushed off along the corridor to fetch the scientist.

The Bavelize glided towards Vincent. "Does Reign please you?"

Vincent turned back to face the creature. "He's...creative."

The Bavelize made a high-pitched whine that Vincent suspected may have been a laugh. "There's nothing he would stop at. No boundary he wouldn't break," the Bavelize hissed, delight echoing in his ethereal voice. "He will propel this army into greatness."

Before it had finished the sentence, the Bavelize began to fade into stray strands of smoke, disintegrating in the air and leaving his words hanging in the ether.

Vincent calmly paced back and forth in the small library, waiting. There was a knock at the door. He called to enter. The guard opened the door and stepped aside. Reign strode in confidently with a strong presence for such an old man.

Vincent frowned at him. Reign gave a cold, detached laugh. "Sorry to bother you with my presence, Master Wilder. I know my aged face bothers you." His voice was crisp and perfectly enunciated.

Vincent scoffed, "I called you here. Besides if you chose to let your body decay with age before taking the elixir, that's no concern of mine."

Reign laughed again. "It makes a good disguise though, doesn't it?" He didn't wait for a response. "Are you ready to infect the boy?"

Vincent nodded. "Yes. It will be done by this evening."

Reign sighed. "Wouldn't it be better just to let me unleash the creatures I've been making instead?"

Vincent glared at him with intense, burning eyes. "Absolutely not. They're a liability and we need this to be discreet. Besides, this toxin is a lot of fun, don't you agree?"

Reign grinned, showing yellowed teeth. "That I do, Vincent. That I do."

"So go and collect the syringes from the facility in Parador. Use an old cart that nobody will suspect. The boy's name is Soren. He's a little mongrel brat—half Alcheran and half Paradoran. It is essential he gets the disease. Do you understand?"

"If there are others with him?"

"There shouldn't be if Jade did her job properly. If there are, make sure they all get it. And if it's impossible to infect him, you must at least kill him."

Reign locked onto Vincent's stare. "He'll get the sickness. I promise."

Chapter Eight
Medicines and Madness

 SCRUFFY-LOOKING brown dryll was waiting for Soren and Deveron as soon as they stepped out of their house. It ruffled its feathers with a haughty squawk, as if it had grown impatient with waiting for them to get up. It shook a sharp-taloned claw at the boys as Soren approached the bird calmly. He removed the tatty piece of paper attached to its brace. As soon as Soren had it in his hand, the bird shot off into the sky.

The boys huddled together to look at the crudely drawn map that Jade had sent to them. She had kept her word, and Soren's heart leapt in his chest. Now the glory could be his, and she would be mightily impressed with his bravery. It was just a shame his liability of a brother was with him, but there was nothing he could do about that.

Soren committed the map to memory and shoved it into his back pocket. Then, they set off on their journey.

Soren ran ahead, ducking and dodging through the pathways that wound through Fallway's neatly maintained gardens, the early morning sun warm but not yet blistering. He leapt over a small bush, landing gracefully, and continued running without breaking his stride.

"Wait! Soren, don't be mean. Wait for me!" Deveron yelled, trying to run after him but getting his uncoordinated feet caught up in the branches and leaves that stretched across the path.

Soren reluctantly pulled up and turned to see Deveron struggling after him. "You don't have to come, you know. If it's too hard…"

Deveron glared at him. "It's not *too hard*. I just can't run like you." He was out of breath, and his voice shook.

Soren rolled his eyes. "Come on then. It's not too far. Jade said it was just down here." He took off again, but at a slightly slower pace to allow his older brother to catch up to him.

They were soon out of the Fallway gardens and began to head out into the woodland area in the north of Parador. Soren frequently stopped to huff loudly at Deveron in an attempt to spur him along, but the fourteen-year-old merely slowed down further to irritate his little brother.

They continued that way for a few miles farther, Soren running ahead, Deveron deliberately dragging behind to irritate him. Soren's patience with his brother was wearing thin. He thought of leaving him behind many times, but as much as Deveron annoyed him, Soren was thankful for the company. He hoped maybe having an adventure might snap Deveron out of his strange opinions and behaviour. It might make him behave like a real Children of Light soldier, a true descendant of Callista Nienna.

But the harder Soren pushed Deveron into being a warrior, the more he seemed to resist. Nothing about him was built for fighting, not his soft skin and gangly, thin frame or his gentle, poetic soul and unwavering respect for life. He wasn't destined to be a soldier. His life would take another path, and Deveron himself just didn't know what it was yet.

Soren, however, was born a fighter. Every game he played included epic battles, warring queens, noble knights and princes. It was in his veins and in his soul, and he was lucky enough to have been born to the greatest warrior the world had ever seen: Callista, ruler of Alcherys and immortal warlord. She had taught him well. From a young age, Soren had far surpassed all those around him until he was picked up as an apprentice to Raven Lennox, a highly treasured position few ever had the privilege of holding.

Born to different parents, his life would have been considerably different. The Children of Light operated under nepotism, and favour was always given to those who were "well-bred." Callista had her favourites, even amongst her own children, and bestowed honours upon those she valued the most. Soren was a favourite of his mother and so flourished under the diligent tuition of the finest soldiers the Children of Light had to offer. Had he been born to a lesser member, he might never have risen to such heights and his talents might have floundered. Had he been born in the unallied lands or as a general citizen of Alcherys, he could still make it in life but through an agonising process of entering the Children of Light's training academy at Salvatore. The most talented soldiers taught there, but it was notoriously difficult to graduate, and anybody who really wished to make it in the Children of Light prayed they were chosen to be an apprentice to a master instead.

At the age of sixteen, when all Children of Light members took the elixir of life, they were given the opportunity to put themselves up as apprentices in the hope of being chosen by a master. If chosen, they spent twenty years under the one-to-one tutelage of their master and adopted their style and skill set. If not chosen, they were free to train by themselves or enter the Salvatore Academy. Every child in the Children of Light grew up desperate to be chosen by a master. It was every little boy and girl's dream to be picked by their hero, and many trained for every minute of every day until their sixteenth birthdays, when they became eligible.

Deveron, at age fourteen, had already decided he didn't want to become an apprentice or join the academy. He said he wanted to choose his own way in the world. It was something his family found difficult to understand. Soren, on the other hand, was the first child in history to have been taken on as an apprentice before the age of sixteen. He had been picked up by Raven at nearly ten years old, something utterly unheard of, not just due to his age but also because Raven famously rarely took an apprentice. Despite being the most highly established warrior in the nation and being eligible to train new soldiers, he flat out refused to take on apprentices unless he thought they were good enough to warrant his attention.

Raven had trained Soren's other half-brother Deacon Thialdor for thirty years before agreeing to pass him. His training regime was brutal and uncompromising, and he nearly led Deacon to the brink of death and insanity many times, but eventually Deacon made it out alive and now rivalled Raven in fighting prowess.

When Soren was picked by Raven out of the blue, he was both terrified and ecstatic, but Raven had been considerably softer with him than with Deacon, for which Soren was immensely grateful. He'd been training with Raven for four months, and the progress he'd made in that time was staggering. Raven's skill as a mentor and his incredible knowledge of a variety of fighting arts were giving Soren an invaluable education, but also a tendency towards over-confidence.

It was this unwavering self-belief that drove Soren to do things like head out of Fallway to investigate a facility he knew nothing about. Deveron was making it obvious that he didn't think it was the right thing to do. So what if there was an abandoned facility nearby? What did that have to do with them? But, much to Soren's annoyance, Deveron had always taken it upon himself to be his brother's stupidity guard. He would never let Soren go alone.

After thirty minutes of trekking across Parador, Soren came across a fence; old wooden beams and spiked wire standing a metre tall, marking the border. Fallway, as a dual-occupied town, rested perfectly between Alcherys and Parador. It was an independent little bubble which, though patrolled and inhabited by both Alcherans and Paradorans, was officially ruled by neither. It meant that both Children of Light and Brotherhood of Shadow people could come and go freely in Fallway, although Brotherhood citizens had stayed away in recent months now that Callista and Prince Khaled had struck their deal and opened the School of Unity.

The defences on the far side of Fallway were far more developed, almost impossible to cross in fact, for the safety of those in Alcherys. Khaled, who felt little threat from the Meraxans, did not insist on anything like the severe level of security for the Paradoran border. He knew how the Eternal War worked. If either the Brotherhood or the Children attacked Parador, the other would defend every time. They had reached a situation where neither side even tried anymore, and the borders were left largely undefended.

Soren vaulted the fence easily, his athletic limbs powering him over without any real exertion. Deveron hovered on his side of the fence, as if he was unsure how to even start climbing.

"Come on. What's the matter with you?" Soren snapped, becoming impatient.

Deveron frowned. "I'll never make that."

"I just did it, so you can do it. Your legs are way longer than mine."

Deveron shook his head. "I can't do it, Soren. There must be another way."

Soren sighed and rolled his eyes. He slipped his brown jacket off his shoulders and laid it carefully over the spiked wire. "Come on! At least the spikes can't catch you now."

Deveron tentatively patted the jacket and when no vicious points poked through the material, he swung his leg over. His long legs made it over the fence easily, and he pulled his second leg over with a smile.

"That was easier than I thought." He grinned at Soren, who scoffed haughtily.

"You didn't even need my jacket! You were easily tall enough!"

"Yeah, well, I just wanted to be sure."

Soren grumbled under his breath as he carefully pulled his jacket off the wire. "If my jacket's got holes in it now, you're buying me a new one."

Deveron turned away, but Soren still caught his grin.

"Hey, Soren, want to play hide and seek?" Deveron asked.

Soren laughed. "No way. I've fallen for that before. It's not fair. You cheat."

Deveron held his hands out in mock indignation. "What? I refute that."

"You'll use your power to detect me. How can I hide from that?"

Deveron laughed. "You better remember that. You can't hide from me." He spread his fingers wide and screwed his face into a snarl, trying to scare Soren.

Soren raised one eyebrow but couldn't help his lips curling into a laugh.

The plains of Parador were beautiful, gently sweeping meadows with small woodlands dotted around and the odd small lake or stream trickling through the grasslands. The two boys enjoyed the rising sun on their skin and Soren swung his jacket over his shoulder. It was mid-morning, but the temperature was already high and the warmth of the sun coated them like a blanket.

Soren soon had a skip in his step, jumping lightly over the occasional roots or rocks on the woodland floor. He turned it into a game, seeing how far he could leap over the obstructions. Deveron cheered him on, daring him to go further and faster. Soren rose to the challenge gladly, throwing his jacket to Deveron and flinging himself over every rock he found, until his back foot caught the tip of a larger boulder and he fell flat on his face.

Deveron doubled over with hysterical laughter. Soren, unhurt but dirty, stood to face him, preparing to be embarrassed and angry, but he couldn't help a grin from spreading across his own face.

They continued and Soren enjoyed the laughter that had been scarce between them lately. He leapt as far and as high as he could, allowing himself to trip just to make Deveron laugh. When his energy began to run out, he slowed to a walk and they looked out over the peaceful meadows.

Soren glanced at Deveron and smiled as the sun rays glittered on his skin. Deveron wasn't really one for the outdoors. He tended to stay indoors with his head tucked inside a book, but even he couldn't deny that this was beautiful. Soren knew Deveron never would have experienced this if he hadn't dragged him out here.

They looked far across the rolling fields. If they continued deeper into Parador and veered off towards the east, the grasslands would give way to vast deserts, stretching out towards Meraxor, the Brotherhood's lands. Where the Paradoran desert ended and the rainforests of Meraxor began, nature provided a natural border separating the nations.

The building Jade had drawn on her map wasn't as far as the desert, though. It looked like it was tucked into the woods just over the border. They wouldn't have to go far.

Another half an hour into their walk, the patches of woodland became denser and the trees tucked tightly together. It was the perfect place to hide a secret facility. They made their way through the woods, stepping carefully over the rocks and exposed roots that littered the woodland path.

"Stop!" Soren said and placed a hand on Deveron's chest to hold him back.

"What?" Deveron snapped, pushing Soren's hand away.

"Quiet!" Soren hissed in a whisper. "Look. A clearing." He pointed to an area where the trees opened up and a stone road wound through the woods. They crept quietly closer and peered through the trees. It was a wide clearing where only grass and dotted yellow dandelions covered the ground. Ivy and moss trailed up the front of the building and a quick glance could easily pass over it. But Soren had been looking for the facility, and his keen dark eyes picked out the building straight away.

"That's it," he whispered to Deveron. "I think that's the building Jade drew on her map."

The boys spent a few moments looking over the map and trying to read Jade's scrawled directions and pictures.

"Look, it lies in between the woods and the stream, just like this," Soren pointed to the section of the map where the building supposedly lay. Even Deveron had to admit it looked like this was the right place.

The facility was deathly quiet, and they could see no movement ahead. It certainly looked derelict, just as Jade had said.

"Let's go in," Soren whispered and stepped out into the clearing.

"No! Wait!" Deveron cried, grabbing the back of Soren's shirt and yanking him back into the safety of the bushes.

Soren shook Deveron's hands away. "Get off me! What's wrong with you?"

"We don't know anything about that building. If that really is a Brotherhood facility, we can't just go waltzing in. That's madness!" Deveron's heart was pounding, and his eyes flashed wide with fear.

"But look at it, Deveron. It's clearly empty. Jade said it wasn't in use anymore and that there was loads of cool stuff inside."

"How would she know? Has she actually been inside herself? Who is this Jade anyway?"

Soren's cheeks flushed pink. "Just a girl at school, that's all. She's Paradoran, so that's how she knows."

Deveron rolled his eyes at Soren's embarrassment. "Oh, I get it now. Some little Paradoran girl mentions it, and now you're trying to impress her."

"I am NOT trying to impress her! I just thought it sounded interesting, that's all!"

Deveron laughed. Soren avoided his gaze, his cheeks burning red. Deveron's laughter was cut short as a loud creaking squeal grabbed their attention. The large wooden gates at the front of the building began to slowly swing open with a screech as the rusty hinges rubbed together.

The two boys crouched in the bushes and watched with bated breath. Once the gates were fully open, a small wooden cart pulled out, led by two proud black horses. It was a traditional old caravan, made of wood with curtains drawn across the back. An older man of around fifty years sat at the front, the reins of the two horses clasped tightly in his aging hands. Three guards walked by the side of the cart, wearing grey uniforms with a black symbol stitched on the front—a phoenix surrounded by a flame, the sign of the Brotherhood of Shadow.

The guards at the back swung the gate closed behind them and slid the iron bolts across to lock it with a loud bang. The cart slowly trundled along the path towards where Soren and Deveron were hiding in the bushes. Deveron shrank back into the leafy undergrowth, but Soren crept closer, pulling the leaves aside to get a better look at the cart. His face creased in a curious frown and his heart began to pound with excitement.

"Get back here!" Deveron hissed as quietly as he could, but Soren ignored his frantic orders.

As the cart came right up to them, Deveron quietly crept forwards and made a grab for Soren's trouser leg, hoping to pull his little brother back to safety, but Soren shook his hand away and cast Deveron a mischievous grin. He turned from his brother and stepped out into the clearing, right in front of the two horses.

"Soren!" Deveron yelled in terror.

The two sturdy black mares pulled up short with irritated whinnies and stamped their hooves against the stony woodland path. Deveron was at Soren's side in a second, cursing his brother's recklessness. He grasped Soren by the shoulders and tried to push him aside, but Soren was stronger and shoved him away easily, so Deveron had to make do with standing at his side, fidgeting and twitching nervously.

Every nerve in Soren's body tingled with excitement and fear, but he was desperate to know what treasures the cart carried. The elderly man who sat upon the cart glanced down at Soren and Deveron with narrowed eyes as the three guards rushed up to them, their swords raised and deadly sharp. They surrounded the two boys. When they saw that they were mere children, they lowered the deadly tips of their weapons. The first guard, a tough and sturdy woman of no more than twenty years, eyed Soren and Deveron suspiciously.

"Don't you know not to play in the woods? What are you doing here?" Her tone was crisp and authoritative. Deveron froze under her gaze, but Soren liked the challenge.

His face softened, and he looked up at her with impossibly wide brown eyes. His voice rose in pitch, making him sound younger than he really was.

"Please, missus. Me and my brother are out here all alone. We was just looking for something to eat."

Deveron cast an irritated glance at Soren as he played the uneducated orphan card.

Another guard, a man of around thirty-five years, slim and short, stepped up to Soren and looked him over, his eyes narrowing as they fell on the sword that hung at his waist.

"Why do you have a sword then?" he asked.

"We needs to look after us selves, don't we? Mum and Dad left us all alone. We just needs a bit of food. Maybe you could let us have a look in the back of ya cart?"

It was the wrong thing to say. Instantly, all three guards had their swords raised, pointing at Soren. He raised his hands in surrender and a sly smile crossed his lips.

"There's no way these boys are orphans," the third guard said. "Look at their clothes...all clean and pressed."

"Yeah, and expensive too by the looks of them." One of them prodded at the golden stitching on Deveron's shoulder.

The woman bent down to look more closely at Soren's sword. Her eyes traced down the hilt to the intricate scabbard. The guard's eyes widened at the exotic gilded patterns and engravings before they landed upon a small symbol about halfway down—four daggers pointing inwards with a knot of infinity at the centre. The symbol of the Children of Light.

The guard shouted a warning, but before it had even left her lips, Soren had unclipped the buckle and wrenched the sword, still encased in scabbard (he didn't want to kill anybody, after all), from his waist. He gave Deveron a sharp shove with his left hand, which sent him stumbling backwards.

In his right hand, Soren swung his sheathed sword, enjoying the familiar weight of the weapon he had trained with for most of his life. His veins started to buzz with adrenaline, and he tingled from head to toe, as he always did just before a fight.

He swung his sword in an arc and sent it flying just inches from one of the guard's noses and then brought it reeling back to slam into the face of another. The guard staggered backwards, bewildered and blinking his eyes, just as Soren's foot flew up and caught him across the jaw. The blow sent his eyes rolling back into his head as he blacked out into unconsciousness.

Soren spun around to see the other two closing in on him. Another powerful kick took the woman out, and her body crumpled to the floor beside her companion.

Running and leaping high in the air, Soren brought the sword and scabbard up high and then, on his descent, slammed it into the temple of the male soldier, who couldn't have been a lot older than him.

Soren and the limp guard landed at the same time. Soren's eyes were wide and excited from the thrill of combat. He had taken all three guards down, and he barely broke a sweat.

Deveron, who was still in a crumpled heap on the ground from where Soren had pushed him over, scrambled over to the limp body of the soldier Soren had taken out last. He leaned over the listless, still body and, with a pounding heart, pressed two fingers tentatively to the guard's jugular. He couldn't feel anything. He pressed deeper into the guard's cooling flesh but still could feel no pulse. His breath caught in his throat as cold horror consumed him.

He tore his hand away, recoiling at the idea of touching a dead body, and scrambled backwards noisily. Soren's head whipped around to look at him. Deveron considered shouting at Soren, forcing his reckless little brother to see the damage he had caused, to appreciate the consequences of his thrill-seeking. But despite Soren's self-importance, when Deveron looked into his eyes, he still saw a little boy. He was too young to have such horror heaped upon his shoulders. Deveron knew there were few ways he could protect his little brother, but this was something he could do. He could keep that pain from Soren just a little while longer. He wasn't sure if it was the right thing to do, but he said nothing and kept the guilt and distaste inside of himself instead. When Soren looked over at him, he forced his quivering lips into a smile and heaved a sigh of relief.

Soren flashed him a quick smile in return and turned back to the man on the cart.

"Hey! What have you got in your cart?" Soren piped up, and Deveron cursed his brother again for being so forthright.

The man didn't reply straight away. He inspected Soren carefully first, his cold grey-red eyes examining the small boy. When he eventually spoke, it was in an unusual voice, perfect pronunciation and expression, but somehow cool and detached.

"Nothing you need to concern yourself with, child."

Deveron bristled uncomfortably. He didn't trust the man on the cart.

Soren scoffed, seemingly oblivious to the undercurrent of menace that Deveron was detecting. "Did you not see what I just did to your soldiers? They were armed, and I still defeated them all. I could easily take you down."

The man cocked his head to the side and weighed Soren up again. He held his hands out in surrender but far too slowly for Deveron's liking. "OK, OK. I'm just an old man making a delivery. I don't want any trouble. What can I do for you, young man?"

Soren smirked. "I've heard there are all sorts of treasures kept inside that facility. I want to know what you've got in the back of your cart. What were you taking out of there?" He nodded towards the rear of the cart. The man jumped down from the wagon with surprising agility for his age.

With a theatrical sigh that sounded forced, the man took the children round to the back of the cart. Pulling the cloth curtains aside, he waved Soren in first.

"After you," he said quietly. Soren ignored the slight burning smell that filled his nostrils as he passed the man and stepped up onto the cart. He ducked beneath the material.

"Soren, wait! It might be dangerous!" Deveron called, but Soren dismissed him with a wave of his hand. Deveron had no choice but to join him,. He stepped up into the cart after his brother.

Deveron didn't really know what he'd been expecting to see, but it wasn't a dusty, dark wagon with rotting damp shelves that were mostly empty. He also became aware of subtle smell of sulphur. A number of wooden crates stood in stacks around the edges of the cart, but there was nothing else.

Soren frowned and ran his hand over the top of one of the boxes. He rapped on one with his knuckles.

"What's in these?" he asked, as the man stepped up behind him.

Deveron reluctantly trailed behind, keeping to the back, out of harm's way.

The old man shuffled forwards and patted one of the cases, almost lovingly, with a peculiar spark of excitement in his eyes.

"These boxes," he said as he flicked open a brass buckle, "contain very precious cargo. I'm a scientist developing tonics, vitamins, toxins…poisons…for Meraxor, the greatest nation on the planet. But you know all about that already, don't you?"

Deveron's blood ran cold as the man's intense grey eyes bored into Soren's. It was as if he knew who the boys really were. And had he said poisons? Deveron's heart began to pound in his chest.

He hissed to his brother, who was standing far too close to the stranger. "Soren!" But when the scientist turned to look at him, he straightened up and adopted a polite tone.

"We're really sorry we disturbed you, sir. Maybe we'll just be on our way now. We can see you've got an important job to do."

The man gave an ice-cold chuckle that sent shivers down Deveron's spine. Another waft of sulphur smell drifted over him.

"Don't be silly. You're here now, so you might as well see what I've brought along."

He reached into the wooden crate and pulled out a single glass syringe filled with a faintly pink liquid.

"Do you know what this is?" he said, stepping closer. "It's a precious health boost. Very rare. I distilled it from a flower in the south. Potent and good for building strength in your bones and muscles." His eyes flashed dangerously. "Here, why not let me give you a shot. You won't regret it."

A sneer spread across the man's face, and Deveron knew it was time to leave. He and his brother were in significant danger. He beckoned to Soren, who made to dart away, back to the safety of his big brother and the linen curtain stretched across the doorway, but the scientist stepped in front of him and blocked his way.

"Try it," he hissed and pulled the cap off the syringe, primed and ready to inject.

"Let him get by!" Deveron called out and stepped up to the man who suddenly didn't seem so frail and old anymore. The man sent Deveron staggering backwards with a hard shove to the chest. He fell, and his terrified eyes widened further as he realised he could no longer protect his little brother.

Soren reached to his waist where his beloved sword hung, but he had no time to draw the blade. The man stepped up to him, breathing his hot breath in Soren's face, looking down on him with a menacing glower.

The syringe advanced towards Soren with lightning speed. Deveron watched with horror-filled eyes as the man plunged it into his neck. Within a few seconds, it had happened. The man had injected Soren with whatever had been in the syringe.

Soren panicked and lashed out with all his strength and delivered a hard punch to the scientist's gut, knocking him backwards. The man doubled over with a groan of pain and the glass syringe slipped from his fingers. It shattered on the wooden floor, and the remnants of the pink fluid spilled out into a small puddle.

The man fell to the floor in a heap right beside his spilled potion.

A faint coppery aroma drifted into the air, a mild metallic tint, but Soren had no time to register the smell.

The old man, lying amongst the glass shards, began to laugh, beginning as a dry, quiet chuckle and escalating into mania.

Soren and Deveron stared in fear and confusion, frozen to the spot. The man stopped cackling for a few seconds, just long enough to utter the words "You're infected now." And his high-pitched giggle began again.

Chapter Nine
Pursuit

 T 7:30 AM, the same time as Soren and Deveron were preparing to explore Parador, Raven Lennox sat in the training hall at Fallway waiting for Soren to arrive for his training session. The room in which he waited hadn't always been a training hall. Once, the spacious single-roomed building had been a checkpoint, a place for traders and merchants to submit their wares for inspection before passing onto the markets. That had been back in the days when Parador ran its own trade instead of being subsidised by Alcherys.

Fallway, despite the lack of major buildings and government offices, was an important part of the Children of Light's nation. Main roads ran through the town. The major trade network between Alcherys and Parador began at Fallway, and Alcherys had the agricultural nation to thank for the vast quantities of food, cloth, spices and medicines they provided.

Trade with Parador was essential to the Children, and Callista knew that relations with their neighbouring nation had to be kept amicable. So she had made a deal with Prince Ezra Khaled. Parador would supply all of Alcherys with goods, and in return the Children of Light would offer protection and access to Alcherys's superior educational facilities, particularly the war academy at Salvatore.

Their deal with Prince Khaled had been profitable so far, and the two nations enjoyed a warm and mutually beneficial alliance. There had only been two Paradoran soldiers who had entered the Academy so far, both young and powerful teens who longed for tuition under the greatest masters of the land.

The older men of Parador had not joined, knowing that the intense twenty-year training regime was of no use to them. The reward at the end of graduation was a dose of elixir and a welcome into the Children of Light's military ranks, something only the young coveted.

Many Paradoran teens and young adults had made a huge decision and packed up everything they owned and made the long journey to Fallway in the hope of meeting Children of Light soldiers and finding a way into Alcherys. As such, Fallway was full of a mixture of Alcheran and Paradoran citizens.

That was why Callista had set up the School of Unity. The children could learn about Alcheran military law and Paradoran nomadic tradition. Some other members of Callista's family had protested the children's enrolment, de-crying it as exploitation. They claimed Callista was using her children as pawns to secure political alliance. Even if that were the case, Soren didn't mind. He relished the opportunity to mix with people outside of the Children of Light and was fascinated by their unusual customs. It didn't stop him from playing up for his teachers, though. That was something he would do no matter where he was schooled. The lure of mischief was too great, no matter how many times his mother scolded him for disrespecting his elders.

Callista made no secret of the fact that Soren was difficult to control, but she ensured his teachers were well-paid. Despite that, he still ended up outside the classroom on many occasions, sent out for being disruptive or disrespectful.

Callista never came down on him too hard, though, as she always said he had to be nurtured into greatness, not bullied out of it. That was only part of the reason though. Raven guessed that deep down she also struggled to be too hard on any of her children these days and had been much gentler towards them in recent years, since Freya's death.

So Raven, who was Soren's half-brother and his mentor, tried to pick up Soren's discipline where he could. Raven had been born to Callista and her second husband, Hayden Lennox—a wiry, tough man who had grown up in the wilderness and for whom acclimatising to life in Alcheran society had been difficult. Raven had inherited some of his father's antisocial tendencies and definitely his brooding intensity.

Now, he lived in Nazaki, the capital city of Alcherys, a two-hour ride from Fallway, but he visited three to four times a week to keep an eye on his young protégé and to maintain his fighting prowess whilst he was away from the capital.

Raven trained Soren extensively for hours at a time, helping the young boy to learn a wide variety of skills and techniques, even though Soren was a difficult child and their training sessions often descended into Raven losing his temper.

Today, Raven had brought his half-brother and closest friend Deacon Thialdor along to help with Soren's training. Born to Callista and her third husband, Sam Thialdor, Deacon had an entirely different nature to his half-brothers. Calm, wise and thoughtful, Deacon was a much-needed calming influence on Raven's temper and a steady, good influence on Soren's behaviour.

Deacon, his wife, Kyra, and their young daughter Dana had moved to Fallway along with Callista to offer their support for her Unity project. Deacon being in Fallway gave Raven another reason to visit the border town. He pretended it was to keep an eye on the development of his ex-pupil, the first apprentice he had ever taken on, but if he was being honest it was because Deacon taught him as much as he taught Deacon. Their friendship had been shaky to begin with, mostly due to the fact that Raven had been a brutal and callous master. Since his graduation, however, Deacon had stood up for himself, and this had allowed a mutual respect to develop between the two warriors. Now, their friendship was solid, and they were rarely apart.

They sat together in the cool, wooden hall, perched upon the sturdy punching bags and protective pads that were neatly stacked around the edge of the room. Deacon sat calmly, his eyes occasionally flicking up to the large timepiece that was suspended on the wall.

They'd been waiting for Soren to arrive for twenty minutes, and Raven glared at the door with an intense frown on his dark features. His knee twitched up and down with irritation. Every few minutes he'd reach up and brush his thick dark hair aside angrily. If there was one thing Raven Lennox would not tolerate, it was tardiness. Soren had learnt that lesson early on.

"I don't think he's coming," Deacon said quietly. Raven shot him an annoyed look.

"What is he playing at? I told him we had scheduled this especially for him. I'm going to kill the little grub when I get hold of him."

Deacon's thin lips broke into a smile which lit up his narrow, handsome face. His chestnut eyes shone warmly. "You won't though, will you?"

"What do you mean?"

"You're far too soft on him. You would never have let me get away with this when I was your apprentice. You'd have beaten me to within an inch of my life."

"I wasn't that bad," Raven replied, his glare still boring into the closed wooden door.

Deacon raised his eyebrows, which Raven saw from the corner of his eye but chose to ignore.

Deacon continued. "You should put a bit of pressure on him. Show him he can't behave like this. Otherwise he'll end up being undisciplined and his talents will go to waste."

"He's just a child."

"Yes, but he could still do with a really good yelling at, don't you think?"

"You're one to talk. Your daughter runs wild most of the time. When you going to clamp down on her behaviour?"

Deacon grinned and fiddled with the wrapping on the handle of his sword. "Dana's a law unto herself. I'd to try to discipline her, but we both know she does whatever she damn well pleases."

Raven chuckled. "You got that right."

"The difference, though, is that Dana does listen when it's really important. She is a cheeky little madam, but she knows when things are serious and she knuckles down when it's necessary, even though she's so young. She understands priorities. Soren doesn't."

Raven heaved a deep sigh. "You're right. He can't get away with this level of disrespect, especially if he's hoping to make one of the elite teams in the future. Let's go and get the little terror, and I'll make him regret it."

Deacon gave a small smile, which he tried to hide from his stern friend, but Raven's eyes were sharp and missed nothing. He let it go this time because he knew that Deacon was right. No matter how strict Raven tried to be with Soren, he had changed drastically in the last twenty years. He was no longer the brutal tyrant he had been when he taught Deacon. He was ashamed to admit that he had been unreasonably harsh with Deacon, almost sadistic in the torturous regimes he put him through. But a lot had happened in Raven's life since then. He had fallen in love and married Estella Baker, a wise and beautiful woman who always calmed his temper. He had become a father, which also helped to ease his temperament, but most of all, mentoring Deacon had taught him that mutual respect was more important in a relationship than being a tyrant. Now that he was training Soren, the young boy was lucky to benefit from Raven's wealth of experience without having to suffer his nasty temper.

Raven and Deacon left the training area and walked back along the main road through the small town of Fallway. Paradoran and Alcheran citizens mixed happily, a perfect testament to the success of the diplomatic mission Callista was operating. A young girl, around Soren's age, shot across the road in front of them and made them both pull up short. Deacon smiled warmly as the little girl sprinted on, oblivious to the inconvenience she caused. Raven yelled angrily after her, "Watch where you're going, you little brat!"

Deacon raised his eyebrows. "Really? You're telling her off just for playing when Soren is allowed to get away with everything short of murder."

Raven scowled at the truth in Deacon's words but said nothing, content to simply glare at every child who crossed their path.

They wound their way through the rough, bumpy streets of Fallway where the buildings were tall and teetered over the narrow maze of passageways. It would be easy to get lost in the rabbit warren of alleyways that branched off the main trade route, but Raven knew the way well.

They ducked under the sheets and clothes that were strung up to dry on washing lines hanging between the buildings. For a small, humble village, it was remarkably clean, thanks to the citizens' fastidious belief in cleanliness and hygiene. Residents swept their paths and washed their doors and shops rigorously. The town sparkled in the early morning sun, the warm rays lighting up the richly coloured shop fronts and house doors.

Raven was fond of the discrete nature of the town. He could wander the streets for hours and never cross paths with another person. He liked the anonymity. Deacon, however, found it claustrophobic and missed the beautiful open courtyards and gardens of the capital. He had never understood Raven's desire to avoid others at all costs.

Soren was just like his mentor and far preferred the narrow streets of Fallway, but his reasoning was almost definitely more mischievous. The winding passages gave him a convenient escape route after he'd caused trouble.

After winding through the maze of houses, Raven eventually led them to a large wooden building with dark beams and pristinely painted beige walls.

Raven stepped up to the oak doorway and rapped loudly with his knuckles. A meek young woman in a simple white dress answered. Upon seeing Raven, she dropped her eyes to the floor and bowed before waving them inside. It was obvious she knew who Raven was and was intimidated by his reputation, but it was in the way her cheeks flushed pink at seeing Deacon that showed her shyness was more than that.

Her dark eyes flicked up at Deacon for a split second as he passed her, but when he gave her a polite smile she immediately looked down again. Even if he hadn't been married to Kyra, one of the most beautiful women in all of Alcherys, Deacon Thialdor was a noble of the highest order, son of Callista and Sam Thialdor, a high-ranking elite soldier. In Children of Light tradition, the elite tended to marry the elite. It didn't stop the maid from blushing at his handsome features—his strong jawline, deep red hair, sharp nose and chestnut eyes. It didn't stop her heart from pounding at the sight of his toned, strong frame.

They continued along the corridor, leaving the maid to cast longing glances at Deacon's retreating back. At the end of the long hallway, a small staircase led to the first floor of the house. Raven and Deacon ascended the flight of steps. Raven's irritation burned in his throat as they walked along the landing to Soren and Deveron's bedroom. If the insolent little brat was still lazing in here, Raven would skin him alive.

Raven marched up to the door and pushed it open without knocking. The door swung inwards, and Raven prepared himself to drag Soren out by the scruff of his neck, but the room was empty.

Deveron's books were scattered across the floor. Raven tutted and pushed them aside with his boot, frowning at the stylised art prints that slid out, all fancy brushstrokes and complementary colours. It meant nothing to Raven; he didn't see the point in art. Soren had picked up the same attitude from his mentor, as was obvious from his side of the room, which was bare and lacklustre. His bedclothes were in a state of disarray, casually slung aside when he got up, but aside from that, there were few possessions except a few packs of cards and various toy knights.

Most of Soren's belongings were back at their permanent residence in the capital city of Nazaki. He said he'd been content to leave them there, as eventually his family would return to their castle. Deveron, on the other hand, had put up quite the resistance. He had insisted that he tied his identity to his hobbies and his tastes. He said that music and art were where the human life force was at its strongest. Crossing his arms in the haughty way he did, he had proclaimed that his love of books and music was what made him who he was.

Raven could never understand how your identity could be found outside of yourself, and he had rolled his eyes at Soren, who had grinned back.

Deacon smiled as he looked over the beautiful prints of sunsets and land-scapes that lay scattered on the floor, but Raven wandered over to Soren's side of the room, feeling more comfortable with the simplicity of his apprentice's belongings.

It was then that he saw the note, lying squarely on Soren's pillow, a piece of folded paper with Raven's name on the front. Raven snatched up the note and fumbled it open quickly, his eyes growing wide as he read the words, scribbled roughly in Deveron's handwriting.

Raven,
Soren has insisted we go to find some Brotherhood facility in Parador, just over the border.
I couldn't stop him, so I had to go with him. Please, please, come after us. I can't make him see sense. You can.
Come quickly,
Deveron

Holding the note out to Deacon, Raven began to pace back and forth. Deacon saw his half-brother's face crease in a mixture of horror and anger and took the note from his hand and read it. Raven clenched his hands into fists as he muttered obscenities under his breath. He marched to the back of the room and then suddenly turned and made a run to the door, barking a loud expletive, but Deacon stood in his way and stopped him with a firm hand to his chest.

"Wait! We can't just go. We'll need backup. Besides, we can't march on Paradoran soil, it could start a war. We've got to go to Mother."

Raven suppressed a flare of impatience, but he took a deep breath and nodded. The two men took off towards the Fallway town hall where they knew Callista would be holding council.

The town hall at Fallway was small by Nazaki standards, but was still the largest building in the town. Its circular main hall had high ceilings, criss-crossed with old wooden beams. The thick oak floors echoed underfoot. It was a far cry from the impressive cavernous senate room of Nazaki, but Callista was fond of the rustic hall and enjoyed holding meetings here. At the far end of the hall was a stage, upon which the head of the council often made speeches and the local children sang and performed.

Whilst the Children of Light resided at Fallway, the town hall was being used as a makeshift senate room, but Fallway's citizens still used it often. Today, the room was decorated with hundreds of paper birds that the children had made in memory of a young girl who had recently passed away from a cruel, debilitating sickness.

The delicately crafted birds were beautiful in all the stunning, bright colours and upon each one was a personal message. After the memorial service in two days' time, the birds would be set alight. Paradoran tradition stated that as the birds burnt away into nothingness, the smoke would carry the messages up to Heaven where the girl would read them and feel the love of those left behind.

It was a beautiful sentiment, and Callista gently ran her fingers across the delicate birds that hung from strings from the ceiling. The memorial would be a happy time, as the citizens of Parador did not believe in mourning the dead; they believed in celebrating them. Those who had made it into the paradise of Heaven were viewed as privileged, and they deserved messages of hope and love, not grief.

Callista's eyes clouded in a mist of tears as she read one of the birds.

I'll never forget your laugh. May you laugh in Heaven now.

Callista would participate as a guest of their town, but she didn't feel any of the warmth and comfort the Paradorans felt. As they smiled and sent notes of joy and love to Heaven, she would hide her sadness behind a fake smile, knowing the awful truth—that death meant death and that the departed would never read those words. But doing this made the people happy, so she would do nothing as they burnt their birds, and would say all the right things at the right times.

From the corner of her eye, she caught Kyra Thialdor, her best friend, daughter-in-law and adviser, watching her closely. Callista fiddled with one of the birds and plastered a smile across her face. "These are lovely, aren't they?"

Kyra muttered an unconvincing yes, but her gentle eyes remained locked on Callista. The tough facade wasn't fooling anybody, least of all Kyra who knew her far too well. Callista was riddled with grief. How could she not be at a time like this, surrounded by tributes to a teenage girl who had died horribly? It was too close to home.

A little girl collided with Callista and broke her out of her thoughts. She looked down to see Dana, Kyra and Deacon's daughter, with a cheeky grin on her face, sticky fingers pressed up against Callista's legs. She had smudges of something around her lips, remnants from breakfast no doubt, and her brown eyes twinkled with some new mischief she was planning.

"Hey, what are you up to, sweetie?" Callista asked, bending down to face the four-year-old.

"Chasin'!" she yelled and then sprinted off again as a tall woman with dark curly hair approached.

"I'm so sorry, Callista," the woman said. "I'll keep her away."

Callista shook her head and waved away the nanny's doubts, and she scurried off to chase Dana down. Kyra and Callista shared a grin as they watched Dana running in rings around the nanny, giggling and pressing her hands to her face to stifle her laughs. As Callista watched, the delight and humour she felt was slowly replaced by sadness, which didn't pass by Kyra.

"How are you coping here? Really?" Kyra asked softly. Callista frowned, but it was quickly replaced by a forced smile.

"Fine. I love it here in Fallway, and the alliance with Prince Khaled is better than expected. Everything is good for a change."

She knew that Kyra didn't believe her, but her friend knew better than to argue. "Good. How's Kham?"

Callista's smile dropped at the mention of her husband.

"He's good. He's...he's..." She heaved a heavy sigh. "Actually, no, he's not in a good place. He gets more and more distant every day. Soon there'll be nothing left of the man I married."

Kyra placed a comforting hand on Callista's shoulder, but Callista pushed it away gently. She appreciated Kyra's gesture, but she was uncomfortable with physical contact these days from anyone, including her husband.

"Give him time," Kyra said. "I know he's different at the moment, but it's understandable after everything he's been through. He'll pull out of it eventually."

"Will he, though? It's not that recent anymore, is it? Freya died five years ago. I've stood beside him, supporting and nurturing him as much as I could, even though I was hurt too. I don't know what else I can offer him, Kyra. I feel like our marriage is in tatters. He is like a ghost with the kids as well. He can't connect with anybody. I'm really worried we're losing him."

"Callista, you've been married for over twenty years. The things you two have been through would stretch any marriage to its limits, but you've stayed strong through it all. You'll come out of this blip in one piece too. I'm sure of it."

Callista stared blankly into the distance, her eyes glazing over. "I hope so. I really do. My other marriages never lasted. We grew apart naturally or re-alised we were more like friends than lovers. And that's fine, for both parties. I can live with that. But even the suggestion of letting Kham slip away from me..." She shuddered. "Not Kham. What we have is different. I cannot bear the thought that Vincent has won, that he's finally done what he always aimed for and driven a wedge between us."

Kyra looked away with a slight frown on her pretty features and began fiddling with a golden paper bird that glittered in the afternoon sun.

Callista forced a smile across her lips. "Anyway, enough about me. How's life at Fallway treating you?"

Kyra smiled. "I like it here. It's a lovely town, and the people are kind. I love that I can soak up a bit of Paradoran culture. And Dana's happy too. She can't wait to start at the School of Unity. I think the nanny will be pleased too. Dana's a handful, and she could use a rest!"

Callista smiled. "I'm glad you like it here. And how are things with Deacon?"

Warmth and contentment flooded into Kyra's eyes and she opened her mouth to speak but was interrupted as the doors to the hall flung open. Raven and Deacon stormed in without introduction.

Callista rolled her eyes. "For goodness sake, boys, can't you even knock?"

Raven mumbled something about no time and marched up to her, kicking aside a paper bird that had fallen to the floor. Deacon was accosted by Dana, who threw herself at him, wrapping her arms around his leg.

Callista tutted at Raven. "What's the matter with you?"

"It's that damn son of yours again."

"Which damn son of mine?"

"Which do you think?"

"Hmph. Soren? What's he done now?"

Raven thrust Deveron's letter into her hand. "He's gone into Parador."

Callista stared blankly at her son. "What?"

"Little brat wanted to explore a Brotherhood facility over the border. Look at that letter."

Callista frantically unfolded the note, her mind racing. "They've gone alone?"

Deacon nodded. "We found this when Soren didn't turn up for training. We came straight here. He should have been with us thirty minutes ago, so they can't be too far ahead."

Callista waved a hand in the air angrily. "Let me get this straight. My ten-year-old and fourteen-year-old sons have gone into unallied territory. Alone."

Raven nodded and clenched his fists at his side.

"I'm going to throttle that little pain in the backside," Callista hissed as she grabbed her sword and scabbard from a small table at the side of the hall.

"Come on. We need to go after them. Now." She began marching to the door, followed by Raven and Deacon.

"Callista! Do you want me to come?" Kyra called after them.

"Yes!" Callista called back over her shoulder. "We might need your healing skills."

"Wait!" Kyra cried, as she gathered her bag of medicines and herbs. The three warriors waited by the door impatiently. "Should I send a dryll to the capital for backup?"

"There's no time. If we go now, we can catch up with them before they get into too much trouble."

"What about Kham? He's only at the farm. I could get him in ten minutes and be right back."

Callista hesitated. "No, leave him there," she said and pulled the door open, preparing to go outside.

"Callista! They're his sons. He'd want to at least know!" Kyra cried, running up behind them.

"No!" Callista called over her shoulder. "There's no time."

"But...!" Kyra tried to call after Callista when Deacon stopped her with a warm smile and a shake of his head.

"She doesn't want him to come. I think it's best to drop it." His voice was soft and warm, and he leaned in to place a gentle kiss on her lips. "Come on, we need to catch up to them."

Kyra turned to give Dana's nanny instructions, but she was already prepared.

"It's OK. You go. I'll look after her for as long as you need."

"Thank you!" Kyra called over her shoulder as Deacon grabbed her hand and together they ran after Callista and Raven.

The four Children of Light members saddled their horses as fast as they could and rode through Fallway and out towards the border. Jumping over the wires that marked the boundary between their town and the rest of Parador, the horses galloped across the open meadows, covering the distance in good time. Callista's stallion powered ahead, its strong athletic limbs working as fast as Callista's heart was beating. Ice cold terror was coursing through her veins at the thought of two of her children out in unallied lands alone. Brotherhood spies were everywhere. Who knew what Soren and Deveron might stumble into out there?

Soren was capable, but still just a child. Against a mob of adults, he wouldn't stand a chance. Although Deveron was older, he was no soldier. He wouldn't be able to protect himself in a fight, let alone his younger brother.

Callista's chest constricted with fear. She couldn't lose another child. She just couldn't. She knew her fear and her paranoia were making this into a bigger issue than it would normally be, but five years of grief still clouded her judgement.

The sweeping meadows looked beautiful, but there was no time to enjoy them if they hoped to catch up to Soren and Deveron. After twenty minutes of riding across the fields, they arrived at a copse where the trees were packed densely together. Callista spurred her horse on to pick up its pace. They charged through the woods, leaping over roots and rocks that were dotted along the path.

Deacon saw the clearing first and cried out to the others, his keen hazel eyes picking out the partially concealed building, the Brotherhood facility they guessed Soren had gone to explore. In the clearing in front of the building, a wooden cart had stopped on the road. Callista's eyes widened at the inert forms of three Brotherhood guards lying on the ground. Unconscious or dead, she couldn't tell.

The cackling laughter that came from the back of the wooden carriage made Callista's blood run cold. Yelling for Kyra, Raven and Deacon to follow her, she sprinted up to the cart.

Chapter Ten
Shadow

ALLISTA JUMPED DOWN from her stallion and ran to the cart. With a thundering heart, she pulled aside the linen curtains covering the back of the carriage. The sight that met her eyes was bewildering. Soren stood with his back pressed against the wall of the cart, his eyes wide and afraid. His head shot up when he heard Callista pull the linen aside. At the sight of his mother, tears welled in his eyes. He ran over and threw himself into her arms. Callista caught him, staggering backwards, and held him tightly, her eyes locked onto the stranger who lay on the floor of the cart, cackling maniacally.

Deveron stood at the back of the cart in silence, twiddling his fingers together nervously, terrified eyes locked onto the man on the floor. Raven leapt up into the cart, kicking aside the broken syringe that littered the floor. He stepped in front of Deveron and gently pushed him to the safety of his mother.

Raven's dark eyes fixed the laughing man in a ruthless stare. "Who are you?"

The man stopped cackling and heaved a heavy sigh, propping himself up on his elbows. He gave Raven a sinister smile but said nothing in response.

Soren trembled in Callista's arms. "Mother, he stabbed me in the neck with that syringe, and then he said I was infected," he said in a quiet, quivering voice.

Cold fear crept over Callista as she pulled him away from her and held him at arm's length. "Infected by what?"

Soren pointed to the broken vials with a shaking hand.

"How long ago?"

"Only a few minutes."

Callista planted a kiss on Soren's forehead. "It's OK. I'll find out what's going on."

She gently passed Soren over to Kyra who enveloped the child in warm, caring arms. Callista stepped up to the back of the cart, her eyes keen and blazing and her lips pressed tightly together.

"What's this? Did you really inject my son with something?" she asked, nodding her head towards the shards of glass strewn across the floor.

The man threw his head back and cackled again.

"Raven, bring him here," Callista ordered. Raven thrust a powerful hand around the man's neck, cutting his laughter short. His eyes widened in fear as Raven dragged him by the neck, kicking and spluttering, to the edge of the cart. With a powerful heave, Raven pulled him out of the cart and slammed him onto the woodland soil.

The man groaned in pain and curled up into a ball, but Callista had the point of her sword at his throat in an instant.

"I'll ask again. Who are you, and what have you done to my son?"

"Your *son* attacked me and my men. We were peacefully taking a delivery from one place to another when those boys hijacked us."

"Is this true, Deveron?" Callista asked without taking her eyes off the man.

"Yes," Deveron mumbled through gritted teeth. "Soren wanted to see what they had in the back of the cart so he stopped them."

Callista cast Soren an incredulous glare. "Why, Soren? Why would you do that?"

Soren trembled in Kyra's arms, but a hardened look crept into his expression. "I heard that the Brotherhood had left lots of strange potions and stuff in there, just abandoned." He nodded towards the small stone building. "I got...curious."

Callista gave him a stern frown. "I'll deal with you later," she said ominously and turned her attention back to the man on the floor. She spoke quietly and calmly, keeping her anger at bay. "What are these syringes? What were you transporting?"

His eyes shifted to the left, trying to avoid her. "Just general potions. Health tonics, vitamins. Nothing special."

"Why did my son say he was infected?"

"I don't know. He's lying. I never said that," the man muttered.

"Yes, you did!" Deveron said, leaping forwards. "He did, Mother. He jabbed Soren with that syringe, and then he said he was infected."

Callista nodded to Raven, who grabbed the man by the throat again and dragged him to his feet. He spluttered and clawed at his throat, his face turning a deep shade of red. Raven growled, pressing his face close to the man's, squeezing his throat more tightly, his fingers pressing into the skin.

"It was an accident!" the man squealed. "I had it in my hand and fell. I didn't mean to inject the boy!" Raven released his grasp and the man doubled over, coughing and choking.

"Stand up and look at me," Callista commanded.

The man slowly straightened up and met her gaze, clearing his throat and struggling to regain his breath.

"Tell me the truth now, or we'll have to beat it from you."

They locked eyes. Callista saw a fierce determination burning within him, but still he said nothing. Raven stepped towards the man again and raised his fist.

"OK, OK...," the man murmured. "Just keep that brute away from me." He nodded towards Raven, who stepped back and dropped his hand with a smile on his face.

"My name is Steffan Blythe. I'm a scientist working for the Brotherhood of Shadow. They hired me to produce a serum for them. It's a toxin with unusual properties. I did it because I feared for my life."

Callista eyed him suspiciously. She didn't recognise the man and had never come across him before in her dealings with the Brotherhood. She knew each and every person in their ranks. She made it her business to know. Her people's lives depended on it. Yet here was a stranger claiming to be with the Brotherhood.

He was older than most Brotherhood members too, in his early fifties. He held himself with confidence and charm, even if his body was beginning to stoop over with age. He was tall, and his grey hair was cut short. His peculiar, deep red eyes displayed a burning intelligence that made her wary of his motives. A peculiar hint of sulphur wafted in the air around him.

Callista glanced at Soren, who was twitching nervously and scratching at his skin, as he often did when he was anxious. "What unusual properties? What is this serum?"

"It's a...virus. Yes, I suppose you could call it that."

"A virus? Why is the Brotherhood making a virus?" Callista asked, her heart pounding in her chest.

"So they can release it on your people, I presume."

"Why would you do such a thing? If you knew they were making a virus that could harm thousands of people, why would you work with them?"

"They paid me, and they threatened me. Anybody would have done the same."

Deacon stepped up to them and grabbed Steffan's collar, dragging him nearer. "What does the virus do? What are the 'unusual properties'?"

Steffan tried to push Deacon away, but he wasn't strong enough. He grabbed Deacon's hand, trying to pry his strong fingers away but he couldn't. "I can't tell you. If the Brotherhood found out, they'd kill me."

"If you don't tell us, I'll kill you," Deacon threatened in a quiet, menacing tone.

Steffan laughed, his red eyes shimmering with pleasure, as if he was enjoying this. "Then you'll never find out how to get the antidote, will you?"

Deacon and Callista exchanged a glance. "Antidote?"

"Oh yes. There is a simple antidote which will reverse the effects of the serum, if you get to it in time. But this virus is fast-acting and dangerous, so you'd better hurry up."

"Do you really expect us to believe that? We've got no proof you've even infected him with anything at all."

"Fine. Take your chances if you like. But I didn't inject him with a syringe full of nothing, did I? You can't be sure I gave him the virus, but you can't be sure I didn't either."

"Where is the antidote then?" Callista asked.

"I cannot tell you," he said with a peculiar smile on his thin lips.

"Your far-fetched claims are ludicrous. People don't carry syringes full of deadly viruses around with them. And if they did, they'd have the antidote with them too, if such a thing exists. Raven, search him."

Raven began rifling through Steffan's pockets, turning them out and flinging aside pieces of tissue and scraps of paper that were hidden inside. When he had thoroughly searched the scientist and was content that he had no antidote upon his person, he moved to the cart and searched it. Eventually, he jumped back down, shaking his head.

Deacon slammed the scientist into the side of the cart again, while Callista questioned him. "Why don't you have it with you? What if you accidentally injected the wrong person or yourself? Why not carry the antidote with you?"

Steffan held his hands up in surrender. "I was told not to! Vincent told me to just bring the virus itself. I guess he knew that this very situation would arise, and you would try to take it from me. I'm just an old man. He knew I couldn't fight you off."

"Why send you to inject Soren then?"

Steffan looked to the floor sadly. "He doesn't value me. I told you I am a slave to his wishes. Once my potions are completed, he has no further need for me. He sent me on this mission to infect the boy, knowing you'd probably kill me."

Callista nodded for Deacon to relax his grip slightly but her eyes still blazed. "And we still might. Tell me what this virus is. What will it do to Soren?"

Steffan met Callista's gaze but didn't even flinch this time. His red eyes burned into hers. "I don't know how long you have before the virus starts to work, but its effect on humans is devastating. It'll affect his skin first, bringing up sores and blisters that will burn with an intensity unlike anything he's ever felt. After the sores start to weep, his muscles will weaken and he will begin to feel tired and heavy. He will become pale and sick, and no amount of water will quench his thirst. His blood will thicken, and his little heart will struggle to pump it around his body. Eventually, the dizziness and nausea will stop him from moving at all." He uttered the words with a callous smile, running his unnerving eyes over Soren who tried to match him with a fierce glare whilst keeping his grip on Kyra's robes.

Callista didn't believe a word he said, but she kept her eyes locked onto his, just in case. "Soren, how do you feel? Any signs of a virus?"

There was no reply at first, but then Soren spoke up in a small voice. "I'm itchy, Mum."

Callista dragged her eyes away from Steffan and looked at her son. The skin on his neck was blotchy and red, but this was no ordinary rash. It wasn't spots on his skin, but the beginning of large sores. No matter how much he tried to stop himself from scratching, his nails automatically moved back to claw at his raw skin.

"You bastard." Raven drove a powerful fist into Steffan's face, splitting his lip open. A trickle of blood ran down Steffan's chin, and he flicked his tongue out to lick the blood away. He smiled at Raven who pulled his fist back and hit him again, causing Steffan's cheekbone to rise instantly in a shiny, red bruise.

"Raven," Kyra said gently, prising Soren from her skirts. "Please stop. It won't help anything."

Raven turned and glared at her but stopped hitting Steffan. Kyra walked up to Raven and gently pulled his hand away from Steffan's collar. He reluctantly let go and took a step back.

"Please, Steffan," Kyra said in a honeyed voice so gentle it was like the tone of a flute. Steffan considered Kyra quietly, running his scarlet eyes over her beautiful features. She continued, "The child is innocent. Help us to save him before it's too late. Tell us where this antidote is."

Steffan said nothing, but the side of his mouth curled in a sly grin.

"Raven, make him talk," Callista said. Raven clenched his fists and stepped forwards.

"All right, all right. There's no need for violence." Steffan held his hands up and backed away from Raven. "I'll tell you. There's a facility just inside the border of Meraxor. It's my laboratory where I developed the serum. In there is a research room with a cabinet containing the antidote. You'll find a wooden box with a sliding lid. Inside there will be glass tubes containing individual doses of the cure. It is labelled as Serum Two antidote. Drink one of those and the boy will heal."

Incredulous at the mere suggestion, Callista gave a laugh, but there was no humour in it. "You've got to be kidding. What a transparent attempt to get us into Meraxor. There is absolutely no way we'll just march onto enemy soil. We aren't stupid. Even if we went back and fetched our entire army, it's too dangerous to start a full-scale war right now." Her voice was high-pitched with tension.

"That or let the boy suffer from this horrific disease. Your choice."

Snarling, Raven stepped up close to Steffan. "We could drag you back to Nazaki and make you brew us an antidote."

Another eerie chuckle broke out of Steffan's lips. "If only it were that easy. The recipe is incredibly complex, involving countless elaborate formulae. Many of the ingredients, not to mention the catalysts needed to brew it, are back in my laboratory. And even if I could get my hands on what I need, it takes many months to enable the antidote to mature. The elements must bond, you see." He interlocked his fingers to demonstrate the point. "So, I'm afraid there really is no choice. The boy cannot wait the months for the antidote to brew. If he is to survive, he needs it in the next few days. That means you have no choice but to make the journey into Meraxor."

There was an oppressive silence as the news sunk in around their group. Raven paced around the clearing again, clenching his fists in the way he always did when his anger was building. With a shout of rage, he flew at Steffan, punching him hard on the jaw and knocking him clear of the cart, to land with a thud on the ground outside. Raven followed after him, grabbing hold of the man's collar and pummelling him again and again in a fit of rage.

"This is all your fault! How could you intentionally infect a *child* with something like this? You're sick!"

"Ease up, Raven!" Deacon snapped and pulled his half-brother to his feet. Raven glowered at him with barely concealed fury. He muttered a few obscenities under his breath and pushed past Deacon to continue pacing around the clearing.

Callista had joined them now, her mind twisting and turning furiously, eyes locked onto Deacon's. She hoped he would be the best person to discuss this with. He was more reasonable than Raven, but more realistic than Kyra.

Behind Deacon, Steffan shifted position, moving what Callista presumed were his bruised and aching limbs, but there was something in his composure that unnerved her. Then Steffan attacked. It all happened too quickly for any of them to do anything about it.

Steffan leapt up from the ground with a second syringe in his hand and jammed it into Deacon's upper thigh. With a cry of shock and pain, Deacon whirled around and ripped the needle from his leg, but it was too late and the syringe had been emptied into his bloodstream.

The flicker of demonic delight in Steffan's red eyes intensified as all doubt about his intentions was removed. Yanking the long silver sword from the scabbard at her side, Callista darted forwards and slashed the blade in an upwards arc.

Steel rang through the air. A spurt of blood sprayed from the deep gash Callista carved across Steffan's chest and throat. The front of his clothes stained a vivid crimson, and he slumped to the ground.

Callista's eyes widened and her chest heaved up and down, not from exertion, but from the sudden fright she suffered, seeing her son attacked without warning. Kyra was huddled in the corner with Soren and Deveron pressed to her, hiding their young eyes from the horror before them.

After wiping her blade on the long grass, Callista sheathed it in one quick motion.

"Deacon. Are you OK?" She dropped to her knees before her son and examined his leg where the material of his breeches had ripped in the scuffle. There was only a tiny pinprick where the syringe needle had entered his leg, but the skin around it was already raised and red. He scratched at it a few times then pulled the torn fabric back over it.

"It's fine, Mother," he said, but his voice was quiet.

Raven poked at the scientist with a boot, checking that he was dead. "Does that mean you're infected now too?"

A scoff erupted from Deacon's lips. "Come on. We don't even know that this virus even exists. The guy was obviously crazy."

Callista frowned. "Soren," she called. "Soren, come here a minute."

It took Soren a while to disentangle himself from Kyra's skirts. When he did, he became a sickly green colour as he passed the body with the mangled face staring up at him in the ground.

"How are you feeling now? Still itchy?" Callista asked, placing a hand on his shoulder.

Soren nodded and turned his head aside to show a series of seeping red bumps, inflamed and sore on his neck.

"Has this only come up since he injected you?" Callista inspected the lesions carefully.

"Yes. It burns, Mum. I don't like it."

Heaving a sigh to calm herself, Callista straightened up and waved the others around her. "This is ridiculous. We don't know anything about this virus. Maybe it just brings up a rash?"

Kyra frowned and shook her head. "I don't know, Callista. These sores look dangerous to me. I've got herbs and medicines with me, and I can treat them for a while—but only the symptoms and not the cause."

"Do what you can for now," Callista said. Kyra got straight to work applying lotions and bandages to Soren's neck and Deacon's leg.

Raven crossed his arms over his chest. "There's no way we can trust the word of that madman. We must have medicine at Nazaki that can cure this. I say we head back and check in at the hospital to see what they can do for us."

There were nods of approval from Soren, Deveron and Deacon, but Kyra wasn't convinced. "I know he seemed crazy, but this isn't a usual reaction. Soren's body is rejecting a foreign substance. Deacon, is your skin sore too?"

Deacon pulled aside the ripped material again and gasped as he saw the red blotches that had spread out from the injection site. Callista started grinding her teeth, a bad habit she had picked up when she was anxious.

"Damn it! Why didn't we bring a dryll with us? We could have sent for backup." She slammed a hand against a tree trunk beside her.

"Look," Raven said with more volume than was necessary, "let's all get back to the hospital now, before it gets any worse. We can sort out Soren and Deacon there. We can't put all of us at risk over something we don't even understand. For all we know, it's a cheap Brotherhood trick. It wouldn't be the first time, would it? They've found some plant that induces a fast-acting allergic reaction. That's all it is. I would put money on it. Let's get back and see what our doctors can do."

"I don't think it's that simple, Raven," Kyra said quietly. "I've seen and treated many allergic reactions before, but nothing like this. If it was just redness and swelling, maybe. Even blistering I could understand at a push. But seeping wounds like this? And the likelihood of both Soren and Deacon reacting severely to the same allergen? It's pretty unlikely."

Folding her arms across her chest, Callista tried to keep a lid on her anxiety for her sons. "OK, so have you ever seen anything like this before? Does it resemble a virus?"

Kyra frowned. "I've seen viruses before with similar symptoms but nothing so extreme and fast-acting. What he said might be true. A virus like this will need treating, and soon, or it could just rampage through their bloodstreams."

Something in her words made Callista freeze. "No, no, no," she muttered and began pacing the woodland clearing. "It cannot be. A virus. Blood will turn...leave it thirsty." She stopped suddenly and held her head in her hands. When she pulled her hands away, her eyes were wide and desperate.

"It's happening. It's actually happening. The blood will turn and consume the host. It's the Prophecy of Blood."

"The Prophecy of Blood? From *The Book of Alcherys*?" Deveron said, frowning.

"Yes," Callista said, nodding her head frantically. "It all adds up. I think this is it. It's finally happening."

"Don't be silly, Mother. That's just an ancient story. It doesn't mean anything," Soren said, rolling his eyes. "There are hundreds of little stories like that in *The Book of Alcherys*. The Prophecy of Blood is just another silly tale, right?"

The others watched her in silence with bated breath. Callista leaned down to look Soren in the eyes. "That book tells of our past and our future. It foretells everything that will happen to our people. It is definitely NOT just silly stories. Our nation was built around those prophecies, and we cannot dismiss them."

Soren's cheeks flushed red with embarrassment. "Sorry, Mother."

Callista gave him one last stern look of admonishment before straightening up to face the others. "The time is now. Remember the words of the Prophecy of Blood: *An infusion it begins; a tragedy it ends. The blood will thicken, consume the host and leave it thirsty. To stop the blood's rampage, the young must journey to the heart of shadows, where feathers will destroy the wild.*"

She glanced up. "Steffan said the blood would turn thick and that we would become thirsty. And that word, 'infusion,' never really made sense before, but Soren and Deacon's blood has become infused with the virus. It all fits."

Raven scoffed. "Seriously, Callista. You can't possibly know that this is the fabled Blood Prophecy."

Her eyes imploring, Callista replied, "When you have spent many years as I have studying these prophecies, you learn how to interpret them and how to recognise the signs that they are about to begin. Trust me. I don't like this any more than you do, but to ignore the Book would be a disastrous mistake."

"To walk into Meraxor without an army would be a dangerous mistake," Raven mumbled, turning away from his mother. Soren watched their argument in silence.

"What else would you have me do?" Callista's voice was strained and tense. "Soren and Deacon have a rapid degenerative illness, and no medicine we have can heal them."

"You don't know that! Kyra said she doesn't know of anything, but maybe doctors back in Nazaki do!" Raven shouted.

Kyra shook her head slowly from side to side. Callista's anxiety rose another notch. "We can't risk it."

"But you'll risk marching into Meraxor? What's happened to you, Callista? This kind of recklessness isn't you."

"I DON'T WANT TO LOSE ANOTHER CHILD!"

The tension in the silence that followed was palpable.

All her pent-up stress released, Callista's voice was a mere whisper. 'A *tragedy it ends.*' That's what the Book says. "

Upon seeing his mother so distraught, Raven let go of his anger also. He placed a sympathetic hand on her shoulder. "I know, Callista. Believe me, I know. But doing this puts more of your children at risk. Take Soren and Deacon back to Nazaki. We'll fix them there, or we'll at least be able to do some tests and find out what this is."

There was silence amongst the group, broken only by the sound of Soren scratching fervently at the infuriatingly sore blotches on his neck.

"Look at him, Raven," Callista pointed to Soren. "Look at how fast that rash came up. Whatever he was injected with, it has worked its way into his system incredibly quickly. It's dangerous. I just know it is. If there is any chance of a cure, we need to find it."

"You're not thinking logically. We can't trust any of this—the virus, the antidote, that 'scientist.' We can't make a rash decision based on the word of some insane man we met in the woods. I'd like to remind you that this man just deliberately injected Soren and Deacon with something. Do you really think he has our best interests at heart?"

"Of course I don't! Do you think I don't know how dangerous it would be to go into Meraxor? How stupid? Do you think I'm not suspicious of that man? Of course I am!" Her fists were clenched at her side, and her face was red as she spat the words at her son.

"Mum?" Soren pulled on his mother's sleeve and looked up at her. "Mum, I feel awful."

Callista's face crumpled in pain and indecision for a moment, before she dropped down in front of him, holding his face with both hands. "I know, baby. We're going to sort this."

An air of unsettling fear stirred around the group. It was inevitable that they would have to go, but it didn't make any of them happier about it.

It was Deacon who spoke first. "We have no choice, do we? If 'tragedy' is what awaits us, then we must head into Meraxor. From what this scientist was saying, the laboratory is just over the border. Maybe we could sneak in and steal the antidote."

There was a lot of frowning around the group. Nobody wanted to go to their enemy's lands, and Raven made his thoughts on the situation clear by pacing around the clearing and murmuring obscenities at plant life, kicking leaves and flowers aside.

"Do you really think we could 'sneak in' to a Brotherhood building? They'll have the place on high alert, especially now. They'll soon realise their scientist was killed, and they'll be expecting us. We'd walk straight into a trap."

"Raven, I understand your concerns, and I think you are probably right. It may be a trap. But what else can we do? Would you rather go back to Fallway and risk Deacon and Soren dying without the medicine we need to treat them? This is our only chance. We have to take it. All of us must go to Meraxor. Right now."

Kyra frowned. "If we do have to go, I don't think the children should go. It's far too dangerous for them. They should wait behind."

"They have to come with us, Kyra. We can't leave them to walk home alone. It's too dangerous. Soren hasn't got long. You said so yourself. We wouldn't have time to fetch the antidote and bring it back for him, so we have to take him to the antidote instead. And as for Deveron—if we're about to walk into Brotherhood territory, then his ability is absolutely crucial to our survival. Besides, the Prophecy of Blood states that the *young* must journey into the heart of shadows. That cannot be referring to any of us. It talks of Deveron and Soren."

"I don't want to go," Deveron muttered quietly, stroking his arm nervously.

Kyra wrapped a caring arm around his shoulders. "I'll be there to help you. Like you, I am not a fighter. We'll look out for each other."

A reluctant smile flashed across Deveron's lips, but it was soon replaced by him anxiously chewing on his lip again.

Soren didn't want to go either, even though he'd never admit it out loud. Yes, he had been looking for adventure, but he had never expected things to go so badly. Playing games and sneaking around old buildings was something he could do, but now he was expected to take the long, treacherous journey to his enemy's lands, or face a hideous death. That was too much for him to cope with. But there was no option for him to do anything else. What his mother decided was gospel. There could be no arguing with Callista Nienna when she made up her mind.

His mother marched around, concentrating, with a frown on her face and speaking to herself. "If the Brotherhood or anybody sees all of this, we could be caught out before we get to Meraxor. We need to get rid of it all. The cart, the bodies and the horses."

"Fire?" Raven suggested. Callista nodded firmly.

Callista nodded. "Let's burn the cart and the bodies to the ground. It's the only way to be sure. We'll take the horses with us. The kids would never be able to walk so far by themselves in time."

"The smoke will attract unwanted attention," Deacon added.

"Yes, so we need to escape quickly and hope for the best." Callista took a small flint box from her pocket. "Raven, you stay with me. The rest of you wait over there by the path that will lead us across Parador. Once the fire has begun, we'll join you."

Following behind Kyra, Deacon and Deveron, Soren made his way to a patch of bushes on the far side of the clearing. He was far enough away to be out of danger. Crouching behind a bush, he could watch as his mother and mentor prepared to set the clearing alight.

They moved aside any debris that could make the fire spread if they were unlucky and piled up dry leaves and branches beneath the cart to make a good-sized bonfire. The horses were still tied to the front of the cart, occasionally snorting or shaking their manes. Callista placed a hand on one of the horses' necks and stroked its soft downy fur, before cutting it free and leading it over to Kyra. She set the second horse free as well.

Raven and Callista crouched over the bodies of the three guards on the floor. They shared loaded glances, both of their eyes skipping over towards where Soren crouched in the bushes. He still didn't know if they could see him or not, but they were almost definitely talking about him. So much had happened in the past hour that he hadn't had time to dwell on the three guards that still lay still on the ground, their bodies twisted at unnatural angles.

Soren had been pretty sure he had only knocked them out, but when Callista pressed her fingers to one of the guard's throats to check for a pulse, Soren looked away. He swallowed an uncomfortable lump that rose in his throat, and the sores spreading out from the wound on his neck itched again. He clawed at his lesions and was dismayed to find his fingers wet with blood. Stinging pains pulsed in his skin, his whole neck hot to the touch and throbbing.

He prayed that he had missed the decisive moment when Callista determined the fate of the soldiers, but he got his answer, stark and brutal, a few moments later when Raven scooped up the first guard's body and slung it over his shoulder as if it weighed no more than a sack of straw. Slinging the body casually into the back of the cart, Raven dusted off his hands and went back for another body. All three of them were dead, and Soren's stomach churned with things he didn't understand. Whatever it was that tugged at his insides, he didn't like it.

Callista and Raven loaded up the cart with the three guards' bodies, then went back to fetch the scientist's blood-drenched corpse. Grabbing it between them, they slung him on top of the pile of dead.

Raven made his way back over to Soren and the others. When he was at a safe distance, Callista grabbed an oil lamp that hung at the rear of the cart. She threw the lamp to the ground. The glass shattered and the thick oil spread in a pool across the floor of the carriage. She then took the piece of flint from her box and struck it across the metal. Sparks flew, and she struck it again, holding it close to the pool of shimmering liquid. The sparks caught the oil and ignited in a rush of heat. Flames rapidly consumed the wooden frame. Callista leapt back off the cart and stood back to watch it burn. When the entire vehicle was alight, and the searing heat was too much to stand, Callista ran to catch up with her family.

The small band of Children of Light members scurried away through the last few trees of the woodland and over the rolling fields of Parador and prepared to make the long journey to the Brotherhood's lands.

The man who had told Callista his name was Steffan Blythe waited until the Children of Light were out of the clearing before opening his eyes. The cart was already alight, burning ferociously around him, the blazing inferno singeing his skin, but it did not bother him. The fires of Hell were far more intense and though he had never witnessed them himself, being only half demon, his body was more than accustomed to intense temperatures. He closed his eyes and relished the searing flames and a smile crossed his lips.

For Reign, faking death had been difficult. He had to relax his body as much as possible to make Raven think he had been killed. The slash from Callista's sword had been truly devastating, but Reign's thick Rhygun skin was only designed to bleed like a human's, while his true hide beneath remained undamaged. It was one of the benefits of his species that humans could do little to harm him.

Vincent wouldn't be too pleased that the virus hadn't made it to Fallway, but as far as Reign was concerned, something much better was happening. He had delivered all of the elites—Callista, Raven and Deacon—plus not one but two of Callista's half-breed mongrels directly into Vincent's hands. Forget the virus. Reign's skin tingled at the idea of all the other experiments he could do once he had these Children of Light members in his hands.

Chapter Eleven
The Nomads

HE BAND OF Children of Light members rode through the last few trees of the woodland and over the rolling fields of Parador. Soren could still feel the scorching heat of the blazing inferno behind them and it made his skin itch like crazy. He looked back over his shoulder. Thick, undulating plumes of smoke clouded the air, masking the blue sky. Over the gentle peaks of the Paradoran plains was the flat, grey roof of the Brotherhood storage building. The hot sun glinted in the windows before the cloud of smoke from the burning cart obscured Soren's view.

Absently scratching at his neck sores, he turned back to the vast openness that lay ahead of them. The northern plains of Parador were wide and mostly featureless with grazing meadows and gentle hills as far as the eye could see. There were occasional clumps of trees and the odd stream trickling a winding path through the grass. Each field was separated from the next by a hedgerow, neatly trimmed, running the length of each patch of farmland.

Soren had read a lot about the Paradoran people at school. Most of the maize, corn and barley found in Alcherys had been farmed in Parador, grown in the fields by diligent, hard-working farmers. They laboured day in, day out to produce large quantities of crops to trade with their neighbouring countries. They herded cows, sheep, pigs and horses, and the Paradoran grazing plains were often scattered with livestock.

The people were peaceful and generally wanted no part of the ongoing war between the Brotherhood of Shadow and the Children of Light, but their lands were inconveniently placed between the two warring nations. Alcherys, the

Children of Light's land, stretched along most of the northern border, with the vast Bernian Sea out to the south of Parador. The Brotherhood's territory, Meraxor, flanked Parador along the eastern border.

When the conflict spread across the land, both of the warring nations had wanted to ally with Parador and had sent ambassadors to negotiate an alliance. Parador wanted nothing to do with either army. The Brotherhood had sent troops in an attempt to take their lands by force, but the Children had been watching Parador closely and intercepted their army. They fought them back to Meraxor, and no further attempt had been made to conquer Parador by either army.

They were now at a standoff. Neither nation could take Parador for their own, knowing their enemy watched it closely. But it was too valuable to leave unguarded, so each nation protected it carefully whilst allowing it to remain its own state.

This suited the Paradorans nicely. They didn't need to fight to protect themselves (which was a fight they would never be able to win, as they were an agricultural nation and not a state that indoctrinated their children into fighting before they could even walk). They could just comfortably sit between the two countries and be kept safe.

Even now when Prince Ezra Khaled had worked with Callista to open the School of Unity, he made it clear that it didn't mean Parador's loyalties now lay with Callista. Khaled was smart, and he would take what he and his nation needed without tying himself too strongly to the politics of either side. He enjoyed a civil relationship with Vincent Wilder too and traded with him as much as he did with Callista. Soren never understood that. Why would Khaled want to work with somebody who clearly viewed Paradorans as inferior? He guessed Khaled was playing some sort of dangerous or stupid game by remaining neutral and independent. It meant that Parador could use both countries as and when they needed them. Due to this, Parador had become a relatively wealthy nation in its own right. They allowed citizens of both Alcherys and Meraxor to travel their lands for the purposes of trade, but any unscheduled visits were frowned upon.

Sneaking a sideways glance at his mother, Soren tried to read her expression. Callista was gnawing at her lips nervously as they made their way across the fields.

"We need to keep a low profile. Deveron, keep your sense heightened and warn us if people approach. If they see us, we may be questioned, especially if they see the smoke back there. We'll be hauled to their capital, nearly three hours on horseback from here," Callista said in a hushed voice.

Soren shrugged his shoulders. "So what? You're friends with Khaled anyway, so he'd just let us through."

"Yes, I'm sure he would, but we can't afford the delay. Three hours there and three back. It's too long. Who knows what could happen in that time?"

"What does that mean? What could happen?" Deveron said, his face creased in a concerned frown.

"Nothing, Deveron," The smile Callista forced across her face was obviously fake. "I just want us to get there quickly."

Deveron stopped in front of them abruptly, and Soren nearly bumped into him. "No! You heard what the man in the cart said. He reckons this virus is fast-acting and dangerous. Soren and Deacon are already coming out in sores." Deveron's eyes were wild and flitted frantically between his companions.

Callista shook her head vigorously, as if overcompensating for the worry in her eyes. "Don't worry, Deveron. I know their sores don't look good, but we'll have enough time to get to the antidote. I'm sure of it. It'll be OK."

Soren said nothing but raised an eyebrow at his mother's words. Nobody believed her nonchalant dismissal, and she almost certainly didn't believe it either. She was doing that annoying thing she always did when trying to calm people down. She was downplaying the seriousness of a situation in the hope of tricking them into a false sense of security.

Deveron wasn't in the mood for it. "What? No, it won't be OK, Mum! You said it yourself. *A tragedy it ends.* I don't want Deacon or Soren's blood to consume them, whatever that means!"

Kyra placed a comforting hand on Deveron's shoulder. "I'm sure that's just a metaphor for sickness, Deveron. It can't literally mean his blood will consume him. What would that even mean?"

"Well, I don't know!" Deveron gesticulated frantically. "But what if the virus is contagious, and we've now caught it from them? Out of the six of us, who is the weakest? Who will die first?" He gestured to all of them in turn. "You, Raven? I don't think so! Mum? No way! You're all strong and your bodies can fight it off. I'm just a kid. I'll die first, and you all know it!"

Rolling his eyes and uttering an exasperated sigh, Soren said, "For goodness sake, I'm younger than you. I was injected in the neck, *the neck*. I've got these horrible blotches on my skin, and I'm not whining about it."

Deveron turned on him, shouting in his face. "Yeah, but you're a soldier, aren't you? Your body is strong. Mine isn't, is it?"

Soren smirked. "Well, you're right about that."

"I'd rather be weak than spend hours mindlessly exercising just so I can kill people more easily!"

"Stop it, you two!" Callista snapped. The look in her eyes was so fierce that neither of her sons dared argue. "Yes, Soren and Deacon have both contracted a virus, and we don't know what effect it will have on them. It could kill them in an hour or just make them slightly queasy in six months' time. The only thing I do know is that we need to get to Meraxor and find this serum before their sores spread and the other symptoms start to appear. By my calculations, we should reach the Parador-Meraxor border in around two hours, so let's get going now. Unless you'd like to make it three hours by staying here and arguing?"

Soren and Deveron wilted under their mother's ferocious glare and their heads sank. Callista waved her hand briskly for her companions to follow, and she dug her heels into the stallion's side, making it canter off across the Paradoran plains. Casting each other nervous glances, the boys rode meekly behind her.

The journey was long and tiring. As the sun rose in the sky, the travellers began to feel the heat rising with it. After they had journeyed near to two hours, the landscape began to change. The grass became patchy and then gave way to coarse sand and dust as the meadows gradually turned to desert. It became more difficult for the horses to find their footing, and slips and staggers became more frequent. They were tiring too. By early afternoon, the scorching heat was unbearable and thirst and exhaustion dragged them to a crawl.

The patch of sore, red skin around Soren's injection mark was agonising. It was still small, but it felt as if his skin were being singed, blistering and puckering in the intense heat. The maddening itch had lessened at least, but cool, sticky liquid was beginning to seep from the opening wounds. Soren dabbed at it with his sleeve, but touching it sent shockwaves of pain through his body so he left it to seep, praying it wouldn't get so bad it ran down his back. Just the thought made him shudder.

Deacon seemed to be experiencing the same kind of symptoms as Soren. Every two or three steps, he would bend down to scratch the skin above his knee. Soren saw him pull the material aside to get his nails at the lesions and saw that his skin was inflamed, sore and angry. The sweltering heat from the sun was not helping.

They all covered their heads with fragments of material they could spare from their clothing, but they dared not expose too much skin to the burning sun. The two children had inherited their father's darker skin and had slightly more protection from the searing rays than the four adults, especially Kyra, whose porcelain-white skin would burn within minutes.

Callista's voice cracked when she spoke. "Deveron, any signs of life?"

Deveron shook his head in response. Callista's posture slackened for a moment before she pushed them on again.

Their biggest concern was dehydration. They hadn't been prepared for this journey and had brought no supplies, except for a small skin of water Raven carried with him. They shared this out between them, but it only stretched to a few gulps each and the adults allowed the two children to take the lion's share. Now, with the sun beating down on them so mercilessly, they desperately needed to find a water source or they wouldn't last the remaining few hours ahead of them.

Despite the extra water he'd had, Soren was the first to suffer. His throat was so dry he could barely swallow. He struggled to control the rasping dry coughs that burst from his throat without his consent. His tongue was swollen and thick in his mouth, and his head felt too heavy for his shoulders. No matter how he tried to keep his head upright, it seemed to loll one way or the other, as if his neck were made of jelly. His eyes blurred and images danced in and out of his vision. He could hear a faint voice in the distance calling his name.

"Soren! Soren!"

There was a sharp stinging pain across his cheek. His eyes focused on Raven, whose face was up close to his, his hand still raised from the slap he'd used to bring Soren around. Soren blinked, his head reeling. He was on the ground in Kyra's arms with Raven kneeling before him. He didn't even remember falling from his horse, but the pressure in his skull was oppressive and uncomfortable.

"Callista! We need to get him some liquid and get him out of this sun. Now!" Raven cried.

Callista looked around urgently, but there were only sand dunes in every direction.

"Cover him up. I'll be back," she said and galloped off across the desert on her horse. Soren remained on the ground, cradled in Kyra's arms, blinking in the blinding light of the sun.

"Soren, I need to look at your neck wound," Kyra said gently. Soren sluggishly rolled his head to one side, allowing her to get a look at his neck. The material of his shirt stuck to the wet sores. When Kyra pulled it away, Soren yelped in pain. The silence that followed was unsettling. Soren could only assume that his wound had gotten worse.

Callista was back beside them before they had a chance to discuss anything. "There's nothing that way. As far as I can see, there are just the trees behind us," she said.

"Then we head back home and get Soren some rest and some medicine," Raven said resolutely, but Callista shook her head.

"No. We have to move forwards. We must. We need that antidote."

"At the expense of Soren's life?" Raven barked.

"To SAVE Soren's life!" Callista's eyes blazed. "Is this exhaustion, Raven? Is it dehydration? Are you sure? Or is this another effect of the virus? You can see what's happening to his neck. Maybe this is another side effect. So, yes, he needs water and we'll find him some. But he needs the antidote too, and he needs it as quickly as possible. We have no other choice."

The others stared at her in silence until Kyra said gently, "Callista, Soren's in danger being out here in the heat. He's too young, and his body can't cope with the effects of this virus and the heat. We need to save Soren now. That's most important. If we get him home and into the shade and get him rehydrated, he'll survive."

"No. He can't go home. Not yet. You said it yourself, Kyra. We haven't got the medicine there to treat him. Taking him home is a death sentence. We push on," Callista said.

"But he's your son," Deacon said quietly.

"And I'm trying to save him! Trust me, I do not make this decision lightly. I'm going to find him some water."

She took off again to the sand dune in the west for a final look over the vast desert, the horse's hooves sinking into the fine sand with every tired step. From the way Callista's shoulders drooped, Soren guessed she hadn't found anything. She started to turn and trudge back to the others when her posture suddenly straightened and she squinted into the distance.

"Over there! I think there's something over there! Deveron, quick, come and see."

In a shot, Deveron was at her side, hand over his eyes as he strained to see into the distance. "There's something there. Vague shapes, but I can't make anything out for definite. It's possible there are people."

Soren's focus was drifting, the blur taking over his entire vision now, but he felt the strong arms of his mentor scoop him up. He was jostled onto Raven's back whilst somebody tied him in position with long strips of fabric. Raven slowly and carefully climbed up onto his horse's back, Soren strapped against him.

A steady rocking rhythm began as the horse started to make its way across the sand. Soren was nervous about falling and tried to hold on, but his strength was waning and he soon realised that it was easier, and much more comfortable, to relax his muscles and allow himself to be carried. Raven would never let him fall.

It took a further hour of trekking through the burning hot sand to reach the source of the light, and Soren drifted in and out of sleep, frequently jolted awake by the horse's increasingly jarring steps or by a sharp, stinging sensation in his neck wound. He was snapped out of a doze as Deveron cried out in delight at the tiny Paradoran encampment that had come into view on the horizon.

"Callista, stop," Kyra said. "We don't know anything about these people. They could be Brotherhood."

Lifting his head and blinking the haziness from his eyes, Soren wanted to see his mother, to read in her eyes how she was going to deal with this dilemma. She responded in typical Callista fashion: icy cool, logical and practical.

"I know, but look at their tents, their clothes. They don't belong to any Brotherhood faction that we know. We need to get Soren some rest and some water. We have to take a chance. All of you, have your weapons ready. And, Deveron, make sure your senses are attuned to what's happening around us."

None of the group seemed happy about walking into a camp of strangers, but their desire for food, water and rest overrode their suspicions and fears.

It was a temporary resting site set up by a band of nomadic merchants. They froze when the six Children of Light members rode in. Some of the people had large clay pots in their hands or were weaving fibres together to make blankets. It looked to Soren as if they had all been flash-frozen in a single second, mouths gaping open, eyes unblinking with shock. Clearly they weren't used to seeing other people on their travels, especially in the unforgiving Paradoran desert.

But, despite their obvious surprise, the people were kind and wanted to help as soon as they saw how sick Soren was. Their gentle eyes were warm, their rich brown skin shiny in the heat of the sun. They scurried around, fetching skins of water and ushering them into the makeshift canvas huts that had been constructed for cover.

The Children of Light members took the water gratefully, gulping down mouthfuls of the crisp, clear liquid. It was slightly warm from the sun, but to their parched throats and dry tongues, it was the most delicious thing they'd ever tasted.

After being placed gently on the ground by Raven, Soren could only lie still with little energy to do anything more. Kyra gently lifted his head and poured some of the water onto his parched lips. He opened his mouth, desperate for more, and gratefully drank. When they had all had enough, they sank to the floor of their hut and rested while Callista spoke with the chief of the nomadic tradesmen.

Their leader, a middle-aged man with stern eyes, was named Eradi and when he spoke it was with an air of confidence and dismissal. He kept his distance from Callista, eyeing her across the table with a mixture of suspicion and intrigue. From where Soren lay upon the soft cushions of the hut, he could see his mother and Eradi and watched them closely, unsure what to make of the nomad.

"Where have you come from and why are you out in the desert at such a time?" the man asked her with carefully chosen words and doubting eyes.

Soren heard his mother hesitate, unsure how much detail she should give. It must have been a difficult meeting for her. If Eradi discovered they were from the Children of Light, would his attitude towards them change? Maybe he would even hand them over to the Brotherhood for a reward.

Callista straightened her posture, lengthening her back. "We are travelling to Meraxor. It is vital that we get there soon. My son, Soren, the young boy in there, is sick and we believe there is medicine to help him in Meraxor."

Eradi narrowed his eyes. "You're from the Brotherhood?"

"Yes, we need to get home." Her voice was strained with the lie, though many would not have heard the indecision that Soren heard in her voice.

Eradi's eyebrows furrowed further, and he pursed his lips tightly. "Where have you come from?"

"We strayed out too far from our home. We were looking for something when my son fell ill."

Eradi crossed his arms with a loud, derogatory harrumph. "Why must you lie? I am a merchant. It is my business to have dealings with the Brotherhood and the Children of Light. Did you think I wouldn't recognise the Avalanche uniform one of your party wears? I supply Avalanche with hay for their horses and those fighting dummies they make. You are not Brotherhood."

Soren gritted his teeth and cursed Raven's insistence upon wearing the sword and shield uniform at all times.

Eradi leant closely in to Soren's mother in a move that was more conspiratorial than threatening. "So, why would a group of Children of Light risk life and limb by crossing the Paradoran desert just to get to their enemies? If you are trying to invade, you have chosen your army poorly, and I will not be part of such hostility."

Callista sighed in resignation. "Two of my people have been infected by a virus. My son, as you saw, is very sick with it. We know nothing of what the virus really does or how it will progress. All we know it that the Brotherhood did this to them and the antidote lies in Meraxor. We must get to it before the virus starts to seriously affect them."

His dark eyes softened a little. "Why did you bring the children? Even the mighty Children of Light cannot be stupid enough to assume such younglings are ready for war." Even Soren felt uncomfortable by the undercurrent of sarcasm in Eradi's words, but his mother was calm and composed, ever the diplomat.

"You're right. I did not choose to bring them, but unfortunately my children often bring such misfortune upon themselves. This virus is fast-acting. They both came out in sores as soon as they were exposed to it. There was no time to go home and prepare."

A deep sigh escaped Eradi's lips, and he shrugged his shoulders at Callista. "What can I say? You're looking out for your people. I understand that. But they aren't my responsibility. MY people are my responsibility, and recently we've been a little short on trading deals and therefore...money."

His insinuation was obvious.

"We have nothing with us, only what you see. But back in Alcherys we have resources. We could compensate you generously. If we are to find this antidote and cure my children, we will need your help to get to Meraxor. We must be allowed to rest here a few hours, and if you could spare any provisions for our journey we would be most grateful."

A wry smile crossed Eradi's lips. "I've been let down by Children of Light promises before. How do I know you'll bring the reward back for us?"

"I am no ordinary Children of Light soldier. I am Callista Nienna, ruler of Alcherys and matriarch of the four daggers of eternity. You have my word."

Eradi laughed a high-pitched chuckle. "It doesn't matter what your title is. Children of Light vows are fragile, and those outside of your inner circle are often forgotten. Your 'word' means nothing to me. I need proof you will return. You must leave something with us, something so important you won't forget to come back for it."

Callista held her hands out wide showing her empty palms. "We have nothing of value."

"Your sword." Eradi nodded at the graceful blade that hung by her side.

"No," Callista said firmly.

"Then, you do not want our help enough."

"And you don't want us to survive long enough to bring your reward. I need my sword if I am to walk into my enemy's territory. Or perhaps you can make a thousand gold coins through other means?"

He clicked his tongue in annoyance. "You strike a hard bargain, Callista Nienna. How about I have your ring instead?" He nodded to the golden band on Callista's left-hand. Soren's heart jolted as he heard the words.

"But...that's my wedding ring," Callista murmured.

"Then you'll be wanting it back, won't you?"

One last sentimental stroke of the golden band, and Callista removed it from her finger. Soren wanted to cry out to his mother to put it back on, that they'd find another price to pay, that her marriage to his dad was more important than this stupid antidote.

Callista dropped the ring into Eradi's outstretched hand. He lifted it up to get a good look at the delicately woven gold and gave a whistle of admiration.

"Now this will fetch a fair price. You'd better come back for it, Callista, or it'll end up on the black markets of Belkeep."

"I give you my word I'll return with the money, and that ring had better be waiting for me when I do," Callista said quietly, but there was no mistaking the fierceness in her eyes.

"Oh, don't worry, it will." He chuckled. "I must say, I do find it strange that you are more willing to part with your wedding ring than your sword. What would your dear husband have to say about that?"

"My husband would be pleased that I put the lives of his children above a band of metal."

"Let's hope he does see it that way and doesn't feel as disposable as the other husbands who came before him."

Callista's eyes darkened for a moment, but she didn't rise to the bait. "We'll leave in one hour when my people have rested." She rose to leave, and Eradi called after her.

"I'll ready the cart. We can't take you into Meraxor but will carry you to the border. It will be quicker and less strain on you. And I'll send food and clothes in right away."

Callista turned in surprise, her eyes wide with gratitude. A smile crossed Eradi's face, and he scurried off to gather supplies for them. There was such relief in Callista's eyes that Soren couldn't be too angry at her for what she had done, but Eradi's jibe about her previous husbands had struck a chord with him. The other marriages of Callista Nienna were no surprise to him. All of the children in Alcherys grew up knowing that their matriarch had married many times, and Soren had even developed good relationships with some of her former husbands. But he viewed them as uncles more than anything else. He assumed that, really, Callista had just been good friends with them, and they had decided to have children because that's just what people did.

True love hadn't come to Callista until she had married Soren's father, Kham. That's what Soren liked to believe, but hearing Eradi suggest that Kham could be cast aside put all sorts of worries into Soren's young mind. It turned over and over in his head, making him nervous and jittery, but as soon as he lay down on the soft blankets, he drifted into welcoming darkness. He slept soundly for the entire hour. When he awoke, it was with renewed vigour and ravenous hunger. Whilst he had been sleeping, Eradi's people had brought them platters of dried meats, cheeses and breads. Soren guzzled a skin full of water and an entire loaf of bread, tearing off chunks with his hands and shoving them into his mouth.

Deveron glared at him in disgust. "You eat like a pig," he said, screwing up his nose.

Soren responded by cramming as much bread as possible into his mouth and chewing it noisily in Deveron's face.

Raven couldn't help laughing at his young apprentice. "I guess you're feeling better now then?"

"Yes, I'm fine," Soren struggled to say through huge mouthfuls of bread.

"Good, because we set off soon."

"Great!" Soren smiled, swallowing the last of his bread and jumping to his feet. As soon as he stood, the room around him shook. He struggled to stay upright. Waves of nausea flooded over him, and he forced down the bile that tried to rise in his throat. Every muscle in his body felt heavy, and he found he could barely move his neck for the stiffness and swelling around the injection site.

Kyra frowned and rose to her feet to check him over. "Soren, you look really pale, almost translucent. Let me take a look at your wound." She pulled aside a makeshift bandage she had strapped over it before he slept, but it was already sodden with a horrible mixture of blood and pus. The terrified look in her green eyes told Soren it wasn't good.

"Are you feeling OK?" she asked quietly.

Soren didn't want to delay the journey any longer. He was embarrassed that merely moments before, when sitting down, he had felt fine and now he didn't want to admit how sick he still felt. "I'm fine. I guess I ate the bread too fast."

Kyra held his head in her hands and looked into his eyes. "Look up. Now down. Hmmm. Your reactions are delayed."

He shook her off. "I'm fine, Kyra! Honestly. Let's just go," he snapped and strode out of the hut. He knew that as soon as he left they would talk about him, and his natural curiosity overrode his stubbornness. Pressing his back against the outside of the hut, he strained to listen to what they said about him.

He heard Kyra's soft-spoken voice first. "He's only a child and the virus was administered directly into his veins, so it will be affecting him more and more with each passing minute."

"Do you think that's what this is? It's not just dehydration?" Raven's gruff voice chipped in.

"With rest and nourishment, dehydration should have lessened by now, but he looks worse than ever. I think it's more than that. The virus is starting."

"Then let's get going," Raven said.

Soren hurried away from the hut to stand with Deacon and Deveron and pretended he hadn't heard anything, but the words stayed with him. If what they said was true and the virus really was starting, then he could be in big trouble if they didn't get the antidote soon.

Eradi proved true to his word and a cart was ready to take them to the border. The women fetched handfuls of clothing and offered them to the weary travellers, explaining that the flowing cotton robes would be far lighter and cooler to travel in. The Children of Light accepted gratefully, except Raven who insisted on staying in his deep purple Avalanche uniform. Despite the heat, he said he was comfortable in it. Soren knew it would take more than heat to make Raven dispense with a uniform that he saw as part of his identity. Plus, Soren guessed he had various weapons and supplies in the pockets that he wouldn't have in the fabrics Eradi offered them.

The others happily sacrificed their pockets for the comfort of the light flowing material, although Callista, Deacon and Soren strapped their sword belts over the top of the new clothing.

At last they were ready to set off, and they clambered into Eradi's cart. The journey took half the time by cart, the camels' hooves far more adapted to tread the sand than human feet or horses' hooves. Up and down the sand dunes they travelled until finally they came to a stop.

"This is it," Eradi said, jumping down from the cart to help them out. He pointed to the north-east. "The border is just over this dune."

"Are there guards?" Callista asked.

Eradi shook his head. "It's unlikely. Nobody travels this way. They only guard the main routes, and the way we have travelled was circuitous and sometimes treacherous to those who don't understand the desert. They will not be guarding this part, I assure you. But once you pass into Meraxor, I believe you must turn northwards to find the facility you are looking for. It will be a few more hours on foot."

Callista shook his hand. "Thank you for all your help. We will return as soon as we have the money for you."

"I hope so," he said with a smile, then returned to his cart and rode away.

Preparing themselves for whatever lay ahead, the six Children of Light members set off on the next long part of their journey.

Chapter Twelve
Inferior Genes

 OLD FURY SIMMERED in Vincent's eyes. "You mean to tell me that you, a half-demon, were defeated by a ten-year-old child?"

Reign gave a lopsided grin. "Not defeated, sire, but yes, our plans have been altered."

Vincent slowly approached Reign with barely concealed anger. "Altered? So that batch of precious, not to mention expensive, virus was burnt to the ground, for nothing?"

Another sly smile crossed Reign's lips. "Well..."

"STOP GRINNING! The only reason I keep you around at all is your experiments and the things you produce for me. If you can't even deliver the viruses you make, what in the name of Hell is the point of you at all?"

Reign did his best to hide a smirk, but the corners of his lips still rose. "Allow me to explain, Master. Jade did exactly what was asked of her. When I left the facility, I encountered the Nitaya boy and his brother. Following your orders, I made sure that Soren contracted the illness. I was ready then to continue my journey to unleash the rest of the virus at the town of Fallway. However, before I could continue on my way...shall we say, 'reinforcements' arrived."

Vincent shook his head in annoyance. "Reinforcements?"

"Oh yes. We were joined by Callista, Raven, Deacon and Kyra."

Vincent's eyes widened, but he said nothing. Tilting his head to one side, Reign laughed at the shocked expression on Vincent's face.

"Callista? Raven?" Vincent spluttered. "Are you sure it was them?"

"Of course. I do know our enemies."

"But how did you escape them?" Vincent asked and began pacing backwards and forwards.

Another high-pitched chuckle. "For a start, I'm a Rhygun, remember?"

Vincent raised his eyebrows with scepticism. "Rhygun or not, Callista and Raven could have finished you off."

"They did 'finish me off,' but they didn't reckon with a Rhygun's ability to heal, did they? I managed to infect another of the group before they 'killed' me."

Vincent stopped in his tracks. "Which?"

"Deacon Thialdor." Reign took great pleasure in the words.

Vincent closed his eyes and tilted his head towards the ceiling, soaking in the realisation that Reign could have altered history forever. The difference this could make was monumental. It was truly the twist of fate Vincent had been waiting for.

"So, let me get this straight. Not only will the Nitaya boy get sick, but one of the most senior fighters in the Children of Light is going to fall victim to the Guardian-Ceresecca disease? This is perfect."

Reign clicked his tongue. "It's a shame I couldn't get to Raven or Callista, but Deacon was the closest. Anyway, I decided to take the next part of the plan into my own hands."

"What did you do?"

"I told them there was an antidote in Meraxor, at the laboratory." Reign held both hands up to stop Vincent, who was about to interrupt him with a burst of vitriolic insults. "I know that's a lie, but it does mean is that a whole group of your most high-profile targets is currently just walking onto your land to find an antidote that doesn't even exist."

It took a moment for Vincent to digest the magnitude of Reign's words, but when he did he allowed a rare moment of pleasure and victory to wash over him.

Reign capitalised on the moment and walked slowly around Vincent. "And they're not just walking into any old facility, Master, but the very place where all of our research is being conducted. If we manage to capture them all, imagine what I could learn, what I could take from such quality specimens. Raven Lennox? I could drain everything from him, milk all of his strength dry and utilise it to create stronger weapons than we ever have before. My creatures, the ones I am developing in the southern laboratory, would be unstoppable with just a small dose of Lennox or Nienna DNA."

"No," Vincent snapped. "If we get them, the others are all yours but Callista is mine."

Reign smirked. "Then it's a deal. We need to get them deep into the facility and then strike when they feel confident of their success."

Vincent nodded in agreement. "I'll only post a skeleton guard, enough that they feel a presence and aren't suspicious. Of course, they'll cut through foot soldiers easily enough but the sacrifice in manpower will definitely be worth giving them a false sense of security."

"The longer they are wandering the facility, the stronger the effects of the virus will become. If we can herd them, keep them travelling in circles, make their expedition as long as possible, then the virus will have more time to do its worst. Can I suggest something, Master?" Reign continued.

Vincent's eyes narrowed, but Reign continued. "Perhaps this is the opportunity we've been waiting for. Perhaps this is time to unleash Guardian and see what he can do. He is more than ready."

"Do you really believe he is strong enough to face Raven Lennox and Deacon Thialdor?"

"Yes, I do," Reign replied matter-of-factly. "For the past six months, he has been training every day, just waiting for the chance to get out there and show everybody what he's capable of. The problem is that he's unstable and likely to kill everybody within the vicinity. Therefore, unleashing Guardian on the battlefield would be just as dangerous to our troops as our enemies. However, you've already said that you're only putting a skeleton army into the facility."

"I'm still not convinced," Vincent said. "I want to see him. Go and fetch Guardian."

With a bow that was either genuine or sarcastic (Vincent couldn't tell), Reign scurried from the room.

As soon as he was left alone, thoughts began to run through Vincent's mind. For most of his life, Vincent had been living in the Meraxan capital city of Belkeep, where his luxurious palace provided everything he could ever ask for and where he felt safe and protected by the huge army he employed and the monumental walls that surrounded the city. But ever since this Paradoran fiasco, he had moved out to the western region of Meraxor, so that he could keep a close eye on the Children of Light's scheming in the neutral country.

Parador had always been unallied, and that was the way that Prince Khaled had promised Vincent that they wanted to stay. This new treaty with Alcherys had come as a complete surprise to Vincent and to say that he felt betrayed was an understatement. Once they had opened the School of Unity, it was obvious where Parador's true loyalties lay, no matter how much Khaled bleated his neutrality.

He knew why the prince had done it. It was all down to Kham Nitaya, Callista's damn husband. *Him again.* Vincent's stomach churned. Kham was originally from Parador before he had moved to live with Callista and their half-breed brats in Nazaki. When Freya had died, Kham had milked his relationship with Prince Khaled to wrangle a treaty between Alcherys and Parador.

Well, Kham Nitaya was nothing more than a cockroach, as far as Vincent was concerned. If he had the chance to squash that cockroach again, regardless of the impact upon the Meraxor-Parador relationship, he would do it.

This whole plan with the virus was supposed to be Vincent's crowning glory. This had been his chance to not only infect one of Callista and Kham's children, but also to show Parador and Prince Khaled that the Brotherhood of Shadow were not to be messed with.

Now, thanks to Reign's quick thinking, the results would be far greater. Just the possibility of capturing Callista Nienna made Vincent's mouth water, and this was finally his chance. The fact that it came with the added bonus of utterly destroying her horrid half-breed children was just the icing on the cake.

What was it with Callista and breeding with subpar humans? Raven, for all of his military skill, came from mediocre stock. His father, the fabled Hayden Lennox, had originally come from the primitive and underdeveloped forests of Thos. Deacon Thialdor, with his red hair and pale complexion, was a classic example of Terralian scum, the people Vincent had enslaved for the past fifty years. And now Callista was breeding with the Paradoran, Kham. It made Vincent sick to see her disgusting children, their genes riddled with imperfections.

Well, once she was his, all of their children would be perfect. They would be a beautiful blend of the best of Alcherys and the best of Meraxor, the two superior races of the planet. He closed his eyes to picture the moment he would come face-to-face with Callista again. The last time he had seen her still tore his heart out. The memories of one of the most tragic days of his life burned into his soul forever.

Vincent clenched his teeth and forced the images from his mind. What he was planning here and now would make everything right again. It would bring the balance back to the world. Finally, he could have Callista by his side, and they could rule as the king and queen of the New World. He would wipe the rest of her people off the face of the planet, those who refused to join him, of course. Then Meraxor would exist as the world's greatest nation, as it always should have been. Vincent sighed. No matter how much he wished it, it always felt like there was such a long way to go.

He was dragged out of his thoughts by the door swinging open. Reign marched in with surprising assertiveness. His withered features always misled Vincent. He found himself expecting a frail old man instead of the powerful half-demon, half-human that hid beneath the crinkled skin. Guardian walked behind him, and Vincent was shocked by the change in the young man.

The last time Vincent had seen his son, he had been weak, pale, struggling to handle the life-changing effects of the Ceresecca virus. The change in him was staggering. A weak, feeble frame had handicapped the young Guardian before, but now he was blessed with a powerful, muscled body and a cocky smirk.

"Good to see you, Dad," he said calmly and stretched a confident hand towards his father.

Vincent shook his hand and felt a glow of pride flowing through him. "I can't believe…"

"You can't believe it's me? Time changes people, Father."

"It wasn't time that changed you." Vincent looked his son up and down again, and a smile crept across his face.

Guardian fixed Vincent in a solid, strong gaze and smiled. "What can I do for you? Are you going to let me out of this prison?"

"Not exactly. You need to stay here, but this will be your chance to flex your wings. Soon, a group of Children of Light soldiers will arrive at this laboratory."

Guardian's face crumpled at the mention of their enemies, and he spat on the floor in disgust. "Can I kill them?"

Vincent smiled at his son's new-found bloodlust. "We need some of them to be kept alive. You are not to touch Callista Nienna. She's mine. Reign wants Raven Lennox. Deacon Thialdor will soon change to become like you. Leave him. I want to see what becomes of him. The rest are for you to kill. Kyra

Thialdor...she's nothing. Wipe her out. Soren and Deveron Nitaya are worthless kids. You can kill them too."

Guardian grinned. "I'll need blood to utilise my full powers. Once I drink blood, my strength and my wings activate."

"Then we shall provide you with a small amount of blood to get you started. Beyond that, you can use the blood of one of the victims to fuel the deaths of the others."

Guardian grinned, his eyes blazing with excitement. "It's a deal. I'll take my leave now and lay in wait for them to arrive."

Vincent smiled, impressed by his son's attitude. "Good luck," he said and then added quietly, "Don't disappoint me."

If Guardian heard his father, he didn't break his stride as he walked from the room.

Reign stepped up beside Vincent, chuckling. "This is exciting, isn't it?"

Vincent turned to Reign with a hint of disgust in his eyes. "Let's just hope Guardian succeeds."

With a shrug of his shoulders, Reign walked to a window that looked out over the western region of Meraxor and into Parador. Resting his hands on the frame, he cast his eyes over the open expanse of desert that lay before him. "Even if he fails and they escape alive, Deacon and Soren will still become blood-sucking monsters. They'll kill anybody and everybody around them. It's a win-win situation for us."

"Let's hope so," Vincent said quietly.

Chapter Thirteen
Sinking

F THE FIRST PART of their journey was tiring, the second half was thoroughly exhausting. They had nowhere near as far to travel as they had between the facility and Eradi's camp, but it was made twice as hard by the terrain. Soren wished they still had their horses, but when they had travelled by Eradi's cart they had left the horses behind. The loose sand beneath their feet was so fine that with every step they sunk deeper into the grains, and it took extra effort to yank their feet back out again.

Soren felt much better than he had on the way to Eradi's camp, but now his calves and thighs burned with the exertion. In his training sessions with Raven, he'd been forced to do hundreds upon hundreds of exercises that strained his muscles to their very limit, so he was no stranger to hard physical work. But three hours of trekking across ever-sinking sand was making even his well-trained legs ache.

They had brought plenty of supplies with them, given to them by Eradi and his people, but still the appearance of a small oasis came as a considerable relief. They rushed forwards, dropping to their knees and scooping up handfuls of the cool water, splashing it upon their sweltering faces. It was unlike anything Soren had read about. It wasn't the typical idyllic desert oasis he had been expecting with crystal clear water and vibrant green palm trees dotted around it. This was nowhere near as beautiful. The water was cloudy with silt that stirred up around their hands as they scooped it up, and the only vegetation to be seen for miles were a few prickly brown bushes. Across at the far bank of the oasis were some stone circles scorched black by fire. Soren guessed that Eradi or another tribe of nomadic people had recently made camp here, making use of the available water.

Tiny streams trickled away from the central pool, and the sand beneath their feet was no longer crisp and dry but instead thick and clammy. With every step, water squelched. The sand was waterlogged, and Soren prodded at it with his foot, fascinated by the way the water would rise around his shoe and then sink back into the sand as soon as he released the pressure.

When they had all doused themselves in cooling water and were ready to move on, they trudged onwards, away from the oasis. Soren trailed slowly at the front with Deveron by his side, wondering when they would finally find their way to this dumb laboratory.

There was a cry from behind him. "Deacon!"

They all spun around to see Kyra, standing as still as a statue with a pan-icked look in her eyes. Deacon went to her with a concerned look on his face. "What's the matter?"

She cast her eyes down to the ground where her feet had sunk into the sand. The water beneath the sand had pooled around her feet, as it had with Soren, but he could see the thick, viscous liquid making its way gradually up her ankles and to the bottom of her calves. She wriggled and struggled to yank her feet free.

"Callista! Raven!" Deacon yelled as he ran to her, halting a metre or so before the darker sand that was sucking her in.

They all gathered around her, panicking and reaching out with their hands to try and help her. Callista yanked the sword from her side, and held the scabbard out towards her friend, urging her to hold on so she could pull her free. Kyra looked as if she didn't even see the offer. Her eyes were fixed upon her husband, pleading for him to help her.

She tried to wriggle her feet forwards, attempting to edge closer towards Deacon and to safety, but she only sank deeper into the squelching sand. The more she tried to pull her foot out, the stronger the suction became.

"Hold on, Kyra!" Deacon shouted. "We'll get you out!" Soren had never heard his half-brother's voice so agitated.

The panic in Kyra's eyes intensified as she struggled to get to her husband, her desperate hands stretching out to him. The sand was half way up her calves now and advancing quickly. Soren's heart was beating so hard in his chest that he thought it might burst out of his ribcage. He stood back, watching as a helpless observer. He could almost see the future ahead of them: Kyra getting pulled deeper beneath the sand, Deacon screaming her name, desperately reaching out to her as she sank to her death.

The shakes began to spread throughout Soren's whole body. Tears began to run down his cheeks. He couldn't hold them in anymore. Callista and Raven reached out to Kyra, but her eyes were still fixed on her husband, who stood at the edge, motionless, helpless to reach her. Deacon's eyes were flitting all around him, searching for something, anything, that could help his wife.

Raven pushed him aside and knelt down, holding his hand out to Kyra. "I'm going to get her!" he shouted as he stretched out across the sand towards her desperate hands. He grasped her flailing hand and held onto it with all of his strength. He grunted, pulling at her as hard as he could. "Help me pull her out!" he shouted to the others.

Callista ran up behind Raven and held onto his belt as he reached out as far as he could stretch. Soren leapt into action and held onto his mentor's ankles, helping in the only way he could. Deveron jumped in too and held onto the tails of Raven's uniform.

Deacon's eyes blazed with anger and fear. "STOP!" he yelled. "It won't work!"

He pushed past them all, hitting at Raven's hand on Kyra's. "Let go of her!" The hysteria in his voice frightened Soren. He had only ever seen his half-brother calm and composed. This kind of fear in somebody who was usually so gentle unnerved him.

Raven dropped Kyra's hand and turned on Deacon with fire in his expression. "What the hell are you doing? Don't you want me to save her?" he yelled with the burning aggression that had earned him his reputation as a fearsome warrior.

Deacon squared up to his old mentor. "You won't save her that way! The more you pull her, the deeper she'll sink!" The sand was up to Kyra's thighs, and tears were beginning to roll down her porcelain white cheeks. Her desperation to reach her husband was clear in her eyes.

Raven shoved Deacon back, pushing him hard with both hands on his chest. "Don't be an idiot! Let us get her out!" Raven turned back to Kyra and reached out for her again.

The sound that escaped Deacon's lips was an animalistic howl of rage. "Leave her alone! She's my wife, and I say how we get her out!"

"You're wrong, Deacon." Raven's voice was filled with contempt. "We just need to pull her out. Stop being such a pompous prick. Put your goddamn pride aside, and save your wife!"

Soren cowered beneath the heat of Raven's glare, just as Deveron froze and even Callista halted for a moment. But Deacon squared right up to him.

His voice lowered to a hiss. "You aren't my master anymore, Raven. Your days of bullying and beating me are over. We only see each other now because I consider you a friend. So drop the whole alpha male thing and help me save Kyra."

Raven simmered with a ferociousness Soren had heard about but rarely seen from the mentor he adored. The two men stood facing one another, the master and the apprentice, a battle of personalities so strong that neither would back down. Eventually, it was their mother who dragged them out of their argument.

"Raven, back off!" Callista shouted. "Deacon, help her!"

He didn't need asking twice. Deacon was over to the edge of the quicksand instantly.

"Right, Kyra. Just calm down. I know it feels like it's pulling you down, but it isn't really. It's just resisting when you struggle. I need you to relax."

Kyra's face showed anything but being relaxed as the sand rose to her waist. "Deacon," she murmured.

"I know it's hard. I know. Just try your hardest to relax. Trust me. Relax and it'll stop sucking you. You need to distribute your weight on the top of the sand, not underneath it."

Raven came to stand beside Deacon. He crossed his arms but didn't try to take her hand this time. He couldn't help himself from whispering to his half-brother, though.

"She'll die. Please, let me help you."

With another snarl of annoyance, Deacon ignored his brother. He repeated the instructions to his frightened wife. "Take it easy. Relax. Lie back in the sand. I know it's scary and the last thing you want to do, but if you lie back you can spread your weight out and float in the sand."

Now up to her armpits, Kyra stared at her husband like he was mad, but she finally stopped struggling. Deacon knelt at the edge of the sinking pit and closed his eyes, as if he was gathering his internal strength. "Trust me," he whispered. When her frightened green eyes met Deacon's, Soren knew she did trust him. She relaxed and did as he asked, lying back on the surface of the sand.

"Good," Deacon said, his voice cracking slightly with the fear of seeing his wife giving more of herself over to the life-threatening sand.

Frightened and unnerved by the whole situation, Soren edged backwards. Some part of his mind was telling him that the further away he could remove himself, the less real it would all seem. Deveron was cowering even further back, pale and sweating in the sweltering sun.

Soren looked to his mother instead, but Callista too stood back, a cold look of removal in her eyes. Soren had seen it before. It was what Callista always did when she was shutting herself off from all emotion, trying to pretend she was devoid of feeling. This look had been on his mother's face at least once every day since Freya's death. She was doing it again now, preparing herself for the idea of losing her best friend.

Slowly, Kyra lay back, her long red hair fanning out over the sand. Just as Deacon had promised, her weight rested on the top of the sand, and she miraculously floated.

"That's fantastic, Kyra!" Deacon said. "Now you just need to pull your feet towards the surface really slowly."

"It's still sucking them down," Kyra muttered, but her voice was more confident now than it had been before. "If I can just…" Her face creased into a frown as she struggled to jostle her feet free.

Eventually, the tip of one of her shoes poked out, much to Soren's delight, who jumped up and down, whooping with happiness.

Callista's head dropped, her eyes closed as if the fear had been propping her up like a puppet and now the relief hit her like the strings being cut. Deacon let out a sighing laugh and wiped the nervous sweat from his forehead. He reached forwards, grasped his wife's outstretched hand and gently pulled her towards the edge of the quicksand.

With Callista and Raven's help, they hauled her out, and she collapsed in a tired heap on the safe, dry sand. Deacon's arms were wrapped around her before she could say a word of thanks. Holding her close, Deacon checked her over for injuries, but she was unharmed; just cold and wet. Luckily, when Eradi had given them their new clothes, he had packed a few spare robes in case they needed them.

Callista and Raven turned their backs as Kyra began to undress. As soon as he realised what was happening, Soren screwed his nose up in distaste and turned around, but Deveron remained transfixed. Raven grabbed him by the collar and spun him around with a chuckle as Deveron's face flushed bright red.

When Kyra was changed and had recovered from her ordeal, they set off again. Raven fell into step beside Deacon and clapped a friendly hand on his shoulder, but he got no response from his half-brother. Deacon's eyes were fixed on the horizon, and Soren slowed to let them pass him. He could feel their tension .

"I'm glad she's OK," Raven said quietly. Still no response.

The tension in Raven's shoulders told Soren what expression was on his mentor's face without him even needing to see. He would have bet money that Raven's dark eyebrows were creased in a frown.

"I shouldn't have..." Raven kicked angrily at the ground, unable to finish the apology.

With a sigh, Deacon walked with his hands on his hips and looked at Raven with eyebrows raised. "You should have trusted me."

"I was looking out for you and Kyra." The words were clearly hard for him to say.

Deacon remained defensive, but his tone softened. "You need to find a way to look out for me without being an ass."

"Agreed," Raven said with a wry smile and held a hand out to Deacon.

Deacon accepted Raven's offer of a truce and shook the outstretched hand. Behind them, Soren heaved a satisfied sigh of relief.

The afternoon was drawing to a close. Soren prayed that they would arrive at the Meraxan laboratory soon. With every dune they passed over, he held his breath in anticipation, desperate to see the building rising from the blistering hot sand.

Eventually, when nearly twenty dunes had yielded no such prize and he was almost ready to give up and accept defeat, Soren saw it. A dull grey facility, shimmering like a mirage in the early evening sun. He cried out in relief and allowed his heavy, exhausted limbs to crumple to the ground. Another wave of stomach-clenching nausea washed over him, but he steeled himself and forced the sickness back down. They were finally there. They had made it, and the antidote would soon be in their hands, and they could all go home again, safe and well.

The relief that flowed through his veins was palpable, but he was startled from his joy as Kyra's gentle hand rested on his shoulder. "Soren, you're sick. You need to rest here a moment," she said, loudly enough for Raven and Callista to hear.

Callista spun around instantly. "We can't. I know he's sick, but you know the prophecy: *blood will thicken, consume the host. An infusion it begins; a tragedy it ends.* We can't risk stopping here. We need to get Soren and Deacon to the antidote with all haste."

Kyra frowned at Callista. "He's more likely to run into danger if he is weak and exhausted. He needs to recharge if he's to fight off whatever we find in that facility."

Callista's brow furrowed, conflict written upon her face. "You've got ten minutes, Soren," she said reluctantly before turning away with her arms crossed tightly over her chest. She appeared stern, but Soren knew his mother too well. He knew she felt unable to show weakness. He knew she turned her back when she needed to hide her pain, anxiety, the constant fear that plagued her, especially since Freya.

It wasn't only Soren who suffered from Callista's solemn and strict nature. All of her children felt the change in her, even the ones who had grown into adulthood. Now, when she was at her weakest and pretending to be her strongest, Soren knew she needed the support of the others. But, whether it was selfish or not, Soren just couldn't help her. All he felt when she snapped at him was anger. A quick glance at Raven showed Soren that he wasn't the only one who saw his mother's pain. Raven said nothing, but the tense muscles in his folded arms and the intense frown on his face gave away his thoughts.

Soren's thoughts were broken by Kyra, who knelt before him, her gentle green eyes twinkling with concern and warmth. He immediately felt comforted and relaxed into her calming presence. She fussed over him a while, grinding up herbs that she seemed to produce from a hidden pocket somewhere in her purple robes.

Kyra asked Soren to remove his shirt so she could get a look at his neck and shoulders. He felt embarrassed but knew she was just looking out for him, so he did as he was asked. Kyra looked shocked when Soren removed the clothing, and his weeping crimson sores came into view. They had spread into blisters, raw and open, stretching across his collarbone and onto his chest.

Kyra leant in closer to take a proper look and whispered to Soren. "How much do they hurt, Soren?"

He hadn't been thinking about them so much for the past few hours. The intense heat and exhaustion had taken his mind off the lesions, but now they were open to the rays of the sun again, they were burning once more.

"Sometimes it hurts a lot, and sometimes not so much. It hurts if I put my arms up, but when they're down it's all right."

The concerned look didn't leave Kyra's face. She called her husband over, and Deacon sat beside Soren, his own chestnut eyes running over Soren's wounds. No doubt realising what his wife had called him over for, Deacon pulled aside the torn fabric of his trousers to take a look at his own injury. The small gasp that escaped Kyra's lips told Soren what she saw there. His half-brother's blisters were spreading, just as his own were.

The couple shuffled closer together and shared hushed whispers, taking occasional glances at Soren, which made him uneasy. When they finally stopped their mutterings, he was relieved, until Kyra told him in a quiet voice that they had decided to tell Callista that the symptoms were progressing.

"Please don't tell Mum," Soren pleaded. "She'll worry, and when she worries she tells me off."

Deacon chuckled and ruffled Soren's hair. "We have to, kid. She needs to know what's happening."

Soren groaned as Deacon went to fetch Callista, wishing more than anything that he could cover himself back up and pretend the marks weren't even there. The scar on his wrist had given him enough humiliation for a lifetime. He didn't need another thing to be ashamed of.

Callista was over to him in no time, her brow creased and her jaw clenched. As she looked him over, her expression darkened a shade.

"How do you feel inside?"

Soren shrugged his shoulders. "Not good. I feel a bit sick and tired. I just want to go to sleep, but I'm a bit dizzy too."

Kyra and Callista shared a nod, and Kyra began crushing more herbs in her bowl. Whatever was happening to him, Soren wasn't enjoying it. It wasn't just the sores and the sickness that were affecting him. It was the guilt that he had gotten all of them into this situation. He pulled his shirt back on and tucked his arms around his knees, feeling the comfort of wrapping himself into a small ball.

Callista was hovering uncertainly, watching Kyra making her medicines, but when Soren tucked himself into the foetal ball, her expression softened. She dropped down to his level, smiled warmly and wrapped her arms around him. It caught him off guard because it was rare for his mother to show affection like that, but he hadn't realised how much he needed a hug until she gave it to him. He cuddled her back and enjoyed the mother-son moment until she pulled away, leaving him feeling stronger and more able to take on whatever might be hurled at them next.

Kyra smeared a green, tacky mush over his sores, then did the same on Deacon's leg, explaining that it would take the burn off and hopefully calm some of the redness too. Then she prepared a bitter, watery paste which she made Soren choke down, and he began to feel better. A new energy buzzed within his muscles and his nausea passed. For the moment, at least.

"Deveron, are there soldiers stationed outside the building?"

Frowning slightly in the direction of the facility, Deveron stared for a moment and then nodded. "Yes, but I can't tell how many exactly. Maybe only three?"

"OK. Raven, Deacon get your weapons ready. Kyra, is Soren ready to go?" Callista asked. Kyra gave her a gentle smile and nodded, her waist-length red hair flowing behind her back. Without looking at Soren, Callista marched ahead over a sand dune and disappeared from view with Raven and Deacon right behind her, keen to get on with the mission. Kyra gently helped Soren to his feet as he stretched the ache from his limbs. He did feel considerably better after whatever foul concoction she had given him.

The grey building on the horizon loomed, colossal and imposing. It had clearly been built for purpose and not aesthetics. Ugly stonework and wooden girders stood at bleak, right angles. Soren couldn't help contrasting it with the glorious crystal and birch palaces of Nazaki, the Children of Light's capital city.

The facility was surrounded by bushes and thickets, dotted in patchy rings around the building. Soren guessed they were intended to provide some cover, but they seemed redundant as the building clearly towered far higher than any of the foliage. Callista waved for the others to follow her as she approached and ensured her path wound through the bushes to give them a place to hide if enemies appeared.

Suddenly, Callista dropped into a crouch behind one of the bushes and waved her hand behind her back, frantically signalling for the others to follow suit. Soren dropped to his haunches, his heart pounding as he readied himself for an ambush.

Raven crept up beside Callista, and Soren saw him mouth silently, "What is it?"

She nodded towards the facility, and Raven tentatively peered around the bush. Thirty metres or so in front of them was the large, oak doorway that led inside the building. The facility was surrounded by wood and wire fences that stretched around the perimeter, but they were poorly maintained and many gaping holes gave them a way inside. The main problem was the four guards stationed at the wooden door. Light glinted off their swords and the grey tabards they sported had the black Brotherhood of Shadow logo, the phoenix and the flame.

"Take a look," Callista whispered. Raven, Deacon, Kyra, Soren and Deveron shuffled forwards to take a look at what they were facing.

Soren scoffed. "Hmph, no problem. I could take them."

Callista answered him with a stern glare.

"What? I could," Soren snapped, feeling indignant.

"Nobody doubts your ability, Soren, but you're sick, you're ten years old and you're my son. Not a chance." There was no point in arguing with her, so Soren said nothing and contented himself with huffing angrily and crossing his arms.

"Mother's right, Soren," Raven added. "We need to do this together." He turned to Callista. "Why don't Deacon and I go in and take them out? We could do it quickly before they have time to alert any others."

Callista shook her head. "No. We're in the last section of cover before the gates. You would have to cross thirty metres of open land to get to them. They'd see you coming and sound the alarm before you got anywhere near. We need to find another way."

"Callista, I'm worried about the boys too," Kyra said. "They're too young to go into a Brotherhood facility. Surely, you can't take them with you. I should stay out here and look after them until you three return."

Soren tried to argue, but Deacon and Raven appeared to be happy with Kyra's suggestion.

"I agree," Raven nodded. "They can stay out here, especially with Soren feeling ill."

"I don't feel ill!" Soren called out, but nobody acknowledged him.

The frown of concentration was back on Callista's face. "But if we leave them out here with only Kyra, there'll be nobody to protect them if soldiers come. We are now officially on Brotherhood land. It is far too dangerous to leave them unattended."

"Then I'll stay out here too," Deacon offered.

Raven scoffed in disbelief and rolled his eyes.

"No, we need you," Callista replied. "Raven and I can't go in on our own. The place might be swamped with guards. We need you, Deacon. Also, we need Kyra in case Soren or Deacon get sicker or we suffer an injury. Deveron, your ability to detect life forms could save us from getting into too many tricky situations."

"Screw this stupid *virus*. Take him home and let our scientists check him out and see if there even is anything wrong with him," Raven said.

"You know we can't do that." Callista's voice was quiet but threatening.

"Why not? Because a weird old guy in a trailer said so? Or because an ancient lunatic wrote a book? This is ludicrous, Mum."

Soren felt the tension in their group rise a notch. Raven only called Callista "Mum" if he was angry.

Callista raised one eyebrow at Raven. When she spoke, her words were calm and considered. "If the boys stay out here, they will be unprotected. They come inside, but we ensure they are always behind us, safe."

"Mum, I'm scared," Deveron said quietly. "I want to stay out here. I can keep hidden and use my ability to see if anybody approaches."

Callista smiled at Deveron softly. "But sensing them isn't always enough, Deveron. If they do see you, would you be happy to fight them off? On your own?"

The look of defeat on Deveron's face told Soren that he was in no way comfortable with that idea. He could also tell from each of the adults' faces that none of them were happy about the arrangement, but Callista continued before they could argue. "Now we need to find a way to get inside that building, without alerting the guards."

They huddled together and began throwing out ideas, which Callista rapidly dismissed, her hundred years of combat experience seeing the errors in their plans. After the first few ideas were cast out, Soren lost interest and his attention began to wander. He strayed to the edge of the bushes and peered around the leafy branches to take a sneaky look at the guarded doorway.

What he saw made his heart leap into his mouth.

Standing just before the guards was a slim figure, covered in black with a dark hood that cast a shadow across his features. His shirt was sleeveless, revealing arms that were covered from shoulder to fingertip in tattoos. Black patterns and lines zigzagged, swirled and spiralled across his skin. Words and pictures were dotted amongst the patterns, but Soren couldn't read them from so far away.

Most disconcerting of all was the fact that, despite the hood covering the man's face, Soren knew he was staring straight at him. His heart pounding, Soren gasped and pulled away from the bush.

"Mother!" he hissed as loudly as he dared. "Raven!"

The four adults glanced up. One look at Soren's wide-eyed panic brought them over to him in a hurry.

"What is it, Soren?"

Soren tried to steady his shaking hands enough to point over his shoulder, towards the facility.

Deacon gasped as his gaze landed upon the hooded man, perfectly still and silent, staring directly at them.

"What the...?" Deacon murmured. Callista and Raven exchanged puzzled frowns. Soren dared himself to peer out again. The man still appeared to be staring straight at them, and Soren's heart threatened to leap out of his chest when another strange thought sent icy blood shooting through his veins. Despite being directly in front of the guards, they hadn't seen him. They carried on about their business as usual. How was that possible?

The man slowly raised his forefinger and pressed it to his lips. Then, in one confident, powerful movement, turned and sprinted straight to the four guards at the door. They saw him at the last second, as if a veil had suddenly been lifted from their eyes. They froze in surprise and tensed to draw their weapons, but he was upon them too quickly. He whipped a dagger from his belt and slashed it across the throat of one of the guards and then plunged it deep into the neck of another until it embedded up to the hilt. The man raised his leg and kicked the body away from him, and in one swift movement, pulled another knife from his belt.

The other two guards had drawn their swords now and slashed at him in angry strikes. But he marched straight up to them, ducking to the side to avoid their clumsy swings, as if he had no fear of their blades at all. He thrust the second dagger into the stomach of one guard, ripped it out and plunged it deep into the heart of the second.

It took less than a minute, and all four guards lay dead. The tattooed man turned to where Soren and his family cowered, both fascinated and terrified. He raised one tattooed arm and beckoned them over. None of them moved, whether through fear or shock, and Callista looked to Kyra with her eyebrows raised. With terror in her eyes, Kyra shook her head quickly.

But Callista had a peculiar, glazed look in her eyes, and Soren wondered if she knew the man. She stood, in full view of the facility and cautiously made her way over. Soren leapt to his feet and joined her, running at her heels to catch up. Raven, Deacon, Kyra and Deveron reluctantly trailed behind, sceptical about how this unknown man could take down four guards so easily. Deacon placed his hands on Kyra's shoulders and gently held her back so he could step in front. Raven pushed Deveron to the back and blocked him with his body, his fists clenched in preparation for battle.

As she got closer to the man, Callista straightened up, returning to her practised regal posture. She cleared her throat, and Soren guessed she was preparing to speak to the hooded man, but when she got close to him, he turned and stepped over the bodies of those he had killed. Without a word, he pulled a brass key from his pocket, and unlocked the large door for them all to pass through.

Callista made to walk through, but Raven held her back with a firm hand on her arm. "Mum! Don't be stupid. We can't just walk in there. Who the hell is this guy?"

The look in Callista's eyes as she turned back to her son was fierce and determined. "He killed the soldiers that we couldn't get beyond. He opened a door we would not have been able to open alone. It would be foolish not to capitalise on this chance."

Deacon looked as sceptical as his half-brother. "He could be leading us into a trap."

"Yes, he could. In fact, it is more than likely." Callista concurred. "But we won't know until we take a chance. What other choice do we have? We've already established that we can't go home or stay waiting out here. Whatever the case, we need to get inside that building, and this man just gave us a way in. We take it. All of you, be prepared. It could get nasty in here. Deveron, keep us updated on guards. Raven and I shall go at the front. Deacon and Kyra bring up the rear."

Soren hovered just behind his mother, but his eyes were still firmly locked onto the half of the man's face he could see. Young or old, friend or foe, nothing was clear and everything was making him uncomfortable.

The others didn't argue with Callista anymore, even if their opinions still strayed wide of hers. With more suspicious, apprehensive glances at each other, the six Children of Light members stepped over the bodies of the dead guards. Soren saw a deep shade of green spread across Deveron's face and watched as his brother held onto Kyra when they passed over the bodies, trying not to look down at the bloodied corpses.

Soren confidently stepped over them. It wasn't the first time he'd seen dead bodies. He trained with Raven. Dead bodies were common when on missions with Raven. Soren was far more intimidated by the stranger in black.

They approached the door slowly and nervously, Callista at the front with her silver-blue sword drawn and ready. The man stood back and gestured silently for them to enter the building.

"Who are you?" Deacon asked when they approached, but the man gave no answer. His head was lowered and the hood covered the majority of his face. All that could be seen was a mouth and jaw line with pale skin.

They had no choice but to trust him. They weren't going to get inside the facility any other way. Callista stepped aside to wave the others through the door, her eyes firmly locked onto the man in black.

Deacon and Kyra entered first, stepping through quickly, Deacon with his sword drawn and ready for anything they might meet inside the building. Raven ushered Deveron in next, pushing the scared teenager through the door as quickly as he could force the boy's legs to move. Soren walked up slowly, trying not to stare, but couldn't help his eyes roaming over the man's tattooed arms. Now that he was closer, he could read the words crudely written onto the pale flesh. They were names:

Holly, Silas, Anathema.

None of the words meant anything to Soren, but his mind was working furiously over what it all meant. Were they places? Names of his family? People he'd killed?

Soren had no time to examine the tattoos further before he was ushered hurriedly into the building by Callista. He stumbled through into the facility, with his mind reeling, desperate for another look at the mysterious stranger. Soren turned back just as the heavy metal door swung to a close.

Chapter Fourteen
Angelis

HE LAST SHAFTS of the evening sun were blotted out with a bang, and the small band of Children of Light members were cast into barely lit gloom. They stood in the darkness for a moment, allowing their eyes to adjust to the change in light. The bizarre turn of events that had successfully gotten them into the building was playing on Soren's mind. He had been afraid of the man, wary and suspicious, but at the same time fascinated by his rough tattoos and shaded face.

He turned to his mentor with eyebrows raised, questioning, but Raven shrugged his shoulders, leaving Soren even more mystified.

"Mum," he murmured. "Who was that?"

Callista looked as confused as he was. "I have no idea, Soren. But he really helped us, whoever he was."

None of them had expected to simply walk in. *If only it could be so simple from here on*, Soren thought grimly.

Callista led the way with Soren and Deveron sandwiched between herself and Raven at the front and Kyra and Deacon at the rear. Deveron frequently whispered to Callista, highlighting the presence of guards down certain corridors. Callista heeded his warnings, and they branched off in various ways to avoid conflicts wherever possible.

As he wandered through the corridors, Soren's mind was turning furiously. He was itching for a chance to get into the action.

Training had been so hard lately, and he had pushed and pushed himself to his limits. Now he was dying to show off his new skills, particularly the acrobatic manoeuvres he had mastered. Now that the sickness had passed, he felt like catching this virus was the best thing that had ever happened to him. He had been given the chance to walk right into the midst of the Brotherhood. Callista wouldn't have allowed him this opportunity for years, if ever. All of the sickness, the dizziness, was worth it for the chance to get right into the heart of shadow.

Something hummed inside his soul. There was often a peculiar vibration humming inside of him, bizarre pulsating rhythm, as if a second heartbeat pounded within his chest. But today it was stronger than ever. He took it as a sign of fate. Today was his day, the day he became an adult and fought alongside the best soldiers in the Children of Light. He smiled excitedly at Deveron but received only an annoyed glare in response.

The passageway before them was long and thin with locked doors sporadically dotted along the walls. They walked through the gloom, twisting and turning along the dark passageways for what felt like forever until the corridor finally spread out into a larger hall. Callista and Raven led the way slowly, checking to make sure the children were behind them. They walked into a grand circular room with eight passages branching off from the middle like the spokes of a great wheel. Each corridor looked the same with wide strips, some incredibly long, so the end could only just be seen. Each of them had other doors or passageways branching off from the central hallway.

They stopped in the centre of the room, looking around, trying to make sense of where they were and which path they should take. On the wall facing them was a map of the eight spokes and the central hall. There were no words written upon it to explain what lay down each of the corridors, just basic symbols.

Soren and the others stood before the sign, frowning and scratching their heads.

"So, which way?" Soren asked, but nobody had a solid answer to give him.

"Deveron, can you detect guards down any of these passages?"

Concentrating intensely, Deveron looked down each passage, staring into the empty space and picking up on the auras.

"This one and this one definitely have guards." He pointed to indicate the two passages. "The path with the sword is the most heavily guarded."

"Maybe an armoury?" Raven asked.

Deveron nodded. "Possibly. The others seem clear, but just because I don't detect guards doesn't mean they aren't out of my range."

Another deep frown was etched across Callista's face. "It doesn't make sense. Why so few guards to protect something so important? I think we can only be walking into a trap."

The looks on the others' faces told Soren that they all agreed with his mother. "Mum," he said, "we're prepared for an attack. We can defeat them if they do come."

The smile Callista gave him was a little condescending. She patted his head. "We don't who 'they' are, Soren. If they're just foot soldiers, then, yes, we can take them. Brotherhood members might be trickier. Either way we all need to keep our wits about us."

"So, which path do we take?" Deacon asked.

Deveron joined in. "Well, we don't know what any of these symbols mean, so I guess each is as dangerous as the next. I say we just head down one of the paths I know is safe and unguarded."

Raven scoffed. "If there aren't any guards, it's probably not the right place."

Deveron clearly disagreed. "So, what should we do? Head to the most dangerous places?"

Raven's eyes blazed aggressively. "What's up, Deveron? Are you too scared? I say we try the archway. It'll mean it's a passageway to something important."

"We don't know that," Deveron mumbled. "What about the hourglass? That could indicate something to do with research and the virus. Don't you think so, Soren?"

Soren gave an exasperated sigh and threw his arms up in the air. "I don't care! Just pick a goddamn passage and we'll take it!"

"Soren!" Callista snapped, casting him a reprimanding glare. "Don't speak to your brother like that."

"What? This is stupid! We're wasting so much time. Let's pick one way and take it. If we are wrong, we'll come back here and pick another. It's not a big deal!"

"We can't do that. It'll take forever, idiot," Deveron muttered under his breath.

"Deveron, you watch your mouth too," Callista warned.

Soren stepped towards his brother, eyes wide and threatening, and his hand on the hilt of his sword. Raven stepped between them and gave Soren a hard shove which sent him stumbling backwards with a petulant frown on his face.

"Deveron's right," Kyra said gently, trying to calm the tension. "It would take us forever if we had to search every possible corridor. Deveron knows where the guards are stationed so we can just keep away from them. It will minimise the chance of risk."

"Nonsense!" Soren snapped. "If we run into soldiers, we fight them and move onto the next batch. Right, Raven?"

Raven cast him an admonitory glare, but Soren caught a hint of a proud smile at the corners of his mouth. Callista took over, ending the debate.

"Absolutely not. We think it through properly and make a sensible decision about which to take. We need a smaller pathway, ideally one that would bypass major corridors and allow us to sneak in directly. Kyra, Deacon, you each pick a corridor and do a quick investigation. See what you can find, but don't go too far. Raven, you and I will stay here and try to get our bearings and work out how this building is structured." She sat down and picked up a sharp stone that lay on the floor and began drawing a map in the dust.

Once Callista, Deveron and Raven were engaged in discussing the four remaining passageways, Soren skulked away, scraping his feet along the floor. He skirted around the edge of the circular hall, peering down each corridor as he passed. One of the passages intrigued him, and he stared through the gloom. Above the passageway was a symbol of a feather. It looked familiar, but Soren couldn't figure out where he had seen it before. His birthmark burned again, and he scratched at it absently. He couldn't take his eyes away from the feather symbol, as if it were calling to him. Curiosity got the better of him and overcame his boredom.

He took a glance over his shoulder to check that nobody was watching him. His mother and the others were all engrossed in trying to draw a map in the dust, their voices getting higher and louder as tensions escalated. Nobody even noticed Soren wasn't there. Confident that he could get away with it, Soren darted down the corridor. A recess appeared on his right, and he saw that it was an annexe, another room cut out of the walls. It was a large room, practically empty, with white walls and a single lamp that burned brightly on the eastern wall. In the far corner, there was a wooden doorway, leading God knew where.

There were a few rusty old filing cabinets pushed into the other corners of the annexe and a bookcase that looked as if it might fall down at the slightest touch. Upon the bookcase were rows of ancient texts, many of which Soren had never heard. But nestled amongst them was a tome Soren knew well. All members of the Children of Light knew it inside out: *The Book of Alcherys*.

Soren was fond of the stories within the ancient book, and he had been playing at recreating them all of his life. But to Soren, it was just that—a book of great fantasy tales. He didn't base his every decision on the Book or use it to predict the future as Callista did. His mother felt intimately connected to the riddles and clues within the pages. When Soren had been to see it for the first time in Alexiria back when Freya had died, Callista had taught him about the time when she had found it and how it came to shape their people's entire culture and values.

Callista and many others in Alcherys viewed the Book with reverence, especially when certain predictions came true. It was sacred, written by an unknown people or maybe even a god. But the Book focused only upon the Children of Light. Why would the Brotherhood want a copy? What good would it do them?

Soren took the copy down and thumbed through the pages he knew so well, his eyes scanning over the patterns around their edges. With a pounding heart, he looked over the dark prophecies that had already come to pass: The Severed Bonds, Innocence Shattered. Each of them was vague and difficult to interpret, but once they came to pass, their meaning was undeniable. Each and every word made sense with hindsight, which made the unknown prophecies all the more mystifying. Some of those that were left to come were downright terrifying. They spoke of the hand of God and a power that could destroy Hell. They spoke of creatures so vile and cruel that demons would crumble before them, a battle that would destroy the world as they knew it and people who would transgress the boundaries of dimensions and time itself.

It all made for a fascinating read, a truly magnificent book of fairy tales. If only it was just myth and legend. But the prophecies seemed all too real, especially at the moment when they were in the grasp of one and were powerless to escape the fate it had thrown at them.

Soren flicked to the prophecy that spurred his mother to bring them here now: the Prophecy of Blood. He read it again, trying to ignore the shiver of fear that ran through him.

An infusion it begins; a tragedy it ends. The blood will thicken, consume the host and leave it thirsty. To stop the blood's rampage, the young must journey to the heart of shadows, where feathers will destroy the wild.

Soren closed the book, thoughts jostling for position in his mind. He'd never really believed in the prophecies. He had dismissed them as religious hokum or the ramblings of some ancient madman. But now he was here, he had to admit it looked far more believable. He placed the book carefully back on the shelf and turned to the eastern wall where the torch lit up a collection of scrolls and parchment pinned to the walls. Soren frowned and stepped closer, his eyes scanning over the documents.

The parchments were fragile and ancient. Fixed carefully to the wall with pins, they looked as if they might crumble into dust if he touched them. The edges were frayed and so thin he could almost see the dark wall through the translucent parchment. Like the pages of *The Book of Alcherys*, the Children of Light symbol was painstakingly printed around the edges. Soren frowned. Only the Book had pages like these. Where had these pages come from? They weren't taken from the Book. There was no way he would have ever forgotten those images drawn in scratchy black lines.

The first page showed a creature of the most incredible beauty. A young girl with hair that floated down to her ankles streaming behind her like ribbons in the wind. Her face was delicate with captivating eyes and a soft jawline. There was a gentle, knowing smile upon her lips. Despite the fact it was a mere sketch, Soren could feel warmth emanating from the image. But what struck him the most was the huge wings spread out behind her, arching from her shoulder blades and fanning into long, white feathers. The words "Angelis Ceresecca" were inscribed above her.

He'd had never seen anything like this before. "Angelis" sounded a lot like "angel." He'd heard stories, but angels couldn't really exist, could they? He remembered the carvings of people with wings he'd seen on the building in Alexiria all those years ago, when his mum had first taken him to the ancient city. Strange shivers shot through him from head to toe.

Swirls and spirals, flecks and zigzags spread out from her, like ripples around her beautiful image. Her hand stretched out to him, and he had the strong feeling she was reaching out to him through the ages from whenever or wherever she had come. Soren felt a peculiar pulsating tingle shiver across his body, and he couldn't help stretching his hand towards the drawing. As his fingers came closer, the vibration in his body intensified and warm waves flooded over him. He tentatively brushed his fingers across the image of her outstretched hand and was sure he felt the page hum gently. The patterns danced before his eyes, radiating outwards in mesmerising streams. He was fascinated and ran his eyes over the undulating swirls. When he finally pulled his hand away, the dancing stopped and he immediately doubted that it had ever really happened. Surely that had just been in his mind? *Pictures don't move, do they?*

He allowed his gaze to wander to the next parchment, and a shocked gasp escaped his lips. The same ancient paper in scratchy ink, the same symbols etched around the edges, but in the centre of the page was another picture of the little girl, her tiny, delicate form meek and placid, but only half of her was shown. Her image was cut lengthways through the centre of her body, one eye closed. The other half of her was not a person at all, but half of a symbol, a symbol he knew all too well.

He reached down and yanked his shirt sleeve up to reveal the unusual birthmark on his forearm. It was unmistakable. The symbol on this ancient page was the same as the red mark that he had been born with. It was in much finer detail, but the outline was the same: gently-spiked edges flicking outwards in graceful peaks before tapering at the bottom. On his arm were three ugly raised bumps like scars of some terrible pox, but on the drawing they were beautifully arranged, sitting neatly one across the other, rested on top of what he now recognised as a feather.

His eyes flicked quickly between the parchment and his wrist, trying to make sense of it. How was this possible? This document, like *The Book of Alcherys*, must be thousands of years old. How could the people who scribed it possibly know of his birthmark? He blinked to clear the fuzziness that suddenly clouded his vision, and he swore the symbol on the page glowed and shimmered. Looking to his arm again, his birthmark burned, but it was a welcoming and comforting heat and he was calmed by it.

He was still staring at the three pictures when a click from across the room pulled him from his reverie. His heart leapt as the door at the back of the room swung open. There was nothing Soren could do. Nowhere to hide and no time to run back to his mother. He froze on the spot, paralysed with panic. Four soldiers stepped into the small room, engaged in conversation. The first stopped short when he saw Soren. Soren's hand instinctively shot to the sword at his side.

"What are you doing here, kid?" the first guard asked with a slight smile at the corners of his mouth. "This isn't a place to play." The man's eyes drifted down to the sword in Soren's hand, and they widened in surprise as they registered the sharpened steel on what he must have previously assumed was a toy sword.

The guard frowned and tilted his head to the side, studying the blade, which wavered in the air before him, shaking along with Soren's hand. The others stepped up around the first, their eyes scanning the dangerous weapon in the hands of a ten-year-old.

It was the young female guard that recognised the Children of Light insignia first, and she gasped in surprise.

"Children of Light intruder!" she shouted at the top of her voice. Within seconds, the other guards had drawn their swords.

Soren's heart leapt into action, and adrenaline flooded his muscles. He turned and sprinted from the room, wheeling around the corner and straight into another group of four guards patrolling from the opposite direction. Behind them, far at the end of the wide corridor, he could just make out his mother and the others.

"Mother!" Soren shrieked at the top of his voice. Her head snapped up. Within seconds she was on her feet sprinting towards him. But she was too far back, and they both knew it. She'd never get to him in time. He was on his own.

Staggering away from the guards, Soren forced down the panic threatening to cloud his mind and steadied his shaking hands.

Both sets of guards closed in around him. Soren was completely surrounded.

One of the guards pointed the tip of his sword at Soren, but his eyes betrayed his reluctance to attack. "He's just a kid...," he murmured, but he was immediately dismissed by the others.

"You know the boss's orders. Children of Light must die."

They circled round him, all eight of them, preparing for the kill.

Chapter Fifteen
Control

RYING FRANTICALLY TO RECALL his training, Soren's dark eyes flicked from person to person, his brain racing to find weakness in their stances instead of allowing fear to overcome him. He locked onto one of the soldiers who was smaller than the rest, a teenager, not much older than Deveron.

"Soren!" He heard his mother's cry but didn't dare take his eyes off his enemies for a second.

"Leave him!" Callista screamed. "He's just a child. Fight me!"

Soren recognised their clothing. Simple grey trousers and shirts and a basic leather armour breastplate. These were Brotherhood foot soldiers. Soren had spent his childhood to date pretending to fight them. They had been the enemy of his entire youth after all the stories he had heard about them from Raven. He vividly remembered sitting around the open fire back at Nazaki as his mentor told stories of the nameless and unquestioning soldiers, and of how they fulfilled their orders at all costs. If they had been told to kill Soren, he knew that nothing would stop them.

They closed in around him, their swords drawn and pointed at his throat. There was nowhere for him to go. The first guard slashed at him, a brutal, cleaving strike that would have split his skull in two if he hadn't dodged at the last moment. Another stab thrust at him and he yelped and knocked the blade aside but not before one of the swords behind him slid across the top of his right arm, slicing through his shirt and immediately soaking the material in crimson.

He was certain that was the moment he would die. No amount of training could have prepared him for facing that many opponents and their razor-sharp blades. All of his arrogance deserted him, and he saw himself for what he truly was—a lost little boy.

Fear made all logical thoughts close down, but something else took control in its place, something Soren had never experienced before, something almost magical. His mind sharpened, his hearing became acute and flawless. He could pick out every breath the guards took and could hear hearts beating in eight chests. He could read their thoughts and see in their eyes what they were going to do next.

All panic left Soren and was replaced by a clear-headedness and a firm certainty of exactly how to respond. Whatever force had taken over him began to manipulate his limbs like a puppet. His body moved fluidly of its own accord.

He singled out the weakest soldier. There was peculiar blue tint around her. He darted forwards, sweeping his leg around in a low arc. He took out the small soldier's foot, and she fell to one knee with a grunt. Soren's body moved instinctively, planting his foot firmly on her bent knee. He used it to propel himself high into the air, hurling a vicious upwards kick into her throat.

The force of Soren's foot connecting with the bone propelled him backwards, and he threw himself into a flip. As he flew through the air, he unsheathed his sword. As he came to land, he threw it out in a wide arc. The tip of his blade connected with three soldiers before he had even landed. The sharp point slashed brutally across their necks, blood gushing in rivers down their throats. As they slumped to the floor, Soren landed lightly on his feet.

The remaining four were wary of him, but still they edged closer. Soren could see the fear in their eyes and knew they were just following orders. He quickly sheathed his sword and unclipped it from his belt, encased in the scabbard. He sidestepped a dangerous stab and whipped the hilt of his weapon around to bring it smashing into the guard's temple. She dropped to the floor, unconscious.

Three remained. They positioned themselves in a triangle and moved in for the kill. Soren's senses went into overdrive, and the world seemed to slow around him. Two guards went for an overhead slash at the same time. Soren stumbled backwards to avoid the brutal slashes and had to duck at the same time to avoid a vicious thrust from the other guard.

Summoning all of his strength, he crouched and then leapt into the air. Utilising the athletic prowess he'd carefully honed over his short ten years and the magical effects that mysteriously aided him, he threw himself as high as he could. At the height of his great leap, he lashed out with a spin kick which caught all three guards on the chin one after the other. They crumpled to the floor like dominoes.

The last guard hit the floor, eyes rolling back in his head, as Soren landed lightly beside him like a cat. As soon as the guards were despatched, the peculiar feeling that had flooded through Soren dispersed. He was confused. He was good at fighting—very good—but he knew he wasn't *that* good. However he'd managed his incredible feat of strength, he hadn't done it alone. Someone or something had helped him.

He'd only just finished with the eight guards when Callista reached him, the others close behind her with panicked looks on their faces. They saw Soren standing amongst the incapacitated bodies of eight guards, blood pouring down his arm, his shirt slashed.

As the adrenaline began to wear off, Soren's confusion was quickly replaced with another feeling, something he had never felt before.

His eyes flicked down to the eight guards on the floor. Blood pooled around the slashed throats of the first three soldiers he had taken down. The others could just be knocked out, but those three...they would never return to their families tonight.

As Brotherhood foot soldiers, they weren't valued as human beings. Raven had taught Soren that at a young age. Vincent's attitude towards them was well-known. He considered them easily replaceable, disposable even, but they must still have mothers, fathers or children of their own.

Panic and guilt rose in Soren. Despite all the times he said he wanted action, he hadn't been prepared for this. Bodies were common, but killing somebody himself was completely different. Instead of the pride he had been anticipating on his first kill, he was overwhelmed by how small he felt and how much he needed his mother. Tears welled in his eyes, and he just wanted to curl up in her arms, but he knew it was too late for that now.

He'd wanted this. He asked for it by bragging about being Raven's apprentice. He couldn't cry. He was a man now, a fully fledged warrior. They'd all be so proud of him, and they would expect him to be strong, despite how sick he felt inside. Wiping the tears from his eyes, he straightened his posture and held his head high. Where the fear and guilt had been, a dark anger started to creep in.

Chapter Sixteen
Sickness

ALLISTA FUSSED OVER SOREN awhile, checking the bandage Kyra had applied to his cut. Every now and then her face crumpled in a sad smile, and she pulled him into her arms for a hug. He didn't know which was worse, his mother fussing or the bewildered and unnerved expressions on the others' faces.

Deacon and Kyra glanced at each other with concerned frowns on their faces. Soren saw it and knew his tough facade didn't fool them. The pain and trauma would have to come out sometime, and he knew that Kyra would be chasing him at some point to "talk about it." Soren hurried on before she could attempt counselling him. He really couldn't stomach the thought of that right now.

Deveron looked sickly green as he trailed silently at the back, clearly shook up by what Soren had done, but that was yet another thing that Soren couldn't think about too much at the moment. There was too much bombarding his senses for him to worry about everybody else as well.

Instead, Soren insisted that they continue their search by going on through the room where the Angelis Ceresecca picture was. He didn't know what it all meant, but somehow he knew it was important they followed that path.

Following Deveron's senses, they continued to trudge silently through the cool corridors of the crumbling facility. Each corridor was the same, but Deveron would occasionally stop mid-step and redirect everybody away from approaching guards. It was a miracle they hadn't encountered more soldiers. *A miracle or a trap*, Soren thought grimly.

How big could this building be? The grey walls seemed to stretch on forever, lit by flickering, sickly yellow lamps. Occasionally, they would pass a window, and they could see the gradually setting sun over the Paradoran plains.

Despite the buzz of adrenaline from his terrifying fight, Soren's body was starting to ache again, every part of him weary and weak. His head was spinning, and he had to focus his eyes on one object to keep his balance. He knew he couldn't let his mother see or she'd just worry and fuss over him. He hadn't wanted to let her or Kyra know, but the sore on his neck was getting worse with every passing minute. It had spread down over his shoulder, passing his collarbone and beginning to creep across his chest, tacky and weeping still, raw and sensitive every time his shirt rubbed against it. He was sure he could smell it too, his nose occasionally catching a drift of something pungent in the air. Whatever was happening to him, it was progressing at an alarming rate, and he was afraid. So very afraid. But more than that he was starting to feel angry.

There was a growing tension in his chest, a constricting sense of urgency to his every breath. They needed to get to the antidote, not soon but right now. Everything they did was taking much too long, and it wasn't acceptable. It wasn't fair on him. He couldn't wait much longer because he was sure that the rancid, rotten flesh creeping over his body was a side effect of something more serious. The real virus wasn't attacking his skin. He was quite sure of it. The real virus was working away at his mind, eating into his soul and corrupting his thoughts. There was a brewing darkness that he didn't much like at all, and it was making him unreasonably cross, his temper shortening by the hour.

Casting a sideways glance at Deacon, he wondered whether his half-brother was feeling the way he was. The redness around Deacon's eyes, the constant itching and the cold pallor of his usually chestnut skin told Soren he was suffering too. It didn't make him feel any better. If anything, it made him feel worse.

The building was quiet, almost eerily so, and Soren could tell that Callista was on alert. There was no way she could be relaxed at a time like this, and he could almost read her mind, suspecting there must be more guards somewhere, ready to ambush them from the shadows. A number of times she stepped in front of the boys and put herself in the line of fire, but it irked Soren. He always managed to nip back in front of her, not exactly eager to meet trouble head-on but more irritated that she thought he couldn't protect himself. It was yet another thing that made him angry. He clenched his fists, trying to control the desire to lash out at his companions.

A strong hand clamped down on his shoulder, and Raven grabbed a fistful of Soren's shirt and dragged him back behind the adults. Soren sulked behind Callista and Raven, glaring at their backs as they huddled closer together for what appeared to be a secret conversation. Soren listened carefully, trying to catch their muttered voices.

"What did you make of that?" Callista whispered, but not quietly enough to keep her words from Soren, whose ears pricked up.

Raven frowned. "Of what?"

"What Soren just did with those guards."

"What about it?" Soren could picture the scowl on his mentor's dark features as Raven spoke. "He took all eight down on his own. Impressive."

"Yes," Callista said in a hurried whisper, "but that's my point. It was unnaturally good. He's only ten years old. No matter how talented he is, he shouldn't have the strength to take out eight guards just like that." She clicked her fingers to emphasise the point. "Most of the adults in the Children of Light couldn't do that."

Soren watched as Raven cast her a sideways glance with his eyebrows raised.

Callista held her hands up. "OK, OK, *you* could do that. Few others have such skills."

"Well, I trained him."

"Yes, but you didn't give him your strength, did you?"

Raven gave no response, and the tension that hung between him and Callista wasn't lost on Soren either. What did they mean by "unnaturally good"? He knew that what he had just done was strange, of course, but "unnatural" made him sound like a freak. Maybe that's what he was after all, just like the kids at school said. He scratched at his birthmark, which was itching like crazy again and pulsating so much it felt like his whole forearm was vibrating.

A layer of light grey dust danced in the air as the group walked through the passageways of the facility. An awkward silence hung over them as they reeled from Soren's spectacular victory over the guards, but nobody felt quite as confused or mystified as Soren himself, he was quite sure of that.

He didn't feel much like walking near to his mother after her "unnatural" comment, so he dropped back to Deveron's side instead, but if he had been seeking some comfort, he wasn't about to find it in his big brother.

"Why are you smiling, Soren?" Deveron snapped.

Soren scoffed. "What? I've only just come over here. I'm not smiling."

"You just murdered three people, and yet you're swanning around with your chest all puffed up, like you've done something to be proud of."

"Oh, I'm sorry. Would you have preferred me to have been killed?" Even though he was feeling delicate, he couldn't help the confrontational tone of voice spilling from his lips as it often did when he spoke to his brother.

"Don't be stupid! Of course, I didn't want that. But if I'd just killed those people, I wouldn't be able to live with myself."

Soren kicked at the dust on the floor and plodded along silently for a long time before he answered. "I didn't want to kill them, Deveron. Really I didn't." His voice was small and lacked any of the assertiveness he was hoping for. "I...I didn't even have any control over what I was doing. It just happened to me. Honestly."

It only took one glance at his brother to see that he didn't believe a word Soren said. Deveron stared at the walls with hazy eyes as they walked the gloomy corridors. "It's just...those people. You don't know what it feels like for me to see that. I see people, Soren. I see their energy, their spirits, whatever you want to call it. Those three people you killed, they weren't people anymore. They were just empty vessels. I couldn't see any spirit. You didn't even know anything about them...who they were, what dreams they had for the future. And it's all gone now. You'll never know what their dreams were, and they'll never achieve them."

A peculiar choking bubble appeared at the back of Soren's throat, and he swallowed heavily. "Don't, Deveron. Just don't."

Soren didn't know whether Deveron had heard his brother's words, but he chose to plough on relentlessly. "I know what you're thinking. They're just foot soldiers. So what, their lives aren't worth anything? They're still people, you know."

Soren heaved a sigh. "I don't think they're worthless. Just Vincent does. They die so quickly in his army. Raven told me that. If I didn't kill them, they'd only be blown up or used as target practice."

Deveron's eyes widened in shock. "Does Vincent really do that? To his own soldiers?"

Soren gave a jagged laugh, but it was without humour. "All the time. The foot soldiers don't mean anything in the Brotherhood. They are used for things like this...guarding buildings and distracting enemies. That's what Raven told me. He even said that some of the Brotherhood use them as targets to practice on.”

Deveron had turned pale again and he looked so horrified he couldn’t find any words to respond with.

In truth, Soren was just as disgusted as Deveron, but after what he had just done, was he really any better? Pretending it was all right to kill foot soldiers because of how Vincent treated them made him feel a little better, for a while at least. If he stopped to think about it too much, he would have to accept that this wasn’t a game. This was real, and the consequences of his actions were real. He was no longer playing soldiers. He had become one.

On top of the guilt gnawing away at Soren’s mind, his body was starting to ache again, every part of him weary and weak. He was relieved he was walking behind his mother, so she couldn’t see how clammy he was becoming, how his shirt was sticking to his sores, or the disgusting pus seeping through the material. For now, he’d have to hold his head up high, choke back the tears and pretend nothing was wrong.

Chapter Seventeen
Basement

AVEN! GUARDS UP AHEAD!" Deveron hissed.

Raven dropped to his knees. He waved his hand frantically behind his back, and Soren and the others dropped to the floor. Until now, there had been no signs or even markings on the wall to tell them where they were, but at the far end of the corridor, hardly visible through the gloom, Soren spotted a metal gate. Flashes of movement breaking the dull glow told them it was guarded.

Soren watched in silence as Deveron shuffled to the front. He narrowed his eyes to squint through the gloom, assessing the number and position of the guards. "Five of them," he whispered. "Just wandering back and forth around the gate."

Raven sneered, "They're not expecting anyone. Can we take them?"

Callista checked the corridor again and nodded. "I'll go. You cover me."

She was off, slinking down the corridor before anybody had a chance to argue. She crept through the gloom, sticking to the shadows and pressing her back to the wall as much as she could. Whenever a creak or footstep sounded from up ahead, she dropped to her haunches like a cat ready to pounce. Once the guards had moved on, she crept forwards again.

Soren held his breath, trying to stay as quiet as possible to avoid jeopardising her progress. It wasn't just him; everybody was anxious for Callista. She was the mother of four of them, and Soren knew that none of them could bear the thought of losing her. Their hearts were probably pounding in their chests as hard as his was. But nobody argued with Callista because deep down they all knew it was unnecessary. If anybody could get up to the guards unnoticed, it was Callista. Her natural grace and stealth were perfectly suited for this. Even if spotted, she could easily take the guards out.

Once Callista was within ten metres, she carefully reached behind her back and pulled a long, silver sword from the sheath strapped across her. Electric blue patterns danced across the delicate blade as she quickly pulled it in to her side.

Maintaining a safe distance, Raven crept up behind her. He was not as light-footed nor conscientious as Callista, but he had to be close enough to jump in if she needed him.

Callista's eyes flickered in the gloom, watching the guards' every movement. It happened in a split second. One of the guards strayed too near, and Callista leapt silently out of the darkness. Grabbing him across the shoulders, she yanked him backwards into the shadows, clamped a hand across his mouth to stop him from crying out and quickly swept his feet out from underneath him. He dropped to his knees, and Callista had her silver blade against his throat before he had time to register her presence.

"Is it through there?" she hissed in his ear. "The antidote. Is it through that gate?"

The confused, wide-eyed look that crept into the guard's terrified eyes was obviously not what Callista had been expecting, and her own face crumpled into a deep frown.

"I won't ask nicely next time. Where is the antidote?"

Too afraid to move in case he decapitated himself, the guard trembled in the wake of her gleaming blade. Struggling to force the stutter from his lips, he spoke.

"I don't know about any antidote."

The cynical laugh that erupted from Callista's lips would have been enough to make anybody uncomfortable. "Don't play games with me. You work here. You must know where it is kept."

"I don't! I really don't!" He floundered, his breathing quickening, and then an idea came to him, as clearly as a flash of lightning illuminating a night sky. "Oh! The lab! There's a lab at the end of the hall. That's where the scientists do experiments. Maybe it's there."

Callista's eyes narrowed again, and her head tilted to one side as she considered whether his answer was worthy. He withered under the fierce gaze of the formidable warrior queen and could do nothing but tremble uncontrollably in her grasp.

"OK. Let's say I take your word for it. Can I trust you not to alert the others? If you did, the consequences wouldn't be pretty."

The guard gave a tiny whimper and a hurried nod in response. Callista turned back to the others and whispered to Raven, "Raven, tie him up, quickly."

"What? That's stupid! Just kill him for God's sake!" Raven spat back through clenched teeth.

Callista's eyes flickered over to Soren, and he recognised the unspoken message that flitted between them. Then, she cast Raven a strict glare, and he argued no further. Raven crawled forwards to the guard, getting a rope out of his backpack as he sneaked along the shadowy floor. Callista edged forwards again as another guard approached.

"INTRUDERS!" screamed the first guard, and he shoved Raven as hard as he could with both hands. The attack caught Raven off guard. He toppled backwards, allowing the guard the chance to leap to his feet and sprint into the darkness. Within seconds, four guards were running at them, their swords raised.

Although he was well out of harm's way, it still made Soren jump, and fear clenched at his insides. Panic flooded his mind. He nearly cried out to Raven and his mother, but, as always, she was already prepared.

Callista clicked her tongue in annoyance and stood up straight, her head and shoulders coming into the light. There was a flicker of fear on each of the guards' faces as their eyes landed upon her. The first guard charged towards her, his sword pointing straight at her like a lance. She waited until he was within a metre of her and then side-stepped, avoiding the strike. The momentum carried him past her, and she brought the hilt of her own sword backwards and slammed it onto the knuckles of his hand. He cried out in pain and reflexively opened his hand, dropping the sword to the floor with a clatter.

Callista's fingers shot out to grab his injured hand. She straightened his arm, twisted the limb around and threw him to the floor. She stepped down on his neck, ignoring his writhing and squirming as the next two guards approached her. One grunted and threw a brutal overhead swing, aiming straight for the top of Callista's head. She swung her own weapon up to block it, and narrowly avoided being cloven in two. For a mere foot soldier, the strength in the young man's arms must have been impressive. Soren couldn't miss the way the grey material strained over the man's biceps. He saw his mother's eyes narrow and her stance widen. He heard the grunt of exertion she uttered. She had to push back with all her strength to hold back the deadly blade.

For a terrifying second, Soren thought she might not be able to hold him off and this would be the horrifying, defining moment in his life when he saw his own mother's death. But Callista drew on reserves of strength that Soren never knew she had. She heaved the guard away from her sword and sent him reeling away.

A brutal high kick followed, which slammed into his chin, flinging him backwards. He crashed into the man behind him and the two clattered to the floor.

Raven rolled over and jumped to his feet, ploughing into the battle just as Callista dropped the first five guards. He ripped a dagger from his back pocket and plunged it deep into the chest of the struggling man beneath Callista's foot. The body twitched and a deep gurgling sound escaped the man's lips before he fell still. Raven yanked the knife back out, wiping the blood on his jacket.

Callista came face-to-face with the final man, who was far more cautious after watching the fate of his three companions. Clutching his sword defensively across his body, the man held back, biding his time. Callista advanced slowly, and her determined eyes weighed him up. The panic clear on his face, he began slashing at Callista, flinging swipe after swipe in her direction, just praying one of them would land. Callista ducked and weaved out of their way, waiting for him to make a mistake and leave his guard open. Her chance came as he overswung and left himself wide open. His attention only slipped for a second, but a second was all it took for Callista to jump in and run her sword through his heart. He dropped to the floor with a thud, and Callista breathed a sigh of relief as she yanked her blade out of his body.

She turned back to help Raven with the two guards on the floor. Dagger positioned above the neck of one of the men, he prepared to kill as he held the other, struggling, beneath his knee on the floor.

"Raven!" Kyra's voice echoed through the corridors, louder and clearer than usual. "Stop! They're down. There's no need to kill them!" She struggled forwards, pushing past Soren and Deveron and staring at Raven with wide, imploring eyes, gently placing her hand upon his forearm as he prepared to make the killing blow. Raven growled in anger and raised his eyebrows at Deacon.

Deacon shook his head gently. "Leave them, Raven. By the time they wake up, we'll be long gone. They're no threat."

Raven glanced at Callista and kneeled down harder on the spluttering man's throat, cutting off his windpipe. Callista looked coldly at the guard in Raven's grasp. Callista's well-placed fist to the guard's jaw knocked him out cold, and he crumpled to the floor.

"Fine, we let them live. This time," she said and sheathed her sword.

Raven nodded and delivered a rapid punch to the temple of the man beneath his knee. He too slipped into unconsciousness, and Raven brushed his trousers down with distaste. Callista looked over to the gate and gestured for the others to follow her.

Soren was shook up from the deaths he had just witnessed and gladly shot to his mother's side, but Deveron stood his ground and stared at her with wide eyes. "You killed those people. They were innocent, Mum. Just doing what they were told to do."

Callista frowned. "Sorry, Deveron, but this is a war and there are always casualties. It couldn't be helped." She stepped over the guards' bodies and made her way over to the gate.

Deveron's face was frozen in revulsion. "Yes, it could," he muttered quietly.

It made Soren feel even sadder to see his brother this way. He knew what Deveron was thinking from the haunted look in his eyes: He had seen a lot of people killed right before him today, and the sickening images would be burned into his memory forever.

For the first time, Soren felt the need to comfort his big brother. He clapped a hand onto Deveron's back with a meek smile. Together they crept past the bodies, trying not to look down at the lifeless eyes that seemed to follow them.

They made their way to the metal gate the guards had been watching. It was old and rusted but solid nonetheless. Callista gripped the bars with both hands and tried to force them open. Her knuckles strained white under the pressure, but the gate would not budge. Soren knelt down and looked carefully at the lock. He was hoping he could pry it free, but even when he jabbed his sword's tip into the keyhole, he couldn't get it to open. His patience deserted him quickly, and he jumped back up to his feet.

"Let's just break the damn thing down!" he yelled to Callista, who was still trying to coax it off its rusty hinges.

An admonishing frown from his mother silenced Soren's protests, but Callista nodded to Raven. He stepped back, pulling Soren by the shoulder. Raven then stepped forwards, steadied himself and then thrust a devastatingly powerful kick at the gate. With a loud crash, the door swung outwards and clanged into the wall behind.

Despite all the horror they had witnessed today, Soren felt a rush of excitement watching his mentor do something so powerful and destructive, and he was reminded why he admired him so much. Raven glanced back, gave him a barely noticeable smirk and waved him through.

The others followed into the murky corridor beyond. It was a short passageway that led through the dusty gloom, lit only by a single filthy window. The shaft of dusky light which filtered through the grime landed on the opposite wall and illuminated a poster with the Brotherhood's insignia on it. Just the sight of the phoenix and flame made Soren's stomach lurch with fear. He had seen it countless times in his life, but it brought with it death and suffering and would always be linked with terror in his eyes.

He caught the quick glance Kyra and Callista exchanged, but he guessed their real concern was the second symbol which lay beside it, a skull and crossbones.

With a growing sense of trepidation, the group continued down the passageway to a white door at the end of the corridor. It was starkly different to the rest of the corridor, squeaky clean and newly painted. Nervous sweat glistened on Callista's forehead as she stopped in front of the door. Deacon seemed to sense her hesitation and stepped to her side. Placing a hand on her shoulder, he spoke quietly into her ear, his rich voice warm and comforting to Soren, even if he wasn't speaking to him.

"It's OK. Let me and Raven head in this time. You stay back with the kids and Kyra."

"Be careful," Deveron warned. "I can feel someone in there."

Callista gave a nod and stepped back, holding Soren to her chest with a firm hand to prevent him from squirming free and trying to join them. Raven and Deacon stepped quietly up to the door, shared a silent signal, and Deacon reached for the handle.

Two guards greeted them, their swords drawn and pointed straight at them. There was no time to hesitate. Raven leapt into the air in a spiral kick. His foot spun through the air with crushing force and struck the guard nearest to him on the temple. She was knocked out instantly and crumpled to the floor.

In the confusion, Deacon shot behind the second guard and placed a brutal side kick square in his back. The unexpected blow sent him barrelling towards Raven who took his feet out with a rapid swipe. The guard fell to the floor, his sword clattering on the stone. He had merely a second to try and shout for help. Before he had even opened his mouth, Raven had slammed a fist down on the back of his head, and he fell silent.

Relief flooded over Soren. He counted the times they had managed to avoid death so far, but when he looked over to his brother to share his amazement, Deveron was cringing. "Raven! You just killed him!"

Raven shrugged his shoulders and walked into the room beyond, leaving Deveron aghast. On any other occasion, Soren would have bounded along after them, but the intense violence that followed the warriors was starting to get to Soren. He knew this was what they faced all the time, every day even. Somewhere deep down inside of him, he knew this was what he would become too. Because he was also a soldier at heart, and he would grow up to be a good one. He just knew it. But for now, he was content simply to be a child and to get some reassurance and comfort wherever he could. So he stayed behind with his brother and Kyra.

Deveron's feet were glued to the floor, and he had that same horrified expression again. Kyra appeared beside him and placed a soft hand on his cheek.

"You are different to them. You see the value of every human being. It shows the goodness in your heart. The others are good too, but they have seen and done things that change the way they see life and death. You must understand that. They are not evil. They are doing what they think is right."

"How is killing ever right?" Deveron replied in a hushed whisper, not wanting the others to hear his weakness.

"Don't judge them by your standards, Deveron. You live in a warring nation. There will be times when you witness terrible things, things that may change you into them." She nodded towards Callista, Raven and Deacon. "If you can hold onto your humanity through all of that, you will be a better person than many."

Deveron nodded slowly. "I will. Whatever happens, I will hold onto it. I will never justify killing."

Kyra gave him another beautiful smile and stroked his cheek fondly. "Come on. Let's catch up to the others."

They followed into the room, which turned out to be a large laboratory. The walls were painted in blinding white, and sterile surfaces and equipment filled the large space.

"Let's get started. The antidote must be in here somewhere," Callista said, and they set about searching the laboratory at speed. Soren didn't know how long they'd have before more soldiers came. Had the guards they had spared managed to sound an alarm? It was possible that the entire Brotherhood army was coming for them right now. What if Vincent himself was on his way? There were only six of them, and two were children. They wouldn't stand a chance. They'd be slaughtered on sight.

Deacon started rifling through drawers and cupboards, pulling out papers and tossing them behind him onto the floor. Raven joined him, getting more frantic with every passing second that they couldn't find the antidote.

"Come on, come on," Deacon muttered. "The guards could be here at any moment."

Deveron stood by the door, concentrating on it intensely. "Somebody's coming!" he hissed.

There was a fluster of panic as Soren and Deveron scurried to hide and Raven, Callista and Deacon drew their weapons. They waited with held breath, the adults preparing to strike as soon as the door swung open. Footsteps echoed in the corridor outside, a rustling of fabric, a hushed conversation, then the footsteps moved away, getting quieter as they moved down the corridor and away.

The group let out a collective sigh of relief and then got back to searching, even more frantically than before.

Soren crawled around on his hands and knees looking under cupboards and tables. He was putting on a brave face and joining in, but he wasn't himself. His little trick with the guards on their way into the building had taken a lot out of him, and he was starting to feel the effects of their long journey and the exhaustion it brought. Rubbing his hands over his face, he stopped for a few moments to stop the world from spinning. From the corner of his eye, he saw Raven eyeing him curiously. Soren forced himself to get back to work. Raven started searching faster too.

There was no drawer or cupboard left unsearched, and Callista had even taken to yanking down ceiling panels to search for the elusive antidote.

"He told us it was here. That scientist, Steffan, he said it was here," Kyra muttered.

Callista let out a loud yell of frustration and slammed her sword down on a white tabletop. Resting both hands on the surface, she closed her eyes and lowered her head as the search continued around her.

"Come on, Mum," Deveron urged. "We can't give up yet. It must be here somewhere."

Another growl of annoyance left Callista's lips. "How could I be so stupid?"

Soren stopped midway through, rifling in a drawer of papers for the third time. "Who's stupid?"

"I'm stupid," she repeated, before slamming both hands down with a loud bang and making the others flinch. "There is no antidote here. It's so goddamn obvious, and I didn't even see it."

A deep frown creased Raven's forehead, and a frown on his mentor's face always made Soren nervous. "What do you mean, 'no antidote'?"

"Why hide something like that in a facility that we can get into so easily? If this really is a deadly weapon it should be kept locked away somewhere highly guarded, not in a barely hidden and barely patrolled lab like this."

"Wait," Deacon joined them in the centre of the room, "you don't think it's here at all?"

"No, I don't," Callista replied. "And what's more, I can't believe I was stupid enough to believe an old man on a country lane."

"So," Soren asked slowly, "is there no cure for me at all?"

"I imagine there is, somewhere, but it's probably not here."

A string of expletives left Raven's lips and he began to pace back and forth as he always did when he was anxious. "Well, where the hell is it then?"

There was no answer anybody could give him, and it only made him angrier as he began to pace faster.

"Come on," Deacon said, slapping his brother's back and making towards the door. "We'll search the other rooms."

The others followed him with no argument. What could they do instead? What other options did they have?

Soren's despair only deepened though as time ticked by. With every empty, unguarded room they discovered, Callista became increasingly anxious.

"This isn't working," she snapped at last.

"There must be more rooms to check because—" Kyra was cut off by Callista.

160

"No! There is no antidote in this whole facility. It's too strange that there are so few guards here. We need to get out of here now. Something's not right. I can feel it."

"We can't just leave," Soren said. "We need that antidote or I'll get more ill, and so will Deacon."

"I know!" Callista said, more harshly than was necessary. Soren shrank beneath his mother's glare. "Do you think I don't know that? But look, we are not going to find any antidote here, but if we can get home in time, our scientists might be able to put something together that would save you."

"We don't know that, Callista," Kyra said quietly. "Even if we could get a sample of the virus from Deacon or Soren's blood, our scientists might not have time to study it and synthesize a cure. Medical research takes months or even years. We haven't got that long."

"I know," Callista's voice dropped to a quiet, morose tone. "But it's the only chance we've got now. If it isn't here, we can't spend the rest of our time searching a building that may not even hold the cure. We've got to get Soren and Deacon to a hospital as quickly as we can. There may be a nearer facility in Parador where we can get treatment. It's their only hope."

"Whoa," said Raven. "A few hours ago you said we couldn't go home and get them into a hospital. You said we had to come here for this antidote. If we'd just taken them home straight away, they would have been in the care of medical professionals now."

"I know that, Raven," Callista hissed. "I had to try for the antidote, didn't I? Can you blame me for that? My children's lives are at stake. But now that there is no antidote, we need to head back. I know it isn't great, but what else do you suggest?"

As no better ideas came to Raven, he dropped his gaze from his mother's and went back to pacing.

Nobody had anything to say to Callista, each of them caught up in their own thoughts and fears. Soren was getting irritable and angry, and he wasn't sure why. A deep fury was starting to build in his nerves, making him twitch, feeling as though his skin was burning from head to toe.

"Are you OK, Soren?" Deveron asked when his eyes landed on his brother. As well as the inexplicable anger, Soren had started feeling weak and dizzy again. His stomach was churning When he pressed his hands to his abdomen, the skin was sore to the touch.

The last thing he wanted right now was to hold up the mission even further, when it was so desperate that they return home, so he waved his hand dismissively. "Yeah, of course. Just stomach ache. It's nothing."

Kyra frowned and walked over. She touched his chin gently to get him to look at her, and he flinched away from the lights that flickered on the ceiling. She placed a hand over his chest, feeling for his heartbeat within his ribs. He could feel his heart thumping in a bizarre beat.

"Does anything else hurt?"

He shook his head. "It's just a stomach ache, really."

"Soren!" Callista barked at him. The room fell silent, but then she softened a little. "It's important you tell the truth. Tell Kyra everything you feel."

He shrank under her glare. "OK. I feel sick too, like I might puke. And I'm kind of weak. My muscles don't feel like they're working properly."

"No, no, no," Callista muttered. "Not yet. Soren, we need you to keep going just for a little bit longer. We need to get out of this building and then to home. I know it's a long way. I know that, baby, and I'm so sorry. Do you think you can do it?"

Baby? He'd never heard his mother address him like that, and it scared him. She was different. She was...afraid.

Every nerve in his aching body screamed *no, no I can't make it back home*, but there was no way he could say that to people whose respect he coveted, so he gave a reluctant nod instead and prayed he could hang on for long enough to make it out of there and back home.

Chapter Eighteen
The Cage

SOREN WAS TRUDGING along behind Callista, ignoring the strange alternate waves of anger and sickness that swept over him, when something stopped him in his tracks. It was as if he couldn't move, as if his body refused to work. His feet were planted on the floor, and something in the pit of his stomach stopped him from taking another step.

Around and around his head reeled, and his eyes grew wider until he was sure they were the size of footballs. Something was grating at his insides, a cold discomfort deep in the pit of his stomach.

Deveron clattered into him from behind, and he gave him a gentle shove. "Come on. Keep moving."

Soren staggered forwards a few steps but his feet locked down again, refusing to move. Something strange was happening inside him. A switch had flicked on inside his head and sent ripples of power throughout his entire body, his illness completely forgotten. Every part of him tingled with latent energy that pulsed from head to toe. Looking down at his hands, he expected to see something happening to him, but his skin looked the same as ever. Only the series of red lines and bumps on his inner wrist seemed to pulse with an eerie glow. He dismissed the thought as ludicrous and dropped his hand.

Callista paused halfway down the stairs. "I know how hard it is, Soren, but we have got to go. You won't feel better unless we get back and find something to make you better, OK?"

But Soren's feet were locked in place on the floor. His heart was pounding, and he could feel waves of power coming from somewhere unknown.

There was another wave of energy, as if the air molecules around him vibrated. Suddenly, he knew where it was coming from. Almost hidden in the shadows of a darkened corner was a staircase, tiny and wrought out of iron.

As if pulled by some invisible force he ran over to it, oblivious to the shouts of his family.

He reached the steps, his body slamming into the iron banister. Looking down the winding staircase, which was barely wide enough for one person to fit down, he could just see a light shining dimly through the gloom. The sickness which had been ravaging his body drifted to a footnote at the back of his mind.

Without a second thought, he threw himself down the steps.

Raven gave a growl of annoyance and ran after him, pushing Deveron aside as he thundered by. The others followed, bustling to get down the narrow steps in single file.

Soren burst through a door into a dusty little laboratory. Around the edges of the circular room, barely visible in the gloomy darkness, were bookshelves lining every wall. From the floor to the ceiling, thousands of dusty old tomes rotted on the shelves. The dark wooden shelves split in the middle of the far wall, where a single window allowed shafts of light to illuminate the room. A single pane of glass looked out over the Paradoran lands beyond. Soren could see the patch of woods where they had found the scientist and his wagon of vials. Beyond that, in the distance, was the safety of Fallway and their home.

The light of the moon shining through the window painted the room in a stripe of silver with dust dancing in the air. The shaft landed on an enormous glass tube, wide enough for a person to walk into. There, huddled on the floor of the tube, was a tiny figure. It was a little girl, tucked up in a foetal position, her body shaking with fear. Her face was buried in her knees, long silver hair obscuring her features. She was dressed in a dirty grey sheet which was far too long and pooled around her on the floor.

There was a rectangular glass door in the centre of the tube. It rested on brass runners and was fastened by a number of hooks and buckles, as well as two immense deadbolts which held the door fast shut.

It was a cage.

Mesmerised, Soren walked to the tube and placed both hands on the glass. Wiping away the layer of grease and grime that coated the surface, he peered in. It was her, the girl from the picture he had seen pinned to the wall earlier. How was this possible? Who was she?

His heart pounded as he stared at the small girl. Did she even know they were there? Was she asleep? From the look of her, she hadn't had a good meal in a while. Her pale white skin hung off her bony arms. From what he could see of her face, her cheeks were even gaunter. Her hair and clothes hadn't been washed in a long time and the sheet that was draped over her, which had presumably once been white, was speckled with ash-coloured filth.

Soren's heart thundered in his ribcage, threatening to burst out of his small body. Nothing else in the world existed at this moment. Everything slowed to a standstill as he gazed upon her face. He felt like he had been gutted the second he laid eyes upon her, his entire soul stripped bare by her presence. And he had no idea why.

The others crowded around and peered into the glass. They were speechless as they stared at her tiny body curled up on the floor. Kyra looked as closely as she could through the grime and dust. She knocked gently on the glass. "Hello. Are you OK? Do you need help?"

The girl gave no response.

"She isn't responding to us. Maybe the glass is soundproof. Maybe she's in some sort of trance or deep sleep, but she doesn't look in a good way," Kyra said quietly.

"What should we do, Mum?" Deveron asked, looking at Callista with wide eyes. "Do we help her?"

"Let's just go," Raven said quickly and tried to usher the others out of the room and back down the corridor. "We need to get home."

Callista frowned, clearly torn. "I want to help her, but we haven't got the time. More guards could attack at any moment, and what if Soren or Deacon take a turn for the worse?"

"We can't just leave her here," Deveron implored. "We don't know anything about her. She could be seriously hurt or ill. What if they've been testing this virus on her?"

Raven shook his head, a dark frown on his face. "Come on. She's in a cage in a Brotherhood laboratory. We don't know anything about her. Sure, she could be an innocent prisoner, but she could just as easily be another of Vincent's experiments. Maybe she's locked up because she's dangerous. Don't forget what Vincent is capable of when it comes to human weapons."

They hesitated for a moment as they weighed up the options in their minds. Save the child but put themselves at risk, or save themselves and possibly leave a defenceless child to a horrible fate at the hands of the Brotherhood.

"She's just a child," Kyra said quietly. Callista turned to look at her, and Kyra's bright emerald eyes begged her to do the right thing.

Callista sighed and her head drooped. She looked at Raven, her eyes apologetic. "It's a risk, but she *is* a child. We can't justify leaving her here to rot. Anything could happen to her."

Raven scoffed in annoyance but didn't argue with her. "Let's get on with it then. I've had enough of this damn building."

Callista nodded and stepped up to the glass door. She started to fiddle with the bolts and catches and slid back the small metal fastenings and then signalled to the others to help with the large deadbolts, which were rusty and difficult to move. Raven and Deacon yanked on the left side until the bolt slid back with a loud clang. The girl flinched, her shoulders shuddering, but she didn't look up.

Kyra stood in front of the door, waiting to step inside and help the girl when she was freed. Callista and Deacon wrestled with the bolt on the right side and finally managed to wrench it back with a squeal of metal. Raven and Deacon pushed on their side of the door and it slid back with a bang.

The sound made the girl recoil, and she tilted her head up.

Her eyes snapped open.

Chapter Nineteen
Shockwaves

S SOON AS SHE SAW the people gathered before her, the girl's bright silver eyes widened in terror. She raised both hands, palms facing outwards, and the air rippled with a sonic boom. Kyra was standing the closest to her. There was kindness in Kyra's deep green eyes. She stretched a hand out to help, but the girl saw it too late. The magic had been released.

The shockwave blasted into Kyra and threw her backwards through the air. Her body slammed into the far wall with a sickening thud, and she fell to the ground, her long red hair fanning out around her body.

Soren shrieked. Deacon threw his sword aside and ran over, dropping to his knees beside his wife. He brushed her fiery hair away from her smooth face and gasped as he saw her emerald eyes staring blankly at the ceiling.

"Kyra?" he whispered quietly, pulling her towards him. He wrapped his strong arms around her limp body and called her name again and again. "Kyra, answer me. Wake up! Deveron, can you see her life force? Is it still there?"

Tears trickled down Deveron's face as he concentrated intensely on Kyra's inert form. There was a moment of tense silence as they held terrified breaths waiting for his response. Straightening up, Deveron choked back a sob and slowly shook his head. "No," he whispered.

The air was thick with loss. Callista, Raven, Soren and Deveron stood in shocked silence, staring at Kyra and Deacon, each fighting back their own crushing pain. Soren had tears welling in his eyes and stood close to Deveron, their shoulders brushing together for subconscious reassurance. He looked to

Callista, reaching out to his mother to tell him everything would be all right, but he pulled back as he saw the look on her face. Callista's expression was strangely blank. The horror of losing yet another loved one had wiped all emotion from her.

The sound of thundering footsteps echoed in the corridors above them. It seemed so unfair to Soren that they could come even now. Couldn't they be allowed this moment of peace in which to grieve?

Tiny whimpering cries broke the tension in the room. The silver-haired girl was still crouching on the floor of the glass tube, but now she had her knees tucked up to her chest. She shook her head slowly from side to side, trying to shake away the pain she had caused.

Delicate, weak, gentle, she looked nothing like the dangerous weapon she had seemed just seconds before. Soren stared at her, unable to tell whether it was fear or fascination that held his gaze. His fixation with her ended as he heard heavy breathing behind him.

Deacon was glaring at the girl, his chest heaving up and down with sobs which he forced himself to hold back. What Soren saw in his half-brother's eyes frightened him. Deacon was shaking from head to toe with growing hatred for the girl. He placed Kyra's body on the floor and stared into her beautiful face, the face he'd looked lovingly into every day for the past nineteen years. With gentle fingers, he swept his hand across her face and closed her eyelids. He leaned forwards and placed a loving kiss on her forehead.

Head still bowed in sorrow, Deacon's hand closed around his sword, and he rose to his feet. His hands shook on the hilt of his sword as he fixed the cowering girl in a fierce stare. Without warning, he shot towards her, lifting the weapon high in the air.

Soren was still in a daze, watching the scene before him with horror. He saw Kyra die and Deacon crumple with pain and shock, but he saw it all through distant eyes. But when Deacon lifted his sword and rushed towards the girl, Soren's heart jolted in his chest.

Time slowed to a crawl. Panic flooded his senses and every nerve ending in his body screamed for action. His limbs moved automatically. Before he knew it, he had thrown himself in front of the girl to block her from the descending strike that would surely kill her.

A terrified scream from Callista cut through the air, and a shocked yelp came from the little girl, but Soren ignored their cries.

He braced himself for the impact, for the searing, cleaving agony that would be his last sensation. Standing before Deacon Thialdor's blade was a death sentence, one he had readily walked into. Soren's entire body flushed red hot as adrenaline pumped around his veins, his entire body tingling.

The sword struck him, but instead of slicing through his flesh, there was a loud squeal of metal as the blade bounced off his skin. Soren's breath caught in a gasp, and he forced his eyes open. There was an intense searing pain in his back. Then out of nowhere, two enormous silver wings sprouted from his shoulder blades. He turned and wrapped them around the girl protectively, pushing his utter astonishment aside. He was also coated from head to toe in a peculiar silver hue. He flexed his fingers, turning his hands over, and moved his arm up and down. It felt no different. He could move as he always did, but a strange humming vibration coursed through his veins. Stretching his muscles, he found that he could control the wings just like extra limbs. He unfolded them and turned back so he could see his family standing before him.

Deacon's sword scraped off Soren's invincible wings and clanged as the tip hit the floor. He let out a cry of surprise. "What? How did you...?"

Callista, Raven and Deveron gasped in shock, bewildered by the unexpected shield that had sprung up around Soren, as part of him.

"Soren...how did you do that?" Callista stuttered, transfixed by his shimmering aura and enormous silver wings.

There was no answer because Soren had no idea what had happened to him. He was just as shocked and surprised as everybody else. Whatever had happened, it certainly hadn't been a conscious decision. It was as if something had been activated inside of him, something that had been dormant all along. The little girl cowering behind him whimpered. Soren felt small fingers reach out to touch his arm.

"Move out of my way, Soren." Deacon's voice was quiet but dangerous.

Soren shook his head furiously. He didn't know what was happening, but he knew he had to protect the girl. Even though he didn't know the first thing about her, it was suddenly clear to him that he must protect her at all costs. His nervous system went into overdrive, adrenaline bolstering his senses and his mind focused with crystal clarity.

He stood tall in front of her tiny form, blocking her with his own body, his wings bending backwards to enclose the girl in a cocoon. As Soren moved closer to her to shield her from Deacon, he felt his skin pulsate again and the silver armour shone with renewed vigour.

Deacon seethed at him with tears in his eyes and pointed his sword at Soren's face.

"Move. Now, Soren. I have to do this. If you get in the way, I'll have to kill you too."

Deveron began to whimper and clutched at Callista's arms. Callista tried to beg Deacon to stop, but her pleas fell on deaf ears. She tried to wrestle out of Deveron's grip, but he clung tightly to his mother.

Fear pounded in Soren's heart. Deacon was far stronger than him. There was nothing he could do if Deacon wanted to kill him, but Soren stood his ground. It didn't matter if he died. He knew that he must protect the girl. That was all that mattered. He raised his chin defiantly and planted his feet firmly on the ground.

"Deacon." Raven's voice was sympathetic but with an undercurrent of warning in his tone. "Just calm down."

Again, Deacon didn't respond. If Deacon was hurt by Soren's resistance, he didn't show it. His eyes narrowed. "So be it," he said in a detached voice.

With a grunt of effort, he swung his sword again, slashing down upon Soren. The metal blade rushed through the air. Soren braced himself and felt another wave of vibration pass through him. The shimmer coursed across his body, and he felt indestructible. Another shriek from the little girl behind him seemed to fortify his determination even further.

Deacon's blade screeched as it struck Soren's silver hue and bounced off again.

Soren didn't feel a thing.

"Deacon!" screamed Raven. "Stop this. It's Soren!" He reached out to put a hand on Deacon's arm to calm him.

Deacon turned on him in fury. "He is protecting her. *Her*. The girl who just KILLED MY WIFE!" Tears glistened in his chestnut eyes and dropped onto his pale cheeks. "Why are you protecting Soren? He's with her. He's a traitor."

Raven clenched his fists. "A traitor? Think about what you're saying! He's just a kid. He doesn't know what he's doing. You will NOT take this out on him. So back off because if I have to fight you, I will. You will not hurt our brother!"

Deacon stared at Raven and threw his sword to the ground. He clenched his fists together, pressed them against his forehead and let out a long, blood-curdling scream. "He's NOT my brother! And neither are you!"

With an almighty shove, he sent Raven reeling backwards and bent down to where Kyra's cold, lifeless body lay.

Tenderly, he placed his hands beneath her and lifted her into his arms. Her long hair fell down around his arms like a crimson waterfall.

With a furious glare at the others, Deacon stormed through the door, carrying his wife's body. Within minutes, he was gone, disappearing back into the long, winding corridors.

Raven tried to follow, but Callista called to him. "Don't, Raven. He needs this time." Soren heard the pain in his mother's voice, but her face remained stoic, a practised diplomatic expression which came from years of hiding her emotions. "Also," she said quietly, "we haven't got time to chase him. I can hear the guards upstairs. They'll be coming down any minute. We've got to go."

"Deacon's your son!" Raven shouted at his mother.

"Do you think I don't know that?" she snapped back at him, the facade of coldness slipping. "Soren is my child too. If we hesitate for too long, I'll have to watch as two of my kids are lost. Do you think I want that?"

Despite his years as a hardened general, fearsome and indomitable, there were still some things that could pierce through Raven's armour, and his relationship with his brother was one of them. He was torn between the need to chase one brother down, and the need to protect another. From the pain on his face, it was clear that Raven wanted to argue with his mother, to tell her she was wrong, that there was plenty of time, and sprint after his brother. Soren had seen that look in his mentor's eyes before. Raven wanted to take back what he'd said and tell Deacon how he really felt, how his world would collapse without his best friend beside him, how he felt Kyra's death like the loss of a sister, how seeing Deacon in such pain hurt him too. But Soren knew that Callista was right. Deacon needed to be alone now, and Raven knew it too.

Raven dragged his weary feet over to the window and stared out across the landscape in silence. When Callista tried to organise them again, Raven didn't even look up. Whether he could even hear her words or not, Soren wasn't sure, but his lack of a response threw Callista into a panic.

"Mum," Deveron whispered, his voice cracking with pain. "Guards are coming."

Soren never thought he'd see the day his mother lost control, but the pain of losing her closest friend was affecting her decision-making skills. They needed to get out of there, and soon. With every passing minute, the virus was eating away at Soren's body and mind. It was more important than ever that the rest of them survive and get home to make some sort of cure, but the oppressive sadness in the room was weighing down on all of them and distracting them from the urgency of his illness.

"Please, Mum," Deveron said, more loudly this time. "They're coming."

Soren was beginning to panic. On top of his grief about Kyra, the sickness clawing at him was taking its toll. And as his body became sicker, his mind became more twisted and paranoid. The shouts and cries that had echoed around the room just moments before must have alerted the guards who would be upon them soon. And with Deacon gone and Raven stunned into depression, they would be massively overpowered. They were all hurt and afraid and couldn't move or do much of anything else, but they had to put aside their pain for now and get themselves out alive.

The little girl from the glass cage was still cowering behind Soren and reaching out to him occasionally. Every time her little fingers brushed his arm (which continued to glow with an eerie silver hue), he received a boost of energy. From the way she shuddered, he guessed she felt it too. The next time she touched him, he reached over to hold her hand and was flooded with an unexpected sense of well-being that calmed his anxieties and fears.

Callista, however, was frozen in her indecision, and that made Soren fearful again. She clearly didn't know what to do. She looked suspicious and afraid of the strange girl who had killed Kyra but who now cried beside Soren. It was just like when Freya had died and Callista had shut down emotionally, her own rage and pain threatening to flood her senses.

With a loud bang, the door to the room swung open and smashed into the wall behind. Two guards spilled into the room, swords drawn. Finally, Callista snapped out of her grief and sprang into action. Her reactions were slow, as if she was weighed down by sadness and exhaustion. She tussled with the two guards, blocking and striking, until she managed to cut the first down. The second was easy to drop once they were one-on-one, and within a few minutes the threat had been neutralised. They could breathe easy again and could being to make their way out and to the safety of home.

Although a huge amount of adrenaline pumped in Soren's veins, he began to feel terrible again, weak and sickly. Every part of him was cold and shivers ran in waves across his body. His trembling was becoming uncontrollable. When he held his hands out, his fingers jittered, unable to grasp hold of anything. His skin was pale, beyond pale, almost translucent. He began to worry that he wouldn't be able to hold his sword if the need arose. How would he defend himself without his sword? How would he defend the girl? He wasn't strong enough with his hands or feet, even at the best of times.

A wave of nausea shook him, and his stomach clenched in pain. He instinctively pressed his hands to his belly, but his whole abdomen was sore to the touch. His head felt too heavy, his neck too weak to hold it up. Lights and patterns swam before his eyes and he fought to remain upright, consciously working against the gravity that threatened to drag him down to earth.

He closed his eyes and took a few deep breaths to steady himself. It took a few minutes, but the nausea and dizziness slowly began to pass. When he opened his eyes again, he saw that his body was returning to normal.

The change came over Soren gradually as he knelt on the floor of the castle. The mysterious silver hue around him faded until his creamy brown skin showed through in growing transparent patches. The wings folded in on themselves and disappeared seamlessly into his shoulder blades. Within minutes, the silver aura had gone and he was Soren again, a confused ten-year-old with no idea what had just happened to him.

Chapter Twenty
Ceres

oren's head felt foggy and his mind was a jumbled mess of memories which couldn't possibly have happened. Was there something to do with wings? Had Raven really...? Surely Kyra hadn't...

Deacon! Soren tried to stand up too quickly and lost control of his senses. Warm, comforting arms caught him just before he fell. He relaxed into them, relying on them to keep him upright. Closing his eyes for a moment, he tried to make sense of what was happening. Eventually, he was roused from his reverie by the distant sound of voices. He took a moment to steady himself and to get used to the weak ache in every muscle and the pounding thump inside his head. The contents of his stomach threatened to rise up into his throat, and he fought to keep them down.

The voices grew closer, and amongst the familiar tones Soren heard a quiet whimper. His eyes snapped open and he saw her. A tiny girl, maybe his age but smaller and more delicate. Long silver hair obscured her face. Blinking furiously to get rid of the blur in his eyes, he saw that she was trembling. He felt an overwhelming need to go to her, to wrap her up safe and warm in his arms, but when he tried to struggle to his feet Deveron held him tightly and his mother stood in front of him, blocking his way. He was too weak to fight against them and sank back into Deveron's arms.

Callista sheathed her beautiful silver sword in its scabbard and approached the young girl. She tentatively stretched out a hand, and the others gasped.

"Don't, Mother!" screamed Deveron, releasing his grip on Soren.

She turned to him with a frown and put one finger slowly to her lips. Deveron cast a terrified glance over to the window where Raven stood with his back turned, staring out across Meraxor, but he gave no acknowledgement.

Soren watched as Callista gently brushed a strand of hair from the girl's eyes. The platinum locks parted to reveal eyes of stunning silver, gentle but wide with fear. From her harmless appearance, it was hard to believe what had happened mere moments before. The girl looked up at Callista and began to tremble again.

"You need to come with us now. We've got to get you out of here," Callista said softly, but the girl tucked her legs closer to her chest and buried her face in her knees. Callista and Deveron looked at each other and shrugged their shoulders. They didn't know what else they could try. They didn't want to risk angering her again, but they couldn't leave her either.

Soren didn't know why he did it, but there was a powerful tugging inside his heart. He fought his way out of his brother's grasp and crawled over to her on his hands and knees. He placed one hand over his own heart and reached out with his other hand towards the girl. Her eyes widened, and she flinched. As he laid his hand gently on her shoulder, she gasped and a smile crept across her lips.

She threw herself at Soren, flinging her arms around his neck. He was knocked backwards and nearly fell, but he just managed to keep himself upright and cast his mother a confused glance. The birthmark on his wrist burned, but it was a warm, comforting feeling, not at all painful, just glowing a peculiar silver. He stared at it in wonder and reached out to touch the girl's shoulder.

Where his hands touched her, there was a tingling in his skin, as if an electric current was being passed between them. He closed his eyes and buried his nose in her hair, smelling her sweet, fresh fragrance, and nostalgia washed over him. Her presence was warm and reassuring to him, and he held her like the comfort blanket he'd had since he was a baby. But he didn't understand it. He'd never seen this girl before in his life. How could she seem so familiar?

He held onto her until he felt her relax too. He looked towards Callista and Deveron and saw them watching him, their mouths gaping open in surprise.

"Soren, how come she...?" Deveron began to ask.

"I don't know," Soren whispered.

Callista dropped down next to them, but as soon as the girl saw her she began to cower into Soren's arms, making high-pitched whimpering noises. Callista stood straight back up again and took a few steps back. There was sadness in her hazel eyes. Soren thought, at first, that the girl's rejection upset her. But he knew his mother well, and he recognised that deep-seated, often ignored pain. It was an echo of the loss she felt from frequently losing those she loved. And this journey was particularly hard on her. Soren wondered if his mother could stay strong for much longer, but she had managed it for years. She wouldn't falter now.

"Soren, we need to go now." Beneath the calm overtones there was a hint of panic and despair. "We still need to get out of here alive. If the guards realise we're here, they'll be sending reinforcements. Without Deacon, we aren't strong enough to fight them. Get her to come with us. Please."

Soren nodded and tried to peel the girl away from him, but she cried out and clung more tightly to him. Taking her shoulders gently, one in each hand, he pulled her gently away and looked into her watery silver eyes.

"It's OK," he whispered. "We're here to help you. I promise nobody will hurt you. Nobody."

She hesitated a moment and then nodded her head.

"We need to get you out of here now and take you to our home where you'll be safe," he continued.

Her eyes flickered to the others, and she shrank back against him.

"They're my family. They don't want to hurt you. They're here to protect you."

"What's your name?" Callista asked with a soft smile.

In a barely audible voice, she replied, "Angelis Ceresecca. Ceres."

"Ceres, it's dangerous here. Will you come with us?" Callista asked.

Ceres's eyes flickered from Soren to Callista and back again. She eventually gave a small nod and got to her feet awkwardly.

They began to make their way to the door. Deveron jumped to his feet and scurried across the room to his half-brother. "Raven, aren't you coming? We need to get out of here."

Raven had his back to them, but Soren could see his broad shoulders slump, and his head full of thick, dark hair drooped.

"I know it's hard, Raven, but you have to come with us. We have to get out of here. Soldiers could be here any minute. We need to get out," Deveron said quietly and reached up to place a gentle hand on Raven's back to comfort him.

Raven shook his head. "No. We're not leaving without Deacon."

Deveron closed his eyes tightly, clearly trying to shut out the pain in his own heart. But Deveron understood, as Soren did, that there would be an eternity to mourn those they had lost, but if they didn't get out of here soon, they'd all be dead.

"He's gone," Deveron said quietly.

"No, he must still be nearby. He's sick. He has the virus. If I go now, maybe I can catch up to him," Raven mumbled, but his deep voice trailed away into a whisper. Raven's half-brother was gone, his best friend, the person he spent almost all of his time with, his closest confidante. They'd sworn loyalty to each other, and Soren knew that Raven Lennox would rather be dead than break that vow to Deacon. "I'm not leaving here. This was the last place I saw him. I can't leave."

The day's events were something none of them would ever get over, and they all knew it, but Deacon leaving had hit Raven hardest of all. Soren had never seen him like this, and it scared him. Raven was always a pillar of strength, and he would never give up. But seeing him like this...it sent shivers down Soren's spine.

Raven waited, pining for his brother at the window. Soren was sure the guards would kill him when they came. With his guard down like this, Soren didn't know if Raven would even try to fight at all.

"Raven! We need to go now," Callista said, forcing strength into her voice.

Raven gritted his teeth and squeezed his eyes shut. "I can't leave. Deacon might come back."

"RAVEN!" Callista snapped. "I know your pain." She pulled him around to face her and rested her forehead against his. "I know...but Soren's getting sicker by the minute. I can't lose another."

Raven's head drooped again and he took a deep breath, the inner turmoil etched across his dark features. He took one more look out of the window, across the pitch-black deserts of northern Meraxor. Pulling away from his mother's grasp, he yanked the wooden frame open and called out to the wilderness.

"Deacon! Deacon!" Raven's anguished cries drifted across the empty deserts, but no response came; his own voice merely echoed back at him.

Callista placed a comforting hand on his shoulder. "He'll come home, Raven. When his pain subsides, he'll come back to us."

As if he had finally convinced himself of the futility of pining for his half-brother, Raven gave a final growl of rage. Then, he pushed away from the window and stormed out of the door. Soren and the others followed closely, their only focus now upon getting out alive.

As they rushed back through the building together, Soren pushed down the nausea rising within him and all his aches and pains and thought about how he couldn't believe they had survived this far.

The darkness that now hung over their group was biting at him, but Ceres's touch distracted him from the pain and allowed him to believe, if even just for a moment, that there was a chance of hope and redemption.

They ran back to the hall with the eight corridors branching off, and Callista recognised the path that would lead them to safety. Everything seemed so much easier on the way out, but there was an uncomfortable undercurrent running through the group. Guilt, grief, anger—there was a potent mixture of emotions that could erupt at any moment.

Soren was running over the day's events in his head when everybody in front of him stopped abruptly.

"Mum!" Deveron yelled. "Ahead!"

Callista gave a loud gasp of surprise, and Deveron stepped backwards, trembling. Soren couldn't see what the others had stopped for as they stood in front of him blocking his view. He pushed past Raven to get a look. What he saw made his blood run cold. Standing in front of their exit was Vincent Wilder.

Chapter Twenty-One
Clash of Steel

INCENT'S JET-BLACK HAIR was sculpted on top of his head, not a strand out of place, as if it had been carved out of onyx. His eyes were the same shade of darkness, pitch-black coals burning like they had just been lifted from a fire.

A cold smile danced upon his lips, and all the hatred within his soul was written upon his pale face. When he spoke, his razor-sharp words cut into Soren's heart like an icy dagger.

"You didn't expect to walk onto my land without me knowing, did you?"

Vincent stepped aside and Soren saw two people standing behind him. One of them was a gangly teenage boy he didn't recognise. But his heart stopped when Jade stepped up beside Vincent.

"Jade? What are you...?"

The sly smile that crept across her face told Soren what he needed to know. She spoke in the velvety voice he had liked so much just a few days ago.

"You were so trusting and simple. It was easy to get you to follow what I said. That's why Great-Grandfather sent me. He knew you'd listen to me."

Great-Grandfather? Vincent was Jade's great-grandfather? Soren felt as if he had been gutted. He stared at her, speechless.

Vincent caught the look in his eyes and chuckled. "That's right, Soren. Jade was working with me. Don't tell me you never figured that out? You really are as stupid as she said. I didn't want her to come here today. I told her it would be too dangerous, but she was quite insistent."

Ceres's hand tightened upon Soren's. Clearly, she had met Vincent before and the memories were not pleasant. Maybe Vincent had been the one who had trapped her in her glass cage.

His spine tingled with fear again. Soren had seen the paintings of the man who had killed his sister, the man whom his family had been fighting for decades, but none of the pictures did him justice. His frame was far broader than Soren had ever expected, his presence immense and oppressive, as if he sucked all the oxygen from the room without a word.

The silence in the air was thick and tense. Deveron whimpered quietly behind Raven, who could do nothing but hold his head high and prepare for battle. Soren tried to be brave, to stand tall and show Vincent he was not afraid, but inside he was terrified.

Callista and Raven stepped in front of the children, shielding them from Vincent as much as they could. Soren's grip on Ceres's hand tightened, and the tingles he had felt earlier began to run up and down his fingers again.

"We don't want trouble, Vincent." Callista gritted her teeth.

The grin on Vincent's face was cruel and unnerving. "Did you come here for something? An antidote perhaps?"

Callista's expression darkened, but she said nothing in response.

"Did you have any luck finding it?" he goaded, eyebrows raised in mock concern.

There was a dry cackle from the pale boy standing beside Vincent. The grating, unhinged sound made Soren nervous.

Vincent continued. "Tell me, Callista, didn't you find it strange that such a dangerous potion was being transported by such weak soldiers? And an old man too! Didn't that make you suspicious?"

"Of course it did." Callista's voice was quiet but lacking none of the fiery strength Soren always heard in his mother's tone. "But what other choice did I have? Even if it was a trap, I had to take a risk to get the antidote or two of my children would die. I suspect that's exactly why you did it the way you did."

Vincent's lips curled into a grotesque sneer. "This would be an antidote for the virus that some scientist injected into your mongrel offspring, right?"

Callista met his gaze with stony silence.

"What a terrible incident. Tell me, has Soren started developing the symptoms yet?"

Soren subconsciously scratched the sore on his neck. Vincent caught the slight movement and grinned. "Ah yes, the open sores. One of my favourite stages of progression." He leaned down until he was level with Soren's height. "Just you wait until the later stages though. So much fun."

Callista stepped between Vincent and Soren. "Just tell me where the antidote is, Vincent. Please. This is way beyond a little game now."

The echoing laugh that erupted from Vincent's lips as his threw his head back with hysteria turned Soren's blood cold.

"You still think there's actually an antidote, don't you? Oh, Callista, I do believe you're losing your touch. I'm disappointed, and it hardly seems as fun fighting you now. You used to be so intelligent, so shrewd. I couldn't get a trick past you, but you've really let yourself go. I wonder why? Could it be your age? Are you getting bored of this whole battle? Or are you losing a shred of sanity every time one of your kids dies?"

A shudder ran down Soren's spine, but his whole body flushed hot with anger at Vincent. Beside him, Ceres squeezed his hand in a show of silent re-assurance. It wasn't enough to squash his fury though, and he couldn't help glaring at his enemy with as much intensity as he could muster, as if a mere glance could actually hurt the leader of the Brotherhood.

"There's no antidote?" Callista murmured, her grasp on her sheathed sword faltering at her side.

"Oh, Callista," Vincent said, shaking his head from side to side. "So gullible. I almost feel guilty tricking you. It's like...animal abuse. It was all a trick."

The words were like a punch to Soren's guts. It was a lie. It must be. He could feel the effects of the sickness coursing through him. He could feel the searing burn of the weeping sores on his neck.

"No." Callista shook her head in denial. Raven pushed Deveron gently be-hind him, then stepped up beside Callista. She was clearly struggling to deal with what was happening, weakened not only from their long and stressful journey but also from Kyra's death, Deacon's departure and the stress of com-ing face to face with Freya's killer. Raven relieved her of her job.

"Soren is suffering. We've all seen the effects," Raven said.

"Oh yes, your little boy is suffering, all right."

Soren was starting to worry about his future now. Was this it? Would he really die at a mere ten years old before he even had a chance to achieve his full destiny?

The words had leaked from his lips before he even had a chance to think about them. "If there is no antidote, will I die?"

Vincent gave that sickening, sly grin again and tilted his head to one side to consider the young boy. "Nobody said you would die." He straightened up and turned to Callista. "How different this is from our last meeting, Callista. Although," Vincent scratched his chin in mock confusion, "my guards told me there were six of you. Are you one child down again? I wonder what happened there?" He laughed in a way that betrayed he knew exactly what had happened to Deacon.

Horror coiled in Soren's stomach as he realised what this meant. Deacon had left them all, fleeing into the wilderness, stricken with a disease that would slowly eat away at him and with no antidote to cure him.

There were chuckles again from the thin boy, his hand twitching of the hilt of the sword by his side.

Soren could practically feel the animosity flowing from his mother. Every muscle in her neck and shoulders strained with tension. She was like a coiled spring ready to pop at any minute. Her agitation clearly wasn't lost on Vincent either, and his gaze ran over her body, taking pleasure from seeing her so rattled. When he spoke again, his voice was honeyed and smooth. Soren didn't trust him for one second.

"Callista, this all happened because of our ongoing war. You and I have fought for a century, and it never ends. Must we continue in this way, tricking one another, destroying the lives of all around us? This isn't about anybody else but us two, and you know that. Now you have led me to poison two of your children. The responsibility for that lies with *you*, not me. But, if we were to work something out between us, we could pool our resources and find a way to cure them. I am sick of this infinite battle. Agree to join me, and all of this will end now."

"If only that were possible." Callista's voice was loaded with bitterness.

Vincent rolled his head slowly from side to side, as if he was tired and stiff. "It is possible, *Queen Callista*." He spat the words. "I offer you peace here and now."

He extended a hand, sheathed in a black leather glove, towards her.

Callista hesitated, staring at Vincent's outstretched hand and then laughed out loud. "Are you mad? *Peace*? There can never be peace between us. You weren't interested in peace five years ago when you killed my daughter."

Darkness flashed across Vincent's face. "Now, you know that's not what really happened. Let's not cloud the truth with your venomous lies, *Queen.*"

There it was again, the derision Soren had heard in Vincent's voice the first time he addressed Callista.

"You wouldn't want me to have a chat to your boys about the truth, would you?"

Callista audibly growled at him and spread her stance a step wider, preparing herself for battle.

"So let's end this now. You can't get out of here alive, and you know it." The black-gloved outstretched hand was menacing. Soren was torn on his mother's behalf. Accept the monster's offer and suffer the humiliation of kneeling before Vincent, or refuse and enter a fight she wasn't sure they could win. His own muscles tensed in preparation. With a quick nod to Deveron, he gently pushed Ceres into his brother's arms.

Ceres's eyes widened in protest, but he gave her a smile he hoped was reassuring and stepped up beside Raven to offer support for his mother. Raven's powerful hand pushed him back, but he sprang up again and Raven seemed to accept his determination to help. The tension in the air was palpable as they watched Callista stand her ground in silence.

Vincent lowered his hand. "So, you refuse my offer of peace?"

Callista's furious glare gave him his answer.

Vincent's expression darkened. "Then Freya's death was for nothing, and now your other children shall join her in Hell."

In one smooth motion, Vincent pulled his sword from his scabbard, but instead of swinging it towards Callista, he placed it across his left palm and dragged it across the skin. Blood welled around the gash instantly. With his blazing eyes still fixed on Callista, Vincent held the bleeding hand out towards the thin boy beside him.

With a growl of delight the pale teenager fell upon the cut, hungrily lapping up the blood with his tongue and fixing his mouth on the hand with loud slurping noises.

Soren recoiled in horror and was all too aware of the terrified whimpers coming from Ceres. A burst of energy and determination tingled through his veins.

As the boy drank his blood, Vincent grinned. "Speaking of children, I don't believe you've met my son, Guardian. He's quite...unique. His delightful eccentricities are reproduced in the virus currently working its way through your little Soren's veins. Give it another day, and you'll see Soren become like Guardian. Unstoppable; devastating even."

As Vincent's blood replenished Guardian's system, the change in him was almost instantaneous. No sooner had he slurped down the first few drops of blood than his whole body began to change. His eyes, once a weak blue, blazed red. His skin changed from deathly pale to a glowing pallor and his frame bulked up, muscles appearing from nowhere.

If Callista and Raven were as shocked and afraid as Soren, they didn't show it. They stood their ground admirably until enormous wings burst from Guardian's back.

Muttering a string of expletives, Raven took a step backwards and Callista's muscles tensed even further. Manic glee lit up Guardian's red eyes, and he jittered as if an unstable electric current pulsed through him.

Vincent put a hand on Guardian's shoulder, holding him back. He pointed to Ceres. "That's my angel. I want her back in my basement where she belongs." Guardian nodded impatiently, keen for Vincent to stop talking so he could unleash carnage. "Callista is mine too. Disable Raven. Reign wants him. Kill the children."

As soon as Vincent lifted his hand, Guardian launched forwards, teeth bared, and ripped the sword from his side.

The fight exploded around Soren as Callista and Raven leapt forward to clash swords with Guardian.

Vincent threw his head back in a hysterical laugh and then clapped a hand down on Jade's shoulder. He bent down to her level and grinned. "Oh, go on then. Go get him."

Jade's dark eyes lit up. She yanked a dagger from her belt and marched towards a bewildered Soren. There was no time to ponder the morality of fighting a friend. She was upon him too quickly, slashing and stabbing, her deadly blade flashing through the air with lightning speed he had never known she possessed.

Soren yanked his sword from his scabbard. Her knife flew through the air, and Soren blocked it with a loud clang. But she merely slid down his blade, pulling herself in closer to him, underneath his sword's reach. He jumped back, trying to escape her deadly dagger. If she got in close to him again, he was dead. He needed to keep her at a distance.

They circled one another. He gritted his teeth as his eyes locked onto hers. "I thought you were my friend," Soren hissed.

Jade laughed. "That's why this plan was so easy. You're gullible, Soren."

"Why did you do it?"

"Great-Grandfather asked me to."

"Do you do everything Vincent asks?" Soren asked bitterly.

"Do you do everything Callista asks?"

Soren swung for Jade, but she blocked it easily. "No," Soren scoffed. "You know I don't. I do what I think is right."

Jade slashed at Soren, and he had to duck away to avoid being cut by her lethal blade. He had never guessed she would be this good at fighting, and his confidence began to waver. Maybe he couldn't do this after all. Maybe Jade would kill him, and Guardian would kill his mother and Raven, and then he would go after Deveron...and Ceres. Just the thought of Ceres in danger made Soren's skin begin to tingle from head to toe.

An enormous burst of strength flooded over him. His mind focused, and he flung his sword as hard as he could at Jade. She managed to block it, but her eyes widened in fear and surprise.

"You'll never beat me, just like your mum will never beat my great-grandfather," Jade snapped, but Soren could see she was losing her composure. He used it to his advantage, slashing and swinging wherever he could, trying to keep her at a distance and catch her off-guard. Jade was losing, and she was getting angry about it.

"Just give up, Soren! You're going to turn into a monster anyway now that you've got the virus. It's time you accepted that the Brotherhood should rule Alcherys. Callista's time is over."

Nipping under an overhead swing, Jade was suddenly right in front of Soren's face. He had nothing to block her knife with. A flash of hope shot through his mind. *Please let the silver shield spring up around me now*, he thought, but nothing came.

She jabbed at him. He dodged, but the blade still caught him. A trickle of warm blood ran down his side, and fear threatened to cloud his mind. He hadn't been prepared for this. No matter how much he thought of himself as a warrior, this was too hard. There was no time to feel sorry for himself, though. Death was but moments away. He jumped back out of her range and then snarled and swung for her. The tip of his sword caught her arm, and her skin opened in a huge gash. She crumpled, the knife clattering to the floor.

Soren stood over her, pointed the tip of his weapon at her chest and tried to fight away the desire to kill her.

"You betrayed me," Soren said quietly. "I thought you were my friend, but instead you tricked me. You made me catch this virus and you put my family in danger. I'll never trust you again. Your great-grandfather is the most evil man on the planet. I think you know that, which makes you evil too."

Jade flinched at Soren's words. She tried to grab for her dagger, but Soren kicked it away.

"Are you going to kill me?" Jade asked.

Soren looked over to his mother and Raven, but they were still engaged in a furious three-way battle with Guardian.

"I want to," Soren said, "but I won't because we're not the bad guys here."

Soren pulled his sword away from Jade, but she didn't move. There was still defiance in her eyes.

That was when he knew that the Jade he had been friends with was truly gone. She wouldn't stop. She would never give up. It was down to him to stop her. Pushing aside the creeping guilt, Soren whispered a quick apology and then slammed the hilt of his sword into Jade's temple.

She crumpled to the floor, unconscious. As she fell, the malicious look on her lips disappeared. Her eyes drifted closed, and she looked like the pretty little girl at school again.

The guilt and regret needled inside of him, but it didn't last long. Within seconds, he straightened his back, flipped his sword back around and took a step towards Raven and Callista. A powerful hand clasped his shirt and yanked him backwards. He yelped in surprise and spun around to see Deveron's eyes burning with a determination he had never seen in him before.

"No, Soren." There was none of Deveron's usual awkward indecision. "Not this time." For the first time—probably ever—Soren listened to his brother. Deveron pushed his new-found authority further. "Ceres needs you here."

It was the correct thing to say, and Soren knew he couldn't argue. With a firm nod to his brother, Soren grasped Ceres's hand and felt the comforting buzz of energy ripple through him again.

True, he couldn't do anything to Vincent, and he certainly wasn't strong enough to protect Callista or Raven, but he was the only person alive who could protect the little girl at his side. He wasn't sure how he knew, but his destiny as her protector suddenly seemed obvious to him, a lifelong calling that he'd only just realised.

Grasping her hand even tighter, he could only watch, heart pounding and breath held tight, as his mentor and his mother faced their attacker.

Callista and Raven were two of the strongest warriors alive, but even with their decades of training, they were struggling to land a blow on Guardian. His speed was mind-blowing. Every time they slashed or stabbed at him, he flapped his enormous wings and slipped away easily, laughing all the time, enjoying the game.

Each strike missed and with every failed attack, he would nip behind them and deliver a brutal punch or kick to the back of his enemy. It made Soren's blood boil to see Guardian playing with his family like this, but it was terrifying too. In his eyes, Callista and Raven were invincible. Seeing them brought to their knees shook everything he thought he knew about the world.

Callista flipped and twisted, her sword slashing through the air so quickly she was just a blur of silver. Yet still, she couldn't land a single blow on the blood-sucking creature.

Guardian held his sword up high, seemingly wanting the battle to last longer, enjoying the ride. Soren was pretty sure Guardian could end the battle instantly if he swung that blade, and he prayed for Guardian to revel for longer, just long enough for Callista and Raven to gain the upper hand. Though how they would manage that was beyond him.

Vincent stood silently at the back of the room, hands clasped together behind his back. The same dark, analytical coolness was back in his eyes as he watched the battle dispassionately. Soren wondered why he didn't jump into the battle himself. It would definitely be an easy win for them then. Maybe he was giving Guardian a chance to show what he could do. Well, what Guardian could do was mightily impressive.

In one gut-wrenching movement, Guardian swung his sword in a brutal overhead strike. The descending blade missed Callista's head by inches. She spun away, a deep frown creasing her forehead.

The terror of nearly losing his mother and leader must have hit Raven as hard as it hit Soren because Raven's determination stepped up a notch. He flew at Guardian, furiously flinging devastating kicks and punches at the teenager. Only one of them would have knocked Guardian out, if they had made contact. But attacks scraped by him or flew wide. With each miss, Raven became more desperate and more careless.

Soren had seen Raven fight countless times, and his judgement was usually impeccable. Never had Soren seen him so erratic and out of control. It wasn't just the tension of this fight; it was the loss of his brother too. In recent years, Raven and Deacon had worked together in every battle and had built complimentary techniques revolving around each other.

Now, with no Deacon to rely on, it was like Raven had lost a limb. He flailed around handicapped. It only took one careless stumble, and Raven's guard was down. Guardian wasted no time and plunged his sword through Raven's left shoulder. A howl of agony rang out through the air, and Raven dropped to one knee. Guardian took pleasure in pushing the blade in deeper, the tip poking out of Raven's back.

Soren's breath caught in his throat. Blood was spreading across Raven's Avalanche uniform, the agony written on his mentor's face. It was all too much for Soren, and he couldn't catch his breath.

Callista shrieked in fury and swung for Guardian, but he ripped his blade from Raven, causing another bloodcurdling scream, and met her blade midstrike. Their eyes locked together; Callista's intense and burning with passion, Guardian's whimsical, almost joyous.

Guardian threw a kick in Raven's direction and caught the crumpled warrior in his damaged arm. Raven yelled again, and blood ran over his fingers down his forearm. Callista couldn't stop her eyes flicking towards her son, and that was when Guardian saw his chance.

Yanking his blade away from Callista's, he tore it across her upper arm, slicing a deep gash in the flesh. In a moment that made Soren admire his mother more than ever, Callista winced and adjusted her grip on her sword, but she didn't falter. She carried on facing him, steely and more determined than ever.

"Impressive." Vincent's callous tones cut through the air. "Guardian, leave her to me. You, feast on Raven, but leave him alive for Reign."

Guardian's eyes lit up with excitement, and he fell upon Raven's inert body with ravenous hunger. Grabbing Raven's shoulder with both hands, he sank his razor sharp incisors deep into the exposed wound before him.

Soren's heart leapt into his throat, his stomach churning with horror. All rational thoughts were overridden by sheer panic. He tried to dart over to his help his mentor, but Deveron's arms closed around his upper arms, locking him firmly in an embrace.

"Stop it! Get off me!" Soren cried, trying to wriggle free from his brother's prison, but Deveron's arms held fast.

"No, Soren. You can't." Deveron's voice was quiet and sad.

The hysteria flowing through Soren intensified, and tears began to fall onto his cheeks as he screamed at Deveron for holding him back, at Callista for not doing something to help, and at Raven for not fighting back.

No matter how loudly Soren's tormented screams rang through the air, Guardian was oblivious. His head tipped backwards and forwards, as he gnawed at Raven's wound with sickening thirst, tearing chunks of flesh away, and lapping at the freely-flowing gore.

Powerless to help his mentor, Soren couldn't bear to watch anymore. He turned in to his brother's arms, burying his head against Deveron's chest and weeping into his shirt. The steady, gentle rhythm of Deveron comfortingly stroking his back was at stark odds with the furious heartbeat he could hear within the fourteen-year-old's chest. For the first time in his life, Soren appreciated his brother's love for him, even in the face of his own terror, but that thought just made him cry all the more.

Soren was yanked from his flooding sorrow by a furious battle cry as Callista launched herself at Vincent, her sword slicing through the air. But despite the malicious chuckling coming from Vincent, he was ready, as always, for the attack. His own sword, seemingly drawn from nowhere in a split second, blocked her incoming strike with a loud clang of metal.

Soren dared to turn his head, consciously steering his eyes away from the hideous sight of Guardian drinking Raven's blood, to watch his mother enter a furious battle with Vincent. The two titans, both legends in their own right, were humbling to behold. With strength, speed and skill unrivalled, they moved in a blur, deadly weapons flying through the air with awe-inspiring accuracy.

As he followed her every move, Soren realised he was seeing his mother as he had never seen her before. Usually, her grace and power in battle were humbling, but at the moment she looked flustered and out of control. Tears streamed down her face, and her eyes blazed with furious darkness. Soren knew this battle was about far more than Vincent stopping them from leaving the facility. This was about what happened to Kyra and how it had affected Deacon.

This was about torturing a little girl in a basement and infecting children with deadly diseases. This was about allowing a vampire to feast upon Raven. And more than anything, this was about Freya.

So when she threw herself at her enemy, it was with a ferociousness that would make most soldiers quake with fear, but Vincent was made of much stronger stuff and he met her attacks with a cool-headedness that made Soren feel sick. They clashed with devastating force, but they were evenly matched and they both knew it. They always had been or else one of them would have been victorious in the eternal war long before now. Neither could win on skill alone.

But from the look in Vincent's eyes, Soren could guess exactly what he was thinking. He didn't need to beat Callista; he just had to keep her busy. With every passing second, Raven's lifeblood was being drained from his body. Raven Lennox, who was not just Callista's son but also the strongest commander in the second generation of the Children of Light. With his submission and capture, Callista would be irreparably damaged. All he had to do was keep her busy while her son's blood was drained, his spirit crushed, and her nation was broken apart.

Soren knew this was what he was doing, and Callista knew it too. She dragged her eyes away from Vincent for a split second to look pleadingly at Raven, whose body was becoming paler by the second. But a split second was all it took.

Vincent took advantage of Callista's diverted attention and hooked his blade under the hilt of her sword. With one almighty yank, he ripped her blade from her grasp and sent it flying to land with a clatter on the far side of the corridor. Her surprise paralysed her, and it was easy for Vincent to knock her down with one powerful, well-aimed punch to the side of her head. She crumpled to the floor, and Vincent was immediately above her with the tip of his sword pointed at her throat.

"It's over, Callista. You've been defeated and you know it. This war will end today. You were given a chance to make peace, but you wouldn't take it. So I have no choice but to finish you."

Callista growled at him. "You can kill me, but the war doesn't end with me. My soldiers, my family, will keep fighting you, forever. You will never win."

Vincent chuckled. "That's where you're wrong. Without you to lead them, your people will fall apart. While they're mourning, I shall kill them. Every last one. The Children of Light are a plague upon this world, and there can never be peace while even a single one of your filth still lives. I'll cleanse the planet and start again, repopulate with the virtuous, those that deserve to inherit the land."

Even though she was held in place by the deadly point at her throat, Callista laughed. "How exactly will you cleanse us all? My soldiers are strong. You should know that. We've defeated you enough times."

The maniacal smile was back on Vincent's face. "You know that virus your precious Soren and Deacon are carrying? Well, I have a huge stock of it just waiting for your people. When it is released upon your nation, every man, woman and child will be turned into a blood-sucking monster." He chuckled again and nodded towards Guardian, who still lay over Raven, slurping at the blood trickling from his wound. "Your children and your children's children will become like Guardian, insane with an uncontrollable lust for each other's blood. In that frenzied bloodlust, there are no family bonds. Friendships will mean nothing, and all that will matter is where the next blood is coming from. Will your *diplomacy* and *decency* be enough to stop them from tearing each other apart? I won't need to defeat you. I'll just unleash this disease and let you kill each other."

Callista squirmed, and Soren saw the fear in her wide eyes. What Vincent said was true. The Brotherhood could never hope to defeat the Children of Light in battle, but with chemical warfare...

Vincent stroked the blade across Callista's throat almost tenderly. "You are so proud of that lovely little school you set up, aren't you? The one where Paradorans and Alcherans can mix. Well, in a few days' time, my undercover spies—you know, all those 'Paradoran' kids who you so graciously let in—will carry hundreds of syringes full of this virus into your little school. They will work their way through it, injecting as many of their classmates as they can get their hands on. From there, the disease will spread across the entire nation of Alcherys. Isn't it beautifully ironic that your project to unite Alcherys and Parador against Meraxor will be the thing that brings you both down?

"And the best thing is that even if the plan doesn't work, even if something were to stop the school from being attacked, the damage to the Children of Light has already been done. How will your people cope when their leader is dead, their top-ranking commander captured, another top soldier has vanished and their favourite little soldier has turned into a monster?"

He chuckled again, but there was no joy in his voice. A deep sigh escaped his lips. "I know you think me a devil, Callista, but I assure you I never wanted it to end up like this. I didn't want to kill you or any of your people. If peace without any bloodshed at all were possible, I would take it in a heartbeat, but I learnt a long time ago that you are the most stubborn woman the world over and you can never be made to see sense. You can't even see when somebody is offering you a better life. The Children of Light—Ha! Isn't that a misnomer?—are like cockroaches, always there, hanging on to an obdurate existence."

His eyes were glowing with a furious insanity. "And what do we do with pests? With insects? We wipe them out to save the superior species. It is tragic, but we all know it has to be done. So now I shall kill you, as I killed Freya. And afterwards, I shall kill your other children too."

With hands that trembled, Vincent raised the sword high in the air, preparing to plunge it through her throat and end the war once and for all.

Soren grabbed at his head in despair. "Mum!"

Then, he heard a tiny voice beside him. "No. No more." Ceres's silver eyes, previously so gentle and afraid, glowed with determination.

Taking a step forwards, she planted her feet on the floor and clasped both hands together. Her eyes drifted to a close, and her body hunched over as if she was suffering from an intense stomach ache. Soren gasped as two enormous snow-white wings fanned out from her shoulder blades.

Sparkling silver coated her from head to toe and as she straightened up, tall and regal, her presence suddenly commanding instead of cowering, her silver hair streamed out behind her.

Before he had time to register what was happening, Soren was swept along with her. Her hand, suddenly firm and assertive, grabbed his and all the power and energy he had felt before was flicked on like a light switch. His own wings burst out of his back once more, and Soren and Ceres moved as one. He had no control; she was operating his body for him. In perfect unison, they raised their heads, palms facing outwards. Pulsating power flowed through Soren, starting in his chest and then flooding down his arm like a turbulent river.

Blinding white beams of light shot out of their hands, flying through the air like spears, and then splitting into three rays. Each of the strands struck a target in the chest. Vincent was flung backwards, his sword clattering uselessly to the floor beside Callista. With a sickening thud, he hit the wall and slid down into a twitching sleep.

The second beam struck Jade, and her body was swept away, as if a tsunami had hit her, sending her flying into the wall beside her grandfather. The third beam thudded into Guardian. The effect was instant. Although he managed to maintain his position on top of Raven, his powerful wings withered and disintegrated, grey feathers exploding around him and drifting to the floor. The muscled, powerful body the virus had given him shrivelled as if somebody had deflated a balloon, and his glowing skin was replaced with the unhealthy hue he had been cursed with his entire life.

As all of his strength was stripped from him, he crumpled to the floor, coughing splatters of blood, his face pressed into the stone tiles.

Arms still outstretched and twitching from the sudden outburst of power, Soren was frozen to the spot, his mouth gaping. He couldn't even begin to explain what had just happened, but he could still feel the vibrating pulse in his fingers and could make out, through confused eyes, the silver tinge emanating from his skin.

The next few minutes were a complete blur for Soren. His vision focusing and refocusing, he blinked hard and saw Raven drag himself into a sitting position, his right hand clamped down over his injured shoulder. Soren couldn't be sure, but he thought Raven was staring right at him. A few more blinks and a shake of his head confirmed it. As Soren's vision cleared, he caught a look in his mentor's eyes. Admiration? Shock? Fear?

Whatever it was, it disappeared almost as quickly as it had appeared. Raven pulled himself to his knees and crawled over to Guardian's inert form. Raven snatched up his sword and poked at Guardian, but the weak, pale teenager was no longer a threat, too feeble to even lift his head from the stone beneath him.

Seeing Jade's crumpled body with limbs jutting out at awkward angles made Soren's chest constrict painfully. In his heart, he yearned to run over to her and check she was OK, even though she had betrayed him, but his head screamed for him to stop. It was as if his instincts were trying to protect him from having to witness what he had done to her.

With his breath coming in short gasps, Soren watched her through eyes brimming with tears. Not a single muscle in her body moved. Even from this distance, Soren could see that her chest wasn't rising and falling the way Guardian's was. The awful truth slammed into him and choking gasps caught in his throat. He tore his eyes away, as if she would revive when she was out of sight. A quick glance back ruined that fantasy for him.

"Soren," Deveron whispered behind him.

"Don't." Soren cut him off before he could say the words. "I think I know what you're going to say."

Deveron said nothing more, and his silence told Soren what he needed to know. A tear left his eye and he wiped it away hurriedly.

With clenched fists and a scowl on her face, Callista rose slowly and turned towards Vincent, her sword gripped tightly in her hand.

It was hard to believe that Vincent was such a powerful warlord, based upon the convulsing form on the floor. His eyes were rolling back in his head, froth at his mouth, arms jutting out at strange angles, and he appeared to be in the throes of an intense fit.

Callista's grip flexed on her sword, and Soren could see the indecision in her mind. Every fibre of her being must have been yearning to run straight over and stab him through the heart while he lay so vulnerable, but the Children of Light code of ethics forbade it.

Either way, Soren hoped it would be the end of Vincent Wilder and the Brotherhood of Shadow. They had been defeated. Now that Callista and the Children had Ceres on their side, they would surely be invincible. Even if Soren knew deep down inside that those thoughts were a mere pipe dream, a deep comfort washed over him, and he relaxed muscles he hadn't known he had been tensing.

As all the fear and tension flowed from him, so did the pulsating energy that had bolstered him for the attack. The power sapped straight out of him, leaving him breathless and weak, and feeling as if he had a piece of his soul ripped out. A deep churning began in his stomach as his muscles clenched. He doubled over, shocked by the sudden grinding pain, and was hit by another equally painful agony in his chest. Sucking in deep gasps of air, he began to cough uncontrollably, pressing both hands to his chest in an effort to control the intense pain.

The room spun around him, two, three times, and then he lost control of his limbs and hit the floor.

"Soren!" Callista cried, and the desire for revenge against Vincent was forgotten. She was by Soren's side in an instant, running her hand over his burning forehead and feeling his pale, clammy cheeks.

Through eyes blurred with pain, Soren saw Raven struggle over, grunting at the pain in his lacerated shoulder. Deveron hovered over him with concern and fear etched across his face.

Another coughing fit erupted from Soren, and this time, drops of blood splattered across his lips. It felt as though somebody had planted tiny explosives in his chest and windpipe, and they were detonating, rupturing his lungs.

The light was dimming, his vision waxing and waning, darkness clouding in around him. He forced his eyes open again and saw them all standing around him: his mother, Raven, Deveron and Ceres. *Ceres.* He reached out to touch her delicate hand and received an injection of energy, but it wasn't enough, and his head flopped back down again.

The voices were distant, echoing like he heard them at the end of a corridor. He clung to them, straining to identify each person speaking, desperate to hang onto the consciousness that was slipping away.

"What's happening to him?" *That was Deveron's panicky, high tone.*

"The virus." *Raven's deep grunts.* "It's starting to turn him into a creature like Guardian."

A weaker, quieter voice. "Please save him." *Ceres.*

Soren saw the shadowy outline of his mother flitting before him and tried to grasp her, but somebody held his arms down firmly.

"Mum! We haven't got any antidote for him! We haven't got anything that could help him!"

"I know, Deveron." The cool-headed strength of his mother's voice calmed Soren. "Taking him home is the only thing we can do. Maybe, just maybe, if we get him some sleep and some medicine we can stall the effects of this horrible disease."

Distorted voices at the end of the corridor again, and somebody scooping him up into strong arms. Motion as he was carried quickly.

Soren felt himself slipping into sleep. At least, he hoped it was sleep.

"If we hurry, he might just survive, but I think he'll need something stronger than normal medicine."

A quiet crying.

"Something stronger?"

"It's too strong for his body, this virus. It will break down his delicate system. He's too young."

"Are you talking about giving him the elixir? But he's too young for that."

"You can't be serious."

"It might be the only thing that will stop this virus and keep him alive."

"But...if he takes the elixir now, that means..."

"I know. It means he'll stay this age. If he survives, he'll be stuck in his ten-year-old body forever."

Chapter Twenty-Two
Memories

OREN WAS WOKEN by the light chirruping of birds outside his window. Even though his eyes were still closed, he could feel the early morning sun on his face. He felt slightly hazy and guessed he had been asleep for a long time. He blinked groggily, forcing his heavy eyelids open and trying to ignore the pounding in the base of his skull. His memories were cloudy with chunks of time missing and only a vague recollection of the crazy things that happened at the laboratory in Meraxor.

His vision swimming in and out of focus, he looked up and saw his mother's face. There was the hint of a smile dancing on her lips but, in her eyes, Soren still recognised the familiar sadness that plagued her. Now he knew there would be an even heavier weight dragging Callista down, more lives lost and more darkness in the world. The memories were coming back to him in trickles and splashes. He winced as he recalled difficult moments from the long journey they had undertaken.

Another brief glance around the room brought the other people to his attention. Callista was beside him, her chair pulled right up to the edge of his bed in what he now recognised as a medical room. His father, Kham, stood behind Callista, one hand resting on her shoulder. When Soren locked eyes with his father, he almost flinched. He hadn't made proper eye contact with his father for years. Kham wasn't usually *there* enough to maintain any form of real social contact. This time a smile crept across his father's dark lips, but his eyes, even when they were locked onto Soren, were distant and guarded.

Soren looked to Kham's hand where his golden wedding band still rested on his finger and then flicked to his mother's hand, conspicuously missing hers.

"Mum, did you...?" Soren tried to form a sentence, but his mouth was so dry that his voice cracked and the sound he made disintegrated into nothingness.

"Don't try to speak, Soren. There's plenty of time for that. Save your voice." His mother stroked his hand gently, but the lack of a wedding ring on her finger bothered Soren. He cleared his throat and swallowed a few times to clear his voice as much as he could, but when he spoke his words were still strained.

"Mum, how did we get back here?"

A quick glance to the floor, as if Callista was gathering her thoughts, deciding what he did and didn't need to know. "You passed out back at the laboratory in Meraxor. Do you remember that?"

Flashes of memory came back to Soren, but they were distant, like trying to recall a story he had been told as a toddler.

"I think so." His words were slow and forced, his forehead creased as he struggled to remember. Though his body was still lethargic and aching from head to toe, there was none of the horrific sickness that had plagued him back in Meraxor. Whatever the terrible virus had been, it was gone now. He was sure of it.

Callista continued. "Well, you were unconscious, and we couldn't do anything to rouse you. So Raven and I carried you back to the hospital here in Fallway."

"Carried me?" Soren frowned, his drug-addled brain slow to comprehend. "But, that's miles."

Callista gave a small, humourless laugh. "Yes, it is. It took us a long time and was a difficult journey, but we got you home in time."

"In time?" He knew there was something he was missing, but that part of his memory clearly wasn't functioning. Where there should have been a memory, there was a vague, fuzzy cloud.

Callista and Kham shared a serious glance at each other before turning back to their son. "Do you remember getting sick?"

As soon as the words had left her mouth, the memories flooded back. He remembered how he felt more ill than he had ever felt before, how he had prayed for the ground to open up and swallow him, and how he had been quite sure he was about to meet his death.

He nodded. Callista smiled, clearly pleased that his memories were returning. "That's good, Soren. You contracted a virus when that scientist injected you in the cart in Parador. As we carried you back across Parador, you became more and more sick. We were all quite sure that your time was up." Her words drifted away into a whisper.

"Did you give me the antidote? Did you find it?"

Callista swallowed and broke eye contact for a moment. When she spoke again, her words were slow and deliberate. "Soren, we learnt a lot about that terrible virus from Vincent...from Vincent and his son, Guardian. Do you remember Guardian?"

Another flash of memory: a manic, laughing teenager, hell-bent on murder as he sucked the blood from Raven's neck. Soren shuddered.

"Yes, I remember him."

"That's what you would have become if the virus had taken hold completely. You were beginning to turn that way, into whatever creature Guardian is. That's what Vincent really wanted. The plan wasn't to kill you. It was to turn you into a monster whose bloodlust could never be sated. Soren, there was no antidote. Vincent never made one. He didn't want you to be cured. Ever. So he didn't make a way to reverse the effects. We don't even know if it's possible for the damage to be undone."

"But then how...?"

Avoiding his intent gaze, Callista took a deep breath before beginning again. "Soren, the damage to you was too great. You're only a child after all, and the virus affected you more seriously than it would have affected an adult. With no antidote to give you, there was only one other way to keep you alive."

Soren didn't like the sound of that, not one bit. Whatever his mother was about to say next, he had a deep sense of foreboding about it.

She was choosing her words carefully. "We had to give you something that would make your system stronger, something that would fortify your whole nervous system and strengthen your heart against the effects of the virus. Something more powerful, that would override the poison in your bloodstream."

"Do you mean...?"

Callista nodded with a pained frown. "Yes. We had to give you the elixir."

It took a moment for the words to sink in. "So...doesn't that mean...that I'll always be this age?"

Nobody answered him, but their faces said it all. Soren's whole world span for a moment, and he was forced to re-evaluate everything he thought he knew about the world. He would never grow up and would never become an adult. All the hours he had spent with Raven, training and nurturing his gifts would go to waste because he could never be physically stronger than he was at that moment. How could he fulfil his destiny now? How could he succeed his mother and become the true warrior he had always dreamed of being?

Running his hands over his face, he felt like screaming and releasing all the pent-up anger and frustration inside of him, but at the back of his mind he was all too aware of one redeeming factor. He was alive. After all they had been through, that alone was a miracle.

Pushing aside the anger and pain, he threw back the white sheets that covered him and swung his legs over the side of the bed. Jumping down and steadying himself on shaky legs that threatened to buckle under the strain, he readied his muscles then began to walk backwards and forwards, trying to get some circulation back to his numb feet. It was tough work and his progress was slow, but after twenty minutes of walking, very slowly, around his room, he was beginning to build confidence and strength again.

Soren spoke to his mother and father as he walked, desperately wanting to bring himself back up to speed with everything that had happened.

"Raven? Where is he? Is he OK?" Soren asked, although he was nervous about the response he would get before he had even said the words.

Sadness crossed Callista's face again. "He isn't the same. He's quiet, withdrawn..." Her words drifted off as she bit her lip to contain the tears that she would never allow to fall. In the end, it was Kham who filled in the details.

"Soren, Raven's having a hard time at the moment. He trained with Deacon and tutored and nurtured him for many years. He was always so tough on him, so mean, we all know that, but he needs Deacon. He loves him, even though he won't admit it. Now that Deacon is gone, Raven doesn't know what to do with his time. He has locked himself away for many days, and we haven't seen him at all since you returned. But grief hits everybody in different ways, and that is something you must understand. Raven will deal with this in his own way. When he is ready, he will come back to us."

It was the most lucid and honest Soren had seen his father in years, if not ever. He didn't know how to respond, aside from hugging his dad harder than he ever had before. The feel of his dad's arms around him made Soren's tears flow, and he collapsed into a strong embrace from the father he had never really known.

Still entwined in his father's arms, Soren continued to question the adults.

"Did you take the reward to Eradi?"

"By the time we got back with the reward, the camp was abandoned. They were all gone, and with them, my ring." The sadness in Callista's eyes pulled at Soren's heart too.

"But then how..."

"Never mind, Soren. What's important is that you are safe now. Your mum did the right thing," Kham said.

Soren didn't quite agree, but he wanted to move on. He still had many questions. "But...it wasn't just me that got injected. Did you give Deacon the elixir too? But he already had it at age sixteen, like everyone does, so how...?" His voice drifted off into a whisper as he felt the tension in the air.

He pulled back from his father, but when he looked to his mother, Callista's eyes glazed over. "We couldn't do anything about his illness. He had already fled before we got back to Parador. Even if he had come back here with us, he cannot take the elixir again. Nobody can have it more than once. It would be too strong for the body to handle."

"But that means...he won't turn into a creature like Guardian, will he?" The silence from Callista gave him his answer. "No, Mum! We have to go and find him. There must be something we can do!"

"He decided to leave us, Soren. That was his decision and his alone. He has gone, and we don't know anything about where he is or what he has chosen to do. We can't do anything unless he chooses to come back to us, and even if he does, we don't know what he may have become."

The weight of Callista's words hit Soren like a sledgehammer. There weren't always many consistencies in the Children of Light, times changed and alliances were forged and broken all the time, but Deacon had always been there, for as long as Soren could remember, and for as long as Deacon had been there, so had Kyra. Beautiful, gentle Kyra who cared only for helping others.

"Kyra," he muttered. He wanted to say more, something profound and worthy of his amazing sister-in-law, but none of the words that came to mind did her justice.

"I know, Soren. We need to sort a memorial service, and I just can't. Not yet. We'll talk about it when we're all ready. I promise. But you need to get some rest now."

Rest was the furthest thing from Soren's mind. "But...what about Dana? Who will she stay with?"

Tears welled in Callista's eyes again, and she turned in her seat, shielding her face from Soren. Kham picked up the slack again. "Raven and Estella have taken Dana in. Their daughter, Andromeda, is only a few years older than Dana so they agreed to take care of her until Deacon returns."

"But what if..."

"Soren!" Callista snapped, her head whipping back around. "They will take care of her until Deacon returns."

Soren shrank under his mother's fierce glare, and he knew it would be wise to say nothing more about it, even though his heart ached for little Dana and the isolation and pain she must be feeling.

"There are still so many things I don't understand. When we first got to the facility, there was that man in black. The one who killed all the guards and opened the door for us. Who was he?"

Callista's face darkened. "That's one question I truly cannot answer. I have no idea who that man was, or why he chose to help us. But we can't deny that his assistance was crucial. Whoever he was, he must have been on our side."

Soren's memories shifted and cleared again. He gasped. "Ceres? What happened...? She and I, we did that...thing. Did we...?"

Callista raised a hand in the air, stopping the onslaught of panicky questions. "She's here in Fallway, staying at our house. For now, at least."

"Is she OK? She wasn't..."

A smile crossed his mother's lips as she slowly shook her head from side to side. "She's absolutely fine. She wasn't injured at all...just afraid and confused."

That makes two of us, thought Soren, as his mind raced at one hundred miles an hour, pulling in details from their visit to the facility. The image of Kyra's body flying backwards through the air thudded into his mind again. He swallowed a knot of sickness that threatened to rise in his throat.

"But...she killed Kyra." Sadness flashed through Callista's eyes, but the smile remained fixed on her lips. Hers was a face practised in hiding emotion.

"It's OK, Soren. We have spoken to Ceres. We believe that what happened in the facility with Kyra was an accident. Ceres was frightened and surprised.

She thought we were Vincent's soldiers when she attacked us. We trust that she will not harm us again. We understand now. We know who she is, and what happened to you both back there."

"What...?"

"I think you'd better talk to her."

The confusion swirling in Soren's mind was only outweighed by the startling desire to see Ceres again. It was a desire he hadn't even realised was there until his mother mentioned it. Suddenly, he couldn't bear the thought of not having her beside him.

Chapter Twenty-Three
Nirvana

 IT WAS ANOTHER whole day before Soren was allowed to leave the hospital at Fallway. By that time, he was so jittery that he could barely keep still long enough for the doctors to monitor his health.

When they finally agreed to discharge him, Soren leapt out of bed as if an electric current had been passed through it. All he could think about was seeing Ceres and getting some answers to the countless burning questions he had, but his mother and father insisted he go home and take a shower before being allowed to see her.

No amount of whimpering and whining would make Callista soften, so he resolved to shower as fast as humanly possible. What he hadn't anticipated was the nervousness that would strike when he stepped out of the steaming water and headed to his and Deveron's room to choose his clothes. Somehow, such a simple choice was impossibly difficult. What should he wear? Should he style his hair? How should he act, and what would he even say?

He didn't need to worry because as soon as he got back to his room, Deveron was waiting for him and was surprisingly helpful instead of being his usual antagonistic self. A couple of helpful suggestions later, and Soren was dressed in a plain but handsome shirt and trousers with his hair smartly styled for the first time ever.

Deveron smirked as he straightened Soren's collar and brushed his shoulders down, but whatever snide comment he was thinking went unspoken. Instead, with hazy eyes, he muttered, "I'm glad you're safe."

The words of kindness surprised Soren, and he murmured back, "You too," unwilling to make eye contact.

Deveron smiled and tapped him on the shoulders. "We were nearly done for back there. If it wasn't for you and Ceres…"

More memories clicked back into place for Soren: his mother about to be murdered by Vincent; Guardian crouched over Raven, drinking from his wound; and Jade's motionless body.

"What happened to them? Did we finish them off?"

A frown crossed Deveron's face. "No. After your little trick, you passed out, and we focused on getting you home. We've heard news, though, from spies in Meraxor. Vincent and Guardian both survived. That was his name…that weird kid with the wings who drank the blood…Guardian. Apparently, he was all weak and broken and they took him to a lab. He hasn't been seen since. Vincent is sick—very—but they say he'll live."

Hearing of their defeat didn't make Soren as happy as he would have expected. The question really nagging at his mind was the one he didn't dare ask. As if reading his mind, Deveron answered for him anyway.

"Soren, Jade didn't make it."

He knew that already, of course. He'd known it immediately from the way her body had fallen, from her statue-like form, but that didn't make it hurt any less when he heard the words.

He had thought her betrayal might make his guilt easier to deal with, but it didn't. If anything, it made it worse. Now he had some distance from the situation, he saw it for what it really was—a young girl, desperate to please her great-grandfather, forced to do things she wasn't prepared for. Really, she was innocent in all this, yet she was the one who had died. Not the maniacal dictator, not the bloodsucking monster, but the little girl. The unfairness of it all burned in Soren's consciousness. He tried to ignore the fact that he had been the one who caused her death.

Deveron, showing a remarkable ability to read his brother's silence, clapped Soren on the back again. "Come on, buddy. Let's go see Ceres."

Ceres's chambers were at the end of the corridor, just a few doors down from Soren and Deveron. When they stepped into her room, she was already standing in the centre, waiting for them with a calm, knowing smile.

Soren's legs froze beneath him. He stopped at the doorway, unable to take another step towards her. It was only the gentle shove from Deveron that got him into the room at all. When he turned to yell at his brother, Deveron had already stepped out and shut the door behind them.

Now, it was just Soren and Ceres.

She looked different now to how she had looked back at the facility. Her silver hair was shining and clean, her face fresh. Gentle eyes twinkled at him, and a sweet smile danced on her lips. Warmth and comfort seemed to radiate from her, and Soren relaxed into her presence. She reached out to his hand. At her touch, he felt his soul pulse as it had done back in the laboratory.

Soren's skin tingled from head to toe, and he couldn't drag his eyes away from her. He asked the only thing he could think of.

"Will you stay here? Is that what you want, Ceres?" he asked. "Do you want to stay here with us?"

She replied in a light, delicate voice, like crystal floating on the wind. "My place is here with you. I have never been more sure of anything. And I could not return, even if I wanted to."

"Return where?" Soren asked.

Her voice was so quiet it was difficult to hear her soft tones. "To my place of birth...to Heaven."

Silence.

Soren's mind reeled with the implications of what she said, and his mind flashed back to the images of her that he had seen pinned to the walls in the laboratory.

"I don't understand!" he snapped, louder than he had intended. "Why do you make me feel this way? What's happening? Who are you?"

Ceres's gentle smile calmed him almost immediately. "It is difficult for humans to grasp, and you may never truly understand who or what I am. I'm not like you, Soren. I'm not like any of your people. I have been alive for hundreds of years, and I was designed by the Creator himself. I grew up an eternity away from here in a place filled with joy and goodness. You know it as Heaven. I am an angel, Soren."

The strange revelation should have shocked him, but somehow Soren already knew it to be true. He didn't know why, but everything she told him was familiar, as if he had heard it all in a dream and forgotten it.

She continued, "An angel's soul is tied to Heaven. We are linked to the fabric of that dimension and are not allowed to leave or our souls shall be torn in half. But we live to serve humans. We watch over you and help to steer you to do what is right in your lives. But sometimes you are led astray by darker forces. Sometimes, sending our love from Heaven is not enough and people turn to evil.

"Humans can be weak and are easily influenced. If we do not get to them in time, they can be manipulated by other, darker, forces. I have seen it with my own eyes. I have watched as humans kill one another, as they lie and torment with demons whispering in their ears. There is one group of such people on this earth that are evil beyond all others."

"The Brotherhood of Shadow," Soren whispered, and Ceres nodded.

"My job is to help humans, to protect them from the forces of darkness, but from up there in Heaven all I could do was watch as Vincent Wilder gradually destroyed everything around him. There is a powerful Rhygun working with them, a half-human, half-demon who goes by the name of Reign. And the Bavelize too, the greatest of all evils. I couldn't bear it. I knew I must help the Brotherhood, to guide them back onto the right path. So I decided that I must leave Heaven and journey down to the Human Realm."

Soren frowned. "But didn't you say that angels' souls were tied to Heaven? How did you leave?"

"I can't tell you. It would be too painful. But I can show you."

Ceres stepped towards Soren and placed a gentle hand on his forehead. Lights and flashes of colour swirled in Soren's vision and at last the spiralling fog cleared. But what met Soren's eyes was not the room where he had been standing just moments before. Panicked and flustered, he spun around, trying to figure out what had happened, but he was calmed by the voice of Ceres shushing him, though he couldn't see her anywhere. He took in his surroundings: immense columns of pure white marble and gilded statues everywhere he looked.

The fog cleared some more, and that was when he saw her. Ceres was sitting in the centre of the grand courtyard, surrounded by other angels, all with concerned frowns upon their faces.

"Are you sure this is what you want, Ceres?" asked a tall angel with long, flowing dark hair.

A fierce nod. There were tears in Ceres's eyes but a look of such determination that the others didn't argue with her. "I must do it, and it has to be now or my courage will falter."

"But...," a handsome angel with a stunning golden complexion and dazzling green eyes stammered, his concern clear in his eyes. "But, Ceres, if you do this, you can never come back to Heaven. Is it really worth that? Are the humans worth such a price?"

She looked at him as if he had uttered a blasphemy unlike anything she had heard before. "But of course they are. If we cannot help the humans, what are we here for?"

The handsome angel had nothing to say to that, although it was obvious he wasn't happy with her decision. Reaching behind his back, he pulled out a stunning dagger with golden patterns engraved along the blade and handle. His eyes met Ceres's and they held each other's gaze for the longest time.

"Please, Icarus. You know this is the right thing to do." Her voice rang with the sincere and melodic tones Soren had been captivated by outside of the vision.

Icarus bit his lip and then knelt down beside Ceres. His eyes never left hers as he began to weave his hand through the air above her chest, pulling at invisible strands in the ether around them. Soren couldn't see anything, and it looked strange, Icarus waving his hand around in empty air like that, but before long a strange, floating mist began to swirl around his fingertips.

Ceres's breathing became heavier and her head drooped. Icarus continued twisting his fingers this way and that, grabbing at various strands of the silvery smoke that materialised in thin air. Finally, when he was grasping an entire handful of the eerie threads, he held the dagger at the edge of the clump. He hesitated for a moment, but another nod from Ceres confirmed her wishes.

With one brutal movement, he tore the dagger through the smoky strands. A horrifying wail escaped Ceres's lips and she immediately dropped to the floor as if all the life had been sucked from her. Soren clasped a hand over his mouth in shock, and he yearned to escape the distressing vision, to run away from the horrible truth of what Ceres had done to herself.

Icarus bundled up the silver threads he had cut away from her and took them over to a huge well in the centre of the marble courtyard. The attention he paid to placing the threads safely in the well told Soren what he needed to know, that this angel cared deeply for Ceres.

It was a long time before Ceres could pull herself back up from the floor. When she did, Soren could see the damage that had been done to her. She was a shadow of her former self—pale, weak, and delicate.

The hallucination or whatever it had been began to fade around him, the strands of the vision disintegrating until his familiar home came back into view. As the mist cleared and he was able to finally catch his breath, his eyes locked onto Ceres. He saw her differently this time, no longer as a weak little girl who needed protecting. Now he looked at her with respect and a certain amount of sadness too. It took a fair amount of restraint to stop himself from embracing her in a deep and heartfelt hug, but he held back, simply because there was still so much he didn't understand.

Ceres's eyes welled with tears and she squeezed Soren's hand. "It was the most painful thing I ever had to endure. To leave, I had no choice but to rip my soul in two. One half stayed within me, the other was left in the Kingdom of Heaven. I came here incomplete. It was the only way I could get to Vincent, to help him and nurture him back into goodness. But when I arrived in his lands, he did not welcome me and did not want my help. He saw my wings and wanted to steal my power. He believed that if he took my blood and did experiments on me he could harness my strength and use it for himself."

Soren's eyes hardened and his jaw set angrily. "It is exactly the kind of thing he would do. Vincent always wants power, and he never lets anything get in his way."

Ceres swallowed heavily, and Soren could feel her anxiety. He gently stroked her hand as she continued. "They kept me in that glass cell for ten years, doing many horrible things to me, all in the hope of using my power. I was quite sure that I would die."

Soren gasped. "Ten years! How did you survive?"

"I slept. I put myself into a coma and hid all of the power deep inside of myself, so they could not get to it. But, with my power hidden, I could never hope to escape. I was not strong enough. My family, the other angels back in Heaven, watched from above. As I drifted in and out of sleep I would hear faint whispers of their voices in the night. They were afraid that I would die, and they knew I could not last for long. So they did something to help me."

"What did they do?"

Ceres smiled and reached out to touch his forehead again. He slipped into another vision.

The Kingdom of Heaven was in uproar. The angels huddled together in the temple of Nirvana, engulfed in heated debate. The air was thick with noisy chatter as angels paced back and forth. Occasionally, the sound of concerned voices would halt abruptly and there would be eerie silence as every angel crumpled to the floor in agony at exactly the same moment. They would clutch at their heads and claw at their eyes, raking their fingers through their long silver hair and waiting for the agony to pass. Soren didn't understand why or how, but they all seemed to be feeling the pain of one of their own. When they crumpled in agony, they did it in unison.

One of the angels struggled to his feet and shook his arms and legs out to get rid of the trembling and sickness that had washed over him. He straightened up and stood tall, pushing back his broad shoulders. The others dragged themselves up after him as his booming voice broke the silence.

"How is this possible? How did we let one of our kind be treated this way? By mere humans, no less." His deep blue eyes burned with intensity.

A quiet, female angel answered, her eyes wide and gentle. "Samael, we did not *let* this happen. We would not have let her go if we had known she would suffer this way. The humans are far stronger than we anticipated. The clan she has been captured by—they call themselves the Brotherhood of Shadow—are far too powerful for even an angel to defend against. And the humans are not alone. A dangerous Rhygun is working with them. Ceres was too weak without her full soul to protect her. She didn't stand a chance. If her soul had been full, there would have been little they could do to her, but when she made the decision to go to the Human Realm, she had to split her soul. That's a price she was willing to pay."

"She did that to herself so she could help the humans, and this is how they repaid her selflessness." Samael's handsome face creased into a frown, and he began to pace backwards and forwards, his arms crossed over his broad chest. "In that weakened state she won't be able to get out. She'll be trapped there forever! Without her full soul, all she can do is hide within herself and store up whatever power she has left. She has nothing to protect herself with. One push would be all she could manage, and then she would be totally helpless. We have a duty to look after her!"

Justice, one of the original angels who had first walked the planet, watched quietly from the side of the hall. She had seen countless conflicts upon the Human Realm and watched them tear each other apart and destroy the land and pollute the waters. What the humans did amongst themselves was regrettable, and the angels worked tirelessly to send warmth, love and kindness to them. They tried to inspire strength and courage in the humans, to convince them to do good wherever they could. When a human skirted around the edge of insanity or malice, the angels tried to pull them back to morality. But with the Bavelize so close to the Brotherhood of Shadow, the angels' influence was blocked and evil could reign unchecked.

Justice gave a small cough and the other angels stopped to look at her. "We need to get involved. This is unacceptable."

Icarus's eyes widened. "Yes! Definitely! Let's go to the Human Realm together and free her."

There were tuts of disapproval and a few gasps of shock around the hall of angels.

"No, Icarus," Justice said quietly. "We cannot enter the Human Realm. We would all be forced to tear our souls apart to leave Heaven. All that would do is weaken too many of us. Then none of us could help her, and none of us would be able to return to Heaven with an incomplete soul."

The hall fell silent, but passion still burned in Icarus's eyes.

"Do you know what they do to her? They burn her, cut her, and take her ash. They experiment on her, put their chemicals into her body and test how much pain she can take. We will lose her if she stays there!"

"Yes, but sending others down will bring more loss and death. I cannot allow that, and you know Providence wouldn't allow it either."

"Providence would want Ceres to be safe!"

"He would, but the humans are our priority. You all know that. We cannot allow an action that could lead to war and the death of humankind. The demons could respond by invading too, and then we would have an all-out war on our hands."

The room fell silent again at the mention of demons, but Icarus still wasn't discouraged. "We can't leave her to suffer like that, with nothing to protect her. We MUST go to her!"

"No. We will not enter the Human Realm."

Samael began to argue, but he was cut off by Justice. "However, I agree we cannot leave her with nothing to hang on to. So I propose an alternative, but it may be dangerous. It's never been done before, and we have to do it before Providence could stop us. He would never allow it."

"What do you suggest?" Samael was at the point of desperation, where anything would be worth it to rescue Ceres.

Justice heaved a deep sigh. "I propose that we take the other half of her soul from the Well of Nirvana and send it down to her."

There was stunned silence, until a strong male angel with short silver curls laughed out loud. "You can't be serious."

"Oh, I am," Justice replied, without a trace of humour in her expression.

He was incredulous at the mere suggestion. "We can't take the soul from the well. All of our souls are tied to this realm and could not survive outside of a vessel, a body. If we take the second half from the well, it will perish."

"It will survive long enough for us to get it into a vessel," Justice said quietly, but she bit her lip and her mind was clearly working furiously for a solution.

Samael's face lit up. "Yes! We send it down to Ceres, and then she will be strong enough to break free and can return to our realm safely."

Justice shook her head sadly. "No, we cannot send it to *her*. She is trapped in the basement of a building, being worked on by the Rhygun, Reign. There is no guarantee the soul would find its way to her. There are so many hostile forces surrounding her. What if the energy was intercepted before it reached her? Then an angel soul would be in the hands of humans, or worse, the Bavelize itself. The soul is fragile; it must be stored safely inside a living host."

"Then we should pick a human close to Ceres and implant it in them. When they tend to Ceres, it will be reunited with her," Icarus suggested, his eyes hopeful.

"But a human already has a soul. We cannot give them two and cannot strip them of what makes them *them*. No. We need an empty vessel, a body without a soul...yet."

"Do you mean...a baby?"

Justice's eyes focused with dedicated solemnity. "It goes against our creed. I know it does. We should never interfere with humans like this, but a newly conceived baby could host her soul and grow around it. It would be part of that human, an integral part, but the child would still be human. It would still grow and live as humans do, but would be able to harness the residual power in that part of her soul."

Samael frowned. "How would this help Ceres?"

"Her soul would at least be in the same realm as her body. The two halves of her soul would pull together. Somewhere, somehow, the child would be drawn to her. It is inevitable."

"And what would happen if they meet? Would the child die? Would Ceres get her full soul back?"

"The soul's power might activate in her presence, but it would remain inside the human. Only if the child died, would the soul escape and go back into Ceres. But this way, at least the second half of her power could be available to her."

"What if the child uses her power for evil? What if they never meet?"

"Those are risks we have to take. We have no other option. We will mark the child as they are born, so we can locate the soul if ever we should need to retrieve it."

The tension in the room hung thick in the air.

"All in favour, raise your hand," Justice said quietly, lifting her own hand.

For a moment, it looked as if no hands would rise. Justice remained stoic even as, one by one, the angels lifted their hands. It was a unanimous vote.

"Then we shall proceed to the Well of Nirvana."

The second vision began to fade and, as the mist cleared, Soren's eyes glazed over and all of the sound around him faded into a dull hum. He was beginning to realise what she was saying, and where he fitted into all of this. His attention drifted back into focus as she began to speak again.

"My family were not allowed to simply take the second half of my soul, the half I had left behind, and give it to me. They were forced to steal it, under cover of night, from the Well of Nirvana, where all souls are kept, and discreetly send it to Earth. I was trapped in my cell of glass, and I could not retrieve my soul as it drifted down from the skies. But a soul cannot survive outside of a body. It needed somewhere or someone to hide inside until I could be reunited with it."

Soren's breathing quickened and his heart began to pound.

"My soul drifted, alone in the wind, looking for a body to nestle inside, when it found a woman having a baby. As she gave birth to the baby boy, my soul hid within the child, where it could remain, safe and warm."

Ceres looked at Soren and smiled, her fingers stroking his, and his body pulsed with energy again. "Do you understand, Soren? *You* are the other half of my soul. That power you feel when we are close is the energy of Heaven flowing in your veins. When we met, that power activated, and when we touched it flowed out of us. Soren, you are special. You were destined to meet me and destined to take care of the other half of my soul. You saved me."

Soren nodded, finally understanding. For the first time in his whole life, he knew where he belonged. He knew what his destiny truly was.

He smiled at Ceres. "The prophecy was all true, down to the very last word. *The young must journey to the heart of shadows.* We were the young people the prophecy spoke of, all of us. The Children of Light have the elixir, so we will always be young, and, of course, the heart of shadows must mean the heart of the Brotherhood...Meraxor. And that last bit always confused me. *Where feathers will destroy the wild.* But I see it now. It means your feathers and mine."

With a smile, he reached down and pulled back the sleeve of his shirt to reveal his birthmark. The deep red spikes and slopes suddenly made sense to him. They were feathers. The thing that had marked him as different all of his life finally made sense. He wasn't just a normal child. He was the boy with the soul of an angel.

Epilogue

Deacon Thialdor waded through the knee-length grass, the long tendrils slowing him down, licking at his legs. The crisp air stung his throat when he breathed, and the early morning sun was becoming increasingly painful on his sore, red eyes. He shifted his gaze to the ground and squeezed his eyelids together tightly. Red patterns and lights swirled in his vision and dizziness washed over him.

Cradled in his pale arms was the limp body of his wife. She looked calm, peaceful, as if she could be asleep.

Deacon fought back the waves of anger and despair that rose in his throat, threatening to burst out of him in a primal scream. He hadn't known anything could hurt so much that it would burn into his soul this way. The moment Kyra had died, a tsunami of horror and pain had slammed into him. It shot though his entire body, devastating him in a second. He knew he'd never be the same again. Without her, he was nothing. Without her, he'd never feel alive again.

The surge of emotion had left him cold, and everything was muted and numb. Every glance he took at her beautiful face made him feel emptier, more isolated. And he truly was alone now. He hadn't just lost her; he'd lost them all. The betrayal of his family hurt almost as much as losing his wife. Why hadn't Raven supported him when he'd needed him the most? Bitterness rumbled in the pit of his stomach, darker than anything he'd felt before. At the moment, it was dulled by the pain that masked it, but he knew that, in time, the anger would only fester. He pushed his hatred aside and looked down at his wife.

Despite her light, delicate frame, carrying her body was weighing him down, in more ways than one. Not only did it slow his progress to a crawl, but looking at the face he'd loved so dearly, a face that would never smile at him again, was

215

making his heart darker with every passing second. He didn't want to leave her. He never wanted to be separated from her, even like this, but what more could he do? Carry her with him forever? He knew eventually her body would begin to spoil. He couldn't bear to see that gentle face gradually turn to rot and ruin. But he couldn't leave her here with the hot Meraxan sun shining callously down upon her to be picked at and devoured by scavengers.

There was a river just up ahead, and he shifted her body to allow the circulation to return to his fingertips, which seemed paler than ever, almost blue and getting increasingly colder. He wriggled his digits but no blood flow returned.

He approached the river and stood for a moment, watching the crystal clear water bubbling over the rocks. There was a deeper pool to his right, and he knelt down beside it. He saw his own face reflected in the pool, distorted and twisted as the currents pulled it in different directions. He could just make out a vaguely human shape, paler than it should have been, and two dead eyes, the brown orbs tinged with a sore, red glint.

He had all the time in the world to do this. He wasn't on a schedule anymore. He'd never have a schedule again. But what was there to gain from delaying it? It had to be done, and every passing moment simply made it harder to stomach. He reached out and gently placed her body in the water. She was so delicate and light he thought she might rest on the water tension, but she sank below the surface. Her crystal coffin consumed her features and her red hair billowed around her like an explosion. Within moments she was gone, drifting into icy oblivion.

Deacon's head drooped, his chin resting on his chest as he gulped in a painful breath of air. She was gone. She was really gone.

His head was beginning to spin now and his eyes blurred in and out of focus. A searing agony jolted through his spine, a cleaving and wrenching like something stabbing through the skin and muscle on his shoulder blades. A final explosion of pain, and then two enormous red wings burst out of his back. They arched up behind him and he flexed them back and forth, confused and mystified. They were beautiful, powerful, but a dark omen of what was to come.

It was coming for him, the sickness. There was no avoiding it. The disease they had been fighting would win this battle.

He stood slowly, his eyes two dark voids. With a mighty flap of his new wings, he set off towards the misty mountains ahead, hoping he could get as far as possible from the traitors in the Children of Light before the disease ravaging his body consumed him entirely.

Preview — Genesis of Light

Read on for a teaser preview of the first novella in The Light and Shadow Chronicles: Genesis of Light

The evening was drawing in, the sky just beginning to turn pink as the sun slowly dipped beyond the horizon. It was beautiful. Tom sat up beside her and looked out over the city. "The sky's too red," he muttered, then lay back down again.

"What?" Callista laughed. "How can it be too red? It's beautiful!"

"Nah. Too red," Tom repeated. Callista aimed a playful punch at his shoulder.

"Hey!" he cried out, but his face broke into a smile. They grinned at one another, and Callista felt her cheeks blush as she locked onto his dark eyes. Tom was the first to tear his eyes away.

The smile dropped from his lips. "It really is too red though, don't you think?" he said, nodding back to the landscape.

Callista's heart leapt into her throat when she followed his gaze. This wasn't just a sunset. The sky was blood red throughout, not the scattered, fading patches of pink that usually came with the sun's descent. Something was wrong.

Everything happened in an instant. The sky cracked open. Within seconds, fireballs were shooting through the air and plummeting down to crash into the city. Callista gasped and jumped to her feet, Tom right beside her. Even from this distance, Callista swore she could hear the screams of terrified people as the city was crushed. It was as if the gods themselves were hurling rocks from the sky, decimating everywhere, and everyone, she loved. Tears welled in her eyes, her mouth wide open with horror.

Between the crumbling buildings and blazing infernos, Callista just caught a glimpse of something impossible, unimaginable. She shook her head but when she looked back again it was still there. An enormous creature of towering height, unlike anything she had ever seen before. Skulking through the burning city, it swiped indiscriminately, smashing aside buildings, trees and even people. Callista's stomach churned with horror.

Smouldering stones began to pelt down on her, but thankfully much smaller than the ones obliterating the city. Tom pulled Callista into his arms, trying to protect her, but a rock the size of a penny hurtled out of nowhere and struck her on the forehead. Lights erupted in her vision and the intense agony seared through her like a red hot poker being pressed to her skin. She cried out, and Tom tried to hold his hands above them as protection. A rock hit him, sending him reeling away, clutching his injured arm, blood running down to his fingertips.

Hundreds more tiny stones rained down upon them, some burning hot, searing their flesh when they landed. The ground beneath them lurched, and Callista was thrown off her feet and slung to the grass. Her head spun and her vision clouded. With aching limbs, she tried to lever herself up from the ground, but an agonising gash in her forearm made her collapse back down again.

About the Author

D.M. Cain is a dystopian and fantasy author working for http://www.creativia.org/. The Light and Shadow Chronicles series features a range of books which can be read in any order. The first of these to be written was *A Chronicle of Chaos*. She is currently working on the next novel in the Light and Shadow Chronicles series, *The Sins of Silas*, as well as two complementary novellas entitled *Genesis of Light* and *Origin of Shadow*.

Cain has released one stand-alone novel: *The Phoenix Project*, a psychological thriller set in a dystopian future. *The Phoenix Project* was the winner of the 2016 Kindle Book Review Best Sci-Fi Novel Award.

D.M. Cain is also a member of the International Thriller Writers and one of the creators and administrators of the online author group #Awethors. Her short story *The End* was published in *Awethology Dark*.

Cain lives in Leicestershire, UK with her husband and young son, and spends her time reading, writing and reviewing books, playing RPGs and listening to symphonic metal.

Thank you for buying this book. Independent authors do all marketing and promoting of their books themselves; therefore, if you enjoyed this book, please leave a review with your retailer of choice. I would be most grateful for your support. Thank you.

For background information, character profiles, extra content and sneak peeks at upcoming books in the series, visit http://dmcain84.com/ or sign up for my mailing list here: http://eepurl.com/XevZH.

Author page at Next Chapter Publishing

https://www.nextchapter.pub/authors/dm-cain-fantasy-science-fiction-author-leicestershire-uk.

You might also like:

Assassins by David N. Pauly

To read first chapter for free, head to:
https://www.nextchapter.pub/books/assassins-the-fourth-age-shadow-wars-
epic-fantasy

Lightning Source UK Ltd.
Milton Keynes UK
UKHW011121120121
376872UK00009B/1009/J